22/9

Gordon Lewis

Soho
Hustle

ISBN-13: 9798428504316

A big thank you for Yewweng Ho's involvement in
making it a fun book to work on, Darius Shu for the
cover design, and not forgetting the wonderful Ian
Fitzgerald for his inputs.

Prologue

A lot has changed since the 1980s. Looking back, there's lots to be nostalgic about: the music was better, the hair bigger and the clothes more colourful. But the language was more colourful, too, and attitudes very different. However hard it is being who you are and what you want to be today, it was much more difficult then, and *Soho Hustle* reflects this in unflinching style. It recreates how people spoke and how they thought in sometimes shocking and uncomfortable words, reflecting both the innocence and the ignorance of those times. If you're easily offended, it's probably best if you stop reading now. If you're still reading this – thank you. *Soho Hustle* is a book for people with open minds and big hearts. People like you.

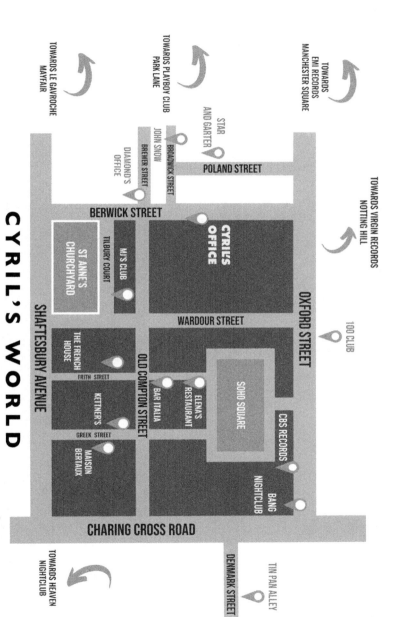

CYRIL'S WORLD

TOWARDS LE GAVROCHE MAYFAIR

TOWARDS PLAYBOY CLUB PARK LANE

TOWARDS EMI RECORDS MANCHESTER SQUARE

TOWARDS VIRGIN RECORDS NOTTING HILL

STAR AND GARTER

JOHN SNOW

DIAMOND'S OFFICE

BREWER STREET

BROADWICK STREET

POLAND STREET

BERWICK STREET

ST ANNE'S CHURCHYARD

TILBURY COURT

MJ'S CLUB

CYRIL'S OFFICE

OXFORD STREET

WARDOUR STREET

100 CLUB

THE FRENCH HOUSE

FRITH STREET

OLD COMPTON STREET

BAR ITALIA

ELENA'S RESTAURANT

SOHO SQUARE

CBS RECORDS

KETTNER'S

GREEK STREET

MAISON BERTAUX

BANG NIGHTCLUB

SHAFTESBURY AVENUE

CHARING CROSS ROAD

TOWARDS HEAVEN NIGHTCLUB

DENMARK STREET

TIN PAN ALLEY

Chapter One

'Tell me why I don't like Mondays'

The Boomtown Rats

It's Sunday night; two heavily-built bouncers stand outside the Bird's Nest disco in Stanmore High Street, north London. The driving beat of Rod Stewart's 'Da Ya Think I'm Sexy' vibrates through the warm, still air. Inside, the multi-coloured disco lights pulse in sync with the driving beat of the music. The club manager leans proudly at one end of the very long bar. Looking around, he's pleased to see the bartenders rushed off their feet; the place is heaving with a young crowd. A mass of four hundred bodies moving together, all possessed by the melody. At the other side of the throning dancefloor sits the DJ booth, protected by a couple of bouncers who are continually eying up the crowd. In the booth, a young, good-looking DJ is enjoying himself as he moves to the music, well aware he has several admirers watching him.

Two girls in leather jackets, headscarves, lacy gloves and extravagant make-up modelling themselves after the up and coming pop sensation Madonna push their way through the crowd and the groupies to get to the DJ booth. The bouncers don't bat an eyelid.

'Hey you, Mr DJ, I wanna talk with you!' one of them shouts, banging her palm on the desk for emphasis.

'What? I can't hear you!' he says, leaning in closer. 'Oh, it's you again. What is it this time?' Cyril takes off his headphones. He's not happy to see the same two girls twice in the space of twenty minutes. The smaller of the two, the redhead, reminds him of a yapping terrier as she continually talks over her friend.

'We told you earlier, it's our friend's hen party tonight and we want the current hits – Duran Duran! Madonna! But you keep playing this old shite,' she exclaims.

'Good music is good music. Doesn't matter when it's released, but you wouldn't understand that!' Cyril fires back. Then he shouts to the bouncers: 'Hey aren't you guys supposed to keep the riff-raff out?'

The burly guys shrug and turn away. Typical. As the redhead begins her yapping again, he puts his headphones back on. He feels a slight twitch of anxiety. Cyril is under pressure to perform well but hates being interrogated about his music. It's something he feels very strongly about.

'You think you're so flash and cool, don't you?' the girl continues when it becomes obvious she isn't getting her way.

'Yeah, you fancy yourself, you prick,' shouts the little terrier.

Cyril ignores them and plays Queen's 'Another One Bites the Dust'. He cranks up the volume with a cheeky grin – his way of giving them the middle finger in a fashion that won't get him fired. The girls shoot him the nastiest look they can conjure and push their way back to their friends.

An hour later the bright white lights come on and the music stops, jolting everyone back to reality. It's one in the morning and time to clear the dancefloor and get everyone off the premises. Voices emerge from the general hubbub of people moving towards the exits; two young men are yelling at each other as three girls look on disapprovingly. The bouncers move in quickly and try to usher them towards the door.

'My sister's not interested in you and stop calling me names!' one of the boys shouts.

'I'll call you what I like, yid. Let's finish this outside,' the other growls aggressively in a way he thinks will impress the watching girls.

My sister's Jewish too, you schmuck,' the first one retorts, pushing the other.

The bouncers step in again to stop the boys from lashing out, and the girls pull them away to avoid further confrontation. Relieved to see the floor empty, the manager walks over to the DJ.

'Cyril, we need to have a chat before you leave,' he says, his bushy eyebrows knitted together with concern.

'Sure, I'm almost done,' Cyril replies as he puts the last record into his box. 'What's up?'

'I had a complaint from the hen party. They said you ignored their requests. This isn't the first time you've upset the customers, Cyril.'

Cyril sighs; 'Look, the problem here in Stanmore is that everyone knows everyone. I know their type. Jewish princesses. They've always got something to grumble about. They can't help it; it's part of their nature. I should know, I'm Jewish!' He shakes his head and lights a cigarette.

'One of the girls says she's an assistant manager at the local record shop, and that you only play EMI records for some unknown reason,' the manager continues.

This makes Cyril a little bit uneasy. 'Well, EMI or not, it's bloody good music. Did you see how much everyone else was enjoying themselves tonight? That red-haired dwarf with the big mouth and her girlfriend. Damn lesbians! Don't know shit about music. And, did you know EMI are the biggest record company with more artists than any other? Of course I'm going to be playing their stuff. It's the law of averages.'

The manager's bushy eyebrows knit even further together in a suspicious frown. 'What's this,' he asks, 'you on a retainer with EMI or something?'

Cyril's laugh in reply is a little too forced. He tells the manager good night and gets out of the place as quickly as possible.

When Cyril arrives home it's almost two in the morning. He unpacks his records from the car and leaves them just inside the front door of the house. His eyes feel full of sand and he can't wait to get to bed, but first he drinks a whole bottle of deliciously cold milk from the fridge. Most people like warm milk before bed, but not Cyril. He creeps up the stairs, avoiding the creaks, and jumps straight into bed.

As always seems to be the case after a gig, Cyril feels his head has only just hit the pillow and it's already time to get up. His mother calls from downstairs. 'Cyril! You're going to be late for work; your breakfast is going cold.' Silence. She calls out again, looking up the stairs and waiting to hear some movement from

Cyril's bedroom.

Slowly and begrudgingly, Cyril opens his eyes. If only mothers came with a pre-installed snooze button. Swinging his legs out of the bed and wriggling his toes, he gets up and draws the cheery Tom and Jerry curtains. *I really ought to change those*, he thinks. It looks like another drizzly Monday morning. The thought of going to work – to his real job – doesn't fill Cyril with any joy; quite the opposite. He turns on the radio to listen to the news but finds it's equally as dismal as the grey weather outside; a spokesman for Margaret Thatcher's government says that unemployment is continuing to rise. Despite this, Cyril gets into the shower, emerging from the steam a few minutes later feeling much more alive.

Cyril does his exercise routine on the bedroom floor, as he does religiously each morning. Got to keep his body in shape. As Cyril exercises, he looks at the pictures he's cut from the music magazines of his favourite rock and pop acts pinned up on his walls: the Sex Pistols, Duran Duran, David Bowie and Adam Ant.

Looking at himself in the full-length mirror, he puts on his Levi's 501 jeans. He pushes back his long, black wavy hair, admiring his toned body. One thing Cyril isn't short of is confidence; he knows he's handsome. He enjoys the attention he receives, especially at the disco where he is guaranteed a fair share of action. A few people have told him he looks like Elvis, and Cyril won't argue with that. He had desperately wanted to be in a rock band but can't sing to save his life. He might not have Elvis' voice, but Cyril's certain he has the same charm. The radio plays Adam and the Ants' 'Prince Charming' as he slips on his freshly pressed white t-shirt. Cyril immediately strikes a pose, pretending to be Adam Ant, and mimes along with the lyrics:

Prince Charming!

Prince Charming!

Ridicule is nothing to be scared of.

Don't you ever, don't you ever

Stop being dandy, showing me you're handsome.

Don't you ever, don't you ever

Lower yourself, forgetting all your standards.

'Cyril! I'm not calling you again,' his mother shrieks at the top of her voice. 'It's almost eight o'clock and I'm leaving for work soon. And we've run out of milk, so there's none for your tea.'

The house phone starts to ring.

'Stanmore, 4468, Gina Gold.'

It's Cyril's father, Alf, who's already at work.

'Has Cyril left for work yet or is he still in bed?' he asks huffily, already fairly certain of the answer.

'He'll be leaving soon,' Gina assures him.

'Sure. Bet he hasn't even had breakfast. Can you ask

him if he still wants to see Tottenham play this weekend? I've had an offer on the tickets.'

Cyril flies into the kitchen, holding his leather jacket in one hand and gulping down a mug of black tea with the other. He takes the phone from Gina.

'Dad, can I pay you next month for the tickets?'

'Cyril, you said that last month and the month before. Cash up front today or I'm selling them.'

Cyril pauses for a minute, weighing things up; 'But I have a date with this new girl I've met. I need the money for tonight.'

'Sorry, son, it's about time you started paying your own way in life. You're twenty-three now.' Alf puts the phone down on Cyril.

'Huh, that's nice. Dad's just hung up on me!' he complains, hoping his mum might have a word with Alf later.

'I left you a soft-boiled egg and some bread soldiers on the table. There's more tea in the pot,' says Gina kindly as she gets ready to leave.

'Dad's put me in a real mood,' says Cyril, angrily drumming his fingers on the kitchen table. 'Did I mention I'm going to quit my job soon?' he adds matter-of-factly.

'Are you sure that's a good idea? You love meeting all the famous people and getting their autographs. And you won't get any more freebie records!'

'Mum, I hate working at the bloody EMI factory. It's not exactly glamorous work – nobody ever had their name up in lights for packing records.' He pauses, considering how much of his hairbrained scheme to divulge at this early stage. 'It's just a stopgap until I've saved up enough money for my own business,' Cyril says finally.

'But you don't save, darling,' his mother replies gently. 'You've still not paid your dad for the season tickets and you've not paid me back for the car yet, either. Your dad would be very cross with me if he knew I'd given you the money.'

'I'm sorry, Mum, I really am. I'll make it up to you when I'm making real money though, I promise.'

Cyril walks out the front door and admires his red 1972 Ford Escort in the driveway. Before turning on the engine, he touches the Spurs football logo on the windscreen for good luck – a ritual he completes every day without fail. He treats his car the same way he treats his many girlfriends: with great care and affection.

With the windows rolled down, Cyril ramps up the volume of his car radio and steps on the accelerator. The news comes on and they're talking about the terrible unemployment figures again. Bored with the constant bad news, he immediately switches the station.

The Boomtown Rats' 'I Don't Like Mondays' plays and Cyril sings along to the chorus – the perfect song for a dismal beginning to the week.

I don't like Mondays.

(Tell me why)

I don't like Mondays.

(Tell me why)

I don't like Mondays.

I wanna shoot the whole day down.

Cyril stops at the traffic lights, banging out the rhythm of the song on his steering wheel. A white Ford van full of builders pulls up next to him. They catch sight of his private performance and start laughing.

'Hey look, he thinks he's that Irish bastard Bob Geldof!' yells the van driver in a strong east London accent.

'What a wanker. And he's a fucking Tottenham supporter!' the driver continues when he spots the Spurs logo on Cyril's windscreen.

'Bet ya he's a Jew,' shouts a passenger, making an obscene face and gesturing with his index fingers to make ringlets either side of his face.

'Chelsea! Chelsea!' chants a third builder.

Cyril is uncomfortable and embarrassed but he tries not to show it. When the lights turn green he sticks his hand out the window, making a tossing off motion and slams his foot on the accelerator; 'Wankers!' he calls out as the van disappears in his rear-view mirror.

As he approaches the EMI pressing factory, the tall security guard with a thick moustache takes great pleasure in ribbing Cyril about his poor timekeeping.

'On the late shift again?' he smirks, opening the gate.

Cyril runs inside, slips onto the production line and begins packing records as if he'd been there all along. But the officious factory supervisor, fully equipped with clipboard and pen, spots Cyril with his head down, pretending to be extra busy packing Cliff Richard's album, *I'm no Hero*.

'Gold!' he bellows. 'You were late again. Just like last week.'

The other workers grin and cast knowing glances at each other.

'What is it this time? The car? Cat died... again? Alarm didn't go off? I've heard just about every explanation going from you, Gold,' the supervisor continues.

'Well, actually...' Cyril begins.

'Stop right there. You've always got some excuse for your shortcomings and I've had quite enough. The truth is, you're just bloody lazy! Are you allergic to work or something?'

Cyril isn't quite sure how to respond. Instead he just looks up at the supervisor with the most pitiful look he can plausibly muster.

'No. Don't give me that. I've had enough of you and your ridiculous puppy dog faces. I've had enough of you point blank! My manager told me I could dismiss you any time after all the warnings I've given you. As they say, you'd better shape up or ship out. And I mean it, Gold!'

Cyril suddenly feels he can't stand to be in the presence of the supervisor for another second. His face snaps into an angry scowl; 'I. Quit,' he snaps, punctuating the second word by dropping a full box of packaged records. It lands with a resounding smack and Cyril is happy to see that the supervisor is a little taken aback.

'You can stuff your lousy job. I'll tell you something else too,' Cyril continues, getting rather carried away. 'This job pays shit money. If it wasn't for the free records I'd have been long gone by now.'

The supervisor is silently incandescent with rage; now he'll never have the satisfaction of sacking the little toe-rag.

Cyril pushes it one step further. 'One day, I'm going to be a famous pop icon and then you'll be packaging my records, you wait and see.'

'Yeah, when pigs fly,' the supervisor manages to say,

despite trembling with fury.

'Send my wages and holiday pay on to me,' Cyril adds with a smile. The supervisor shakes his head in disbelief and the rest of the employees look on, enjoying the unfolding drama.

'Go on, Cyril! You tell him,' one of his workmates calls as Cyril walks out of the factory with a swagger. Cyril waves goodbye to his now-former colleagues as they whistle and cheer in support.

The security guard stops Cyril's car at the gate as he tries to leave. The moustachioed guard has gone home and his replacement looks a lot more serious. He asks for his EMI parking sticker so Cyril pulls it off his windscreen and shoves it into his hand. The guard then proceeds to inspect the car, looking for stolen goods. It's protocol, but Cyril is certain this guy is giving him an extra look over. *Do I have a suspicious face*, he thinks, half amused and half annoyed. Cyril opens his pack of filter cigarettes and drums his fingers on the packet before lighting up. When he gets the all clear and drives out of the EMI factory, it suddenly strikes Cyril that he's now one of the many unemployed people they keep talking about on the news. This doesn't particularly concern him, though; he's just glad to have left the factory behind.

Chapter Two

'Mr Blue Sky'

ELO

Cyril drives with a big smile on his face, feeling a sense of freedom and relief after quitting his dead-end job. He isn't sure where he's going or what to do with the rest of his day. He stops off at a telephone box and calls Hannah at the office where she works.

'Hi, beautiful, what are you doing right now?'

'Cyril! I'm trying to work, that's what. My boss is looking over at me so make it quick.'

'I miss you and I can't wait 'til tonight to see you. Why don't you pretend you feel ill and I'll come and get you? We could have the whole house to ourselves. How about it?'

'You are joking, right? Aren't you at work?' she asks.

'Nope. My boss gave me some time off. I'm so horny for you right now, babe…' Cyril says, quickly moving the subject away from his job.

'What's new?' Hannah chuckles, 'You're always horny, you little devil. I gotta shoot, Cyril. Speak later.'

'Alright, gorgeous. Love you.'

He pulls out his black address book and begins to look up the numbers of his other girlfriends, hoping that at least one of them might be free to hook up. No joy. With a quickie firmly off the table, Cyril tries calling a few of his mates. They're all at work, too. After running out of people to call and change for the telephone, he decides to go home and put his feet up for the rest of the afternoon. He can watch television until Gina and Alf come home from work. Cyril is in two minds what to tell them. Should he be upfront and honest? The main problem with this approach is that his father will expect him to join the family garment business in east London. Cyril loathes the garment factory just as much as he despised working for the EMI. Perhaps a version of the truth will suffice for the time being, he thinks.

Bubbling away in the back of Cyril's mind is a plan. A business idea. He needs money to execute it but the only thing in his bank account is cobwebs. He plops himself down on the sofa and turns on the television. He's watching the screen but his brain is elsewhere. Different possibilities and routes forward disseminate through his mind like a map of the London Underground. When he finally decides which direction to take, Cyril drifts into a satisfied slumber.

Later on, Gina arrives home and wanders into the lounge, waking Cyril as she does so. She smiles but is a little surprised and concerned to see her son home.

'I wasn't feeling good at work – an upset stomach – so they let me come home,' Cyril explains before his mum even has chance to ask.

'Oh, you poor thing. It was nice of them to let you go. Did you get a chance pick up the new record for your dad?'

Cyril pulls out the Frank Sinatra *Greatest Hits* album and hands it to Alf as he walks into the room.

'Dad, this is a special limited export edition album and it's got your favourite on there, "Strangers in the Night".'

Alf is pleased but inclined not to show it; 'I hope you're not looking to wheedle the Tottenham tickets out of me, Cyril. I've already sold them.'

'Why do you always think I'm wheeling and dealing,' asks Cyril, genuinely hurt.

'I'm your father,' he says grimly but with a slight twinkle in his eye; 'I know you better than anybody – including your mother. Anyhow, thanks for the album.'

Later that evening, Cyril helps Gina with the washing up. She does all the talking, which isn't particularly unusual. Cyril's mind is elsewhere.

'Cyril! Cyril! Are you listening? I asked if you liked your dinner tonight?'

'It was great. Thanks, Mum.'

'Is something on your mind? You're very quiet this evening.'

Cyril remains silent.

'Is it something to do with that girl you've been seeing, Hannah?' she tries tentatively. Gina hopes Cyril will open up to her without making her look as though she's prying.

'Hannah's fine. I'm just tired from working late the last two nights at the disco,' Cyril lies. He can't bring himself to tell his mum about the job so he goes upstairs to start planning what he'll do for the rest of the week.

The next morning at breakfast, Alf is sitting reading *The Jewish Chronicle*. 'Your mum says you're thinking of quitting your job, is that true?' he asks. 'The country's in a deep recession and jobs are scarce; you should think yourself lucky that you've got one,' he says pointing to his newspaper.

'Well, I'll be leaving one day, Dad,' Cyril says nervously.

'When you do, come and work with me in the factory. It'll be your business one day.'

'Thanks, Dad, but I want to work in the music

business. I want to manage music acts, find the next Elton John or Diana Ross.'

'What, like Uncle Lew?' Gina butts in.

'No, Mum. He looks after variety acts; comics, jugglers and magicians. I'm only interested in music. Think of late Uncle Brian.'

'Oh, my cousin Brian? He was such a good-looking boy, and lots of *chutzpah*, too.' Gina begins reminiscing: 'When I was a young girl in Liverpool I'd go into his record shop – this was just after he'd started managing the Beatles – and he'd always give a small family discount for the records. Oh, and…'

'Pity he was queer,' Alf cuts in.

'Alf! That's a horrible thing to say. He was lovely, and a good man.'

'I think I have the same *chutzpah* as Uncle Brian,' says Cyril. 'But I'm not gay,' he adds, with a camp flick of his wrist.

Gina and Alf both laugh.

'The *schmatta* business makes good money, son. At least think about it,' Alf says, turning serious again.

Cyril knows his dad wants what's best for him, but he also knows it isn't the kind of business he wants to be in. He stays silent, hoping not to offend Alf while also not giving him false hopes.

'So, you're looking for the next Sex Pistols?' Alf asks,

trying to relate to his son and his wild fantasies.

'No, no. Punk's already dead. Past its sell by date!' Cyril laughs. 'Alright, I'm off to work now. See you both tonight.'

'He's a real dreamer, our Cyril,' Alf continues as the front door closes. 'He doesn't know the first thing about money or business, and that worries me.'

'Don't blame me for that!' Gina says angrily. 'He might have settled down into a proper job if you weren't threatening him with working at your bloody knicker factory all the time.'

'Well you tried getting him that job as a trainee estate agent and look how that turned out!' Alf retaliates. 'You've spoilt that boy rotten, going along with all his fanciful ideas. He's spent all his life ducking and diving and we have to bail him out every time. Anything I tell him goes in one ear and out the other.'

Alf storms out of the kitchen leaving Gina staring sadly out of the kitchen window, watching Cyril pull out of the drive. She knows what Alf has said is true.

Cyril drives into London's West End to begin effecting his plan of setting up a music management business. *No time like the present*, he thinks. If he can get something up and running before his parents even know he's unemployed it might make them worry less.

He's certain that Soho is the best place to be – there are lots of record companies based around the area, as well as his Uncle Lew's artiste management company. Cyril parks his car in one of the old back streets with its century-old three-storey tenements and sets off on his scouting mission. He walks past the many music and theatre companies until he comes to Berwick Street, whose famous fruit and veg market is buzzing with activity. The lively, colourful atmosphere seeps into his skin and Cyril feels as though he's already part of the humming community. The many characters going about their daily business fill him with excitement. He wonders what it's like to be someone important; someone with places to go and people to see.

Soho is different from other parts of London. It morphs and grows throughout the day, beginning with a bright sense of endless possibility in the morning, moving through to an exciting but exclusive hive of activity and mystery in the evening when the red-light district comes alive. It's like a flower opening and closing in the sun.

Cyril strolls along Old Compton Street with his hands in his pockets, passing countless restaurants preparing to open for the lunchtime business. He remembers Uncle Lew talking fondly of his teenage days – how he roamed the streets and hung out in Soho's coffee bars.

It was the fifties then, and the birth of Rock and Roll. Cliff Richard, Tommy Steele and Marty Wilde were the big British stars.

Cyril decides he needs a caffeine rush and makes for Bar Italia on Frith Street, where some of the best coffee in Soho is served by Italian staff. Uncle Lew always used to talk about the Italian influences that form a large part of the culture in the area. Cyril sits at an outside table, orders a coffee and lights up a cigarette. Already he's picturing how Soho is going to become his new world. The bohemian ambiance weaves its way through the crowd and Cyril feels a sense of belonging begin to develop. A smile of satisfaction creeps across his face. After two cappuccinos he decides to discover some of the less frequented back streets. Cyril isn't sure what he's looking for but knows he wants to get a feel for both the shiny exterior of Soho and the grittier, but equally as exciting, underbelly.

Everything he sees is new and intriguing; Cyril feels completely invigorated. He has already forgotten the trouble of the day before and the reality of being unemployed is now being masked by the bright light of possibility. Taking his research to the next level, he walks into a newsagents and leaves with a copy of every music paper and magazine he can lay his hands on.

Cyril remembers a pub nearby he's been in before,

The Star and Garter. What better way to begin his investigations than with a nice pint, he thinks.

'Pint of lager please, love,' Cyril says, flashing a smile at the friendly barmaid. She is chewing gum as though her life depends on it and Cyril can't help but picture a cow chewing the cud. It's a bit of a turn off.

'Are you new round here? Working in the market?' she says, eyeing Cyril up.

'Yeah, but I don't work at the market.'

'What do ya do, then?' the barmaid says flirtatiously. She can see Cyril isn't a run of the mill labourer by the way he's dressed: leather jacket, tight blue jeans and a white T-shirt. He almost looks like a pin-up from a teenage girls' magazine, she thinks.

'I'm in the music business. Well… soon to be anyway,' Cyril says proudly.

'We have lots of important music people coming here. Guess I'll be seeing a lot more of you,' she smiles.

'Maybe one day I'll be important too!' he beams back. 'Can I see a menu please? I'm starving from all this walking around Soho.'

The barmaid goes to the other end of the bar to fetch a menu and hands it to Cyril.

'I actually only work here part time,' she begins. 'I'm trying to be a singer. I can dance too, when necessary. I'm looking to make a record – maybe you can help me?'

'Do you have any demos?' Cyril grins.

'Nothing done professionally, but I have some tapes.'

'Do you write your own songs?'

'No...does it matter?'

Cyril nods politely, as if he's interested, but quickly takes his drink over to a free table. Anyone can sing, but few can write their own music. The pressing factory may have been a dead-end job but it gave him some knowledge of how the music business works. He knows there's nothing much to be gained from cover singers.

After leafing through all the music magazines and enjoying a leisurely pub lunch, Cyril feels ready to get down to some serious business. One of the first things on his agenda is finding a place to work from. Continuing his exploration of the back streets, Cyril finds himself surrounded by striptease joints, girlie bars and sex shops – all adorned with flashing neon lights. His eyes drift upwards to the second and third floor widows, many of which are framed in a red glow; the sex workers are open for business. He feels the afternoon bringing yet another shift in the mood as the prostitutes begin to emerge, looking for work. *This place really is alive*, thinks Cyril with amusement.

He enters Tilbury court, a pedestrianised street about forty metres long between Wardour and Rupert Streets.

Men stroll up and down the strip, deciding which of its many girlie bars and clubs to frequent. The regulars know which ones to avoid, while the tourists and the novices seem less sure.

Cyril is offered many friendly hellos by the front-of-house hostesses. He knows it's just a way of attracting business but he enjoys it all the same. The strip isn't at the height of its activity yet but music is already blasting out of the clubs, mixing into one indistinct sound. He passes Madame J's drinking club and the hostess immediately catches his eye. The girls on the strip are all good looking but this one stands out because of her extravagant dress sense. A glitzy red off-the-shoulder dress clings to her form in a way that is both flattering and refined. She's a big girl with an even bigger personality.

'Hey handsome! Wow, you look just like Elvis … No, are you Nick Kamen, that new model that everyone's talking about?' she exclaims, exaggerating her indecision. 'What a face! And what a sexy arse! Ooh La La!'

'Thanks,' Cyril says with a wink, playing along with the flirtation.

'Come in and meet my girls. They're all very beautiful,' she giggles.

'I like your accent. Welsh, right? What's your name?'

Cyril says bashfully in an attempt to change the direction of the conversation.

'Very observant of you, young man. I am from Wales, yes. I'm Madame J. MJ for short,' she says gesturing flamboyantly to the sign above the doorway. 'This is my club.'

Cyril notices she has rather manly hands and a masculine build, despite her prominent bosom. He realises she's probably a drag queen, or a 'trannie' as he's heard some people call them. He's not as worldly wise as he had thought.

'I love this song – Haircut 100, 'Fantastic Day'. I can make your day better than fantastic if you follow me,' she grins, hoping to entice Cyril inside.

Before Cyril can fumble his way through an excuse to move on, a stunning girl walks out of the club and lights up a cigarette. Her skin is a beautiful light shade of brown, courtesy of her Irish mother and Jamaican father. She leans on the wall and takes a deep drag, appearing not to notice Cyril or Madame J.

'Meet Jazz; I call her Sexy Jazz. She's one of my girls,' Madame J says, jolting the girl into action with a start.

'Who might you be?' Jazz enquires, tilting her head to the side so as not to blow smoke directly at Cyril.

'I'm Cyril, pleased to meet you.' He offers his

hand and Jazz shakes it, laughing. Despite his façade of confidence, Cyril isn't always the smoothest talker when it comes to the very attractive ladies.

'Are you from Liverpool?' he asks, completely unable to think of anything else to say. The blood from his brain is elsewhere.

'Aye, I'm a Scouser.' Jazz gives him a friendly nudge.

'My mum was born in Liverpool. Lost the accent though; she sounds more north London now.'

'Cyril, why not come in and have a Porn Star?' Jazz says, obviously quite adept at dealing with the more nervous customers.

'A what?'

'It's a cocktail!' she points to a brightly coloured list of drinks on the chalkboard next to the door, each sporting an alluring name: Ding Dong, Sex on the Beach, Love Potion 69. *Very clever*, Cyril thinks.

Sensing Cyril might be a dead end in term of custom, Madame J ushers Jazz back inside the club; 'Go on, you. You've had your fag break.'

'You coming in or what, Cyril?' Jazz calls as she disappears down the stairs.

'Gotta make a living, y'know. Can't stand about chatting all day… lovely as you are,' Madame J adds with a kind smile.

'Oh, sorry. I can't!' Cyril stutters, trying not to sound

as inexperienced and naïve as he feels. 'I'm actually supposed to be looking for a small office for my new business, you see.'

'A business? What kind of business?' she asks, curiously. If this Cyril is going to be making competition for Madame J's club, his business is her business.

'The music business. Artist management. That kind of stuff.'

'Oh I see,' Madame J says, relieved. 'Well, you'll want to speak to Mr Diamond Geezer. He works for the one and only Mr Soho... and he owns more properties here than anyone else.'

Madame J knows she won't be doing any business with Cyril today but is happy to help him out anyway. She gives him Diamond's telephone number and he scrawls it in his notebook.

'Tell Diamond I gave you his number – he'll look after you. Now run along, Cyril, you're blocking the view of my customers.' She turns her attention to other potential clients wandering along the strip.

'Thanks, MJ!' Cyril cries, walking away a satisfied customer, though not in the sense most would think.

The next morning, Cyril jumps out of bed before his alarm even rings. It's been a long time since he's felt such enthusiasm for the day ahead. He turns on his bedside radio.

'It's Wednesday morning and the forecast is for a lovely day of blue skies. So we have ELO with 'Mr Blue Sky' up next...'

Cyril loves this song. He hops about his room getting ready, looking extra smart for the day ahead.

'Morning, Mum,' Cyril says as he sits down to his breakfast.

'Goodness, you're up early. I didn't even have to shout at you. Something special happening at work?'

'You could say that.'

'What's with the secrecy, Cyril? You're being very evasive. Oh, before I forget – Uncle Lew and Sharon are coming over for dinner on Friday night. I'm making chopped liver, and your favourite; gefilte fish.'

'Sounds great, Mum.'

'You should invite that girlfriend of yours, Hannah. Or is it Alexandra now? I can never keep track.'

At that moment the phone rings and Alf answers.

'Cyril, it's for you. It's your mate Billy,' he shouts from the hall.

Billy is Cyril's long-time friend and partner in crime. He's known locally as Big Billy, because of his height, although he insists the nickname comes from having something extra in the trouser region. Unlike Cyril,

Billy's already in the music business. Sort of: he's a drummer in a local and not very successful band. Cyril takes the phone and turns away from his parents.

'Are you free at lunchtime?' he whispers down the phone, before Billy even has a chance to say hello.

'Sure. I can tell you all about my new record deal! Hey, what's with the whispering?' Billy asks.

'I'll explain later. You know The Star and Garter in Soho? I'll see you there.'

'Righty-o. Whatever you say, Knickerman.'

'Okay Billy, see you later,' Cyril finishes the call in a normal voice so not to arouse suspicion from Alf.

Alf is always suspicious, though. He looks up from the morning paper; 'Don't tell me you're all dressed up to go skiving off work to meet Billy.'

'No, Dad. I'm seeing him later this evening. Gotta go now.' Cyril grabs the rest of his toast and his keys and shoots out the door before Alf can ask any more questions.

'That boy is definitely up to something. What's with the suit? No one goes to work in a factory dressed like that!'

'Oh, Cyril's a good boy, Alf. It's that Billy I'm worried about; he's a bad influence. Cyril never smoked until he started hanging out with him,' Gina says, quick to defend her boy.

'I think he's on for a promotion at work but he's not telling us in case he doesn't get it,' she continues optimistically.

'Hmm! That'll be the day,' Alf sighs.

Chapter Three

'Sweet dreams are made of this'

Eurythmics

Cyril arrives in Soho at half past eight on the dot and slips into the nearest telephone box to call the mysterious Diamond Geezer. *What a name*, Cyril thinks with amusement. He dials the number, but no one answers. He decides to have a cigarette to kill a few minutes before trying again. Cyril is in and out of the telephone box several times and is now keeping himself amused looking and reading the many sexy escort calling cards stuck on the glass of the telephone box; 'Sexy doll needs a spanking', 'Big Black dominatrix', 'Big tits for hire'…

After an hour of trying, a frustrated Cyril decides to take a walk and get a cup of coffee. He picks up a tabloid and another pack of cigarettes from the newsagents on the way to Bar Italia. Taking a seat outside, Cyril settles in to read his paper and sips his latte. Cyril is quite easily distracted and quickly finds himself lost in the lives of the people bustling around him. He imagines their lives and wonders if they're living their dreams or just stuck in a sad reality. Suspended in the stasis of his observations, Cyril is completely unaware of the passage of time. Before he knows it, eleven o'clock has arrived.

'Shit,' Cyril mumbles, gathering his things and dashing back to the phone box. He hadn't intended on wasting the whole morning. He dials the number again and this time Diamond Geezer picks up.

'Good morning, Mr Diamond… Uh, I mean Mr Geezer. I'm Cyril. Madame J gave me your number. She said you might be able to help me find a small office in Soho for a good deal.'

'Deal?' Diamond snaps, skipping the pleasantries. 'Rooms are cheaper on upper floors. Is that what you're lookin' for?'

'Upstairs is fine. As long as it's cheap.'

'What brings you to the jungle anyway? Looking for a room for your girls?'

'Girls? No! I'm in the music business. Did you say jungle?'

Diamond laughs ominously at Cyril's question. When customers come his way from Madame J, they're usually involved in the sex industry. He agrees to meet Cyril after lunch to show him some of the rooms that are available.

Cyril is pleased with the outcome and feels happy with his progress so far. Next on his to-do list is to set up a business account. He's made an appointment to see a local bank manager, Mr Jones, to see if he can help him out. While he waits, Cyril recognises some famous faces coming and going inside the bank. His excitement begins to build but Cyril tries to concentrate on what he'll say to convince the manager to let his set up a business account and approve a loan.

'Good morning! Or afternoon, rather! Doesn't time fly? Pleased to meet you, Mr Gold!' the friendly-looking bank manager says, extending his hand to Cyril.

Mr Jones is excitable and energetic, which isn't exactly what Cyril was expecting. He had pictured all bankers as dusty old men. When the manager starts talking about how much he loves Soho and working with all kinds of famous people, Cyril knows he's in the right place.

'Are you an up and coming pop star or something? You definitely have that look about you.'

'No, not me. My business is managing artists,' Cyril says with a smile.

'I just had a nice young man like you in here this

morning. He's about your age and already has a top-five best-selling record. George Michael – you might have heard of him?'

'Yes – Wham! George and his mate, Andrew.'

'So, Mr Gold, what can I do for you today?'

'Well, I need a loan of a thousand pounds for my new management business. If you're feeling generous, make it two,' Cyril says with a wink, hoping humour might help his case. 'I'm going to be renting an office to run the business from but I need some money to get started.'

'Have you got any experience working in this sector? Have you managed artists before?' the manager asks.

'Not exactly. I did work for EMI records, though.'

'Good stuff. What did you do there?'

'I was on the factory floor overseeing the packing of records,' Cyril mumbles, knowing this isn't the answer the bank manager wants.

'What do you know about music? Can you write music or play an instrument?' Mr Jones asks, raising an eyebrow.

The manager is starting to sound like Cyril's old school teacher who'd had a lot to say when Cyril told him his dream was to work in the music industry.

'I'm going to manage the artists, not become one,' Cyril replies with a hint of impatience. He hadn't been expecting to be questioned so rigorously.

'You do have a business plan, right?'

Cyril reddens and wishes the ground would swallow him up. He'd been coasting along on a wave of adrenaline until now, but it has just begun to dawn on Cyril how unprepared he is. Mr Jones is quiet for a few moments. He looks at Cyril's bank statements and frowns.

Cyril feels as though he has to say something to win Mr Jones over or his dream will be dead in the water before he's even had a chance to get going.

'Mr Jones, did you give George Michael a bank facility?'

'Yes, but he has a contract with a record company and his music is outstanding – I believe he's going to do very well for himself.'

'I will be just as successful as George one day. I just need a loan to get started,' Cyril says eagerly, hoping that his passion will sway Mr Jones' decision.

'Looking at your bank statements, Mr Gold – you're constantly running on an overdraft. It doesn't look too encouraging,' he says firmly, but not unkindly. 'What does your father do?'

'He has his own business in east London, making women's lingerie for Marks and Spencer's and a couple of other brands,' Cyril says miserably. He wonders how it is that no matter how hard he tries, he always ends up face to face with the bloody garment factory.

'Why don't you go and work for your father before you try setting up your own business? You could save some money and get some proper experience.'

Cyril is beginning to feel like a lost cause. He twists his hands anxiously in his lap.

'I don't like the business my father's in. My passion is music. Surely there must be something you can do for me?' Cyril asks desperately.

'Alright, Mr Gold. Tell you what, I'll increase your credit card limit by a thousand pounds.'

'Isn't that a very expensive and risky way of running a business?'

'Unless you want to ask your father to be the guarantor for a loan, this is really the best I can do.'

'I'll take the credit increment, thanks, Mr Jones. I want to be independent.'

Cyril walks to The Star and Garter feeling somewhat dazed and deflated. Securing a loan hadn't been as easy as he'd hoped. He sees Billy sitting in the corner reading a magazine and wanders over to greet him.

'Big Billy! How you doing?'

'Hello, Knickerman. You look like you've lost a pound and found a penny. What's up? You sounded pretty chipper this morning,' Billy says with a wide grin.

'What you reading?' Cyril says, deftly swerving Billy's questions as he plonks himself down opposite.

'*Playboy* – here, have a gander at the knockers on this!' He opens the centrefold, 'Hot, ain't she? I'd give her one any day of the week.'

'Is that all you think about, Billy? There's more to life than sex, you know,' Cyril laughs.

'Oh yeah? Like what?' Billy replies cheekily.

'Bloody perv. Congrats on the new record contract, though!'

'Thanks, man. What's your news? You said you had something to tell me.'

'I quit my job. I'm starting my own artist management business,' says Cyril, glad to finally have someone to tell.

'About time too. Never understood how you could put up with that officious little prick and his clipboard. I'm glad I got out when I did. It must be nice to move onto something new and exciting, though.'

'I got to listen to music all day and I made a bit on the side selling the records that didn't meet quality control, if you know what I mean.'

'You sly dog! Never told me you were hustling records.'

'It made up for the shit money they paid. If I'd have told you, everyone and their grandmothers would have known. You can't keep your trap shut for more than five minutes.'

'You make a fair point,' Billy agrees.

'Tell me more about this record deal then. Do you get the same share as the other band members, what with you only being the drummer and all?'

'Oi! Cheeky git. I'm just as important as the others. So, yeah, I get the same.'

'If you say so,' Cyril jokes. 'What are you going to do with the advance?'

'Well to start with, I'm getting myself some snazzy gear for my new look. This time next week you won't even recognise me.'

As Billy finishes, Eurythmics' 'Sweet Dreams' begins to play on the jukebox.

'I'm really happy for you, Billy. You're following your dreams. I hope I can do the same.'

'How are you going to find the artists for your new management company?' Billy asks.

'I'll let you know when I've figured it out.'

After lunch, Cyril meets Diamond Geezer on the corner of Brewer and Wardour Streets. He's a tall, bulky man in his late forties. There is a whisper of grey in his jet-black hair, but he's not quite a silver fox yet. Cyril thinks he looks like an ageing rocker rather than an estate agent. Diamond is wearing a dark blue

Crombie overcoat and has his hands deep in his pockets; a domineering figure.

'You only want deals, right? You'd best not be wasting my time,' Diamond says. There's a slight lisp in his south London accent. He looks down at Cyril.

'My budget's pretty tight, Mr… Is it Mr Diamond or Geezer?'

'Depends how much I like you. You can call me Diamond for now.'

Unsure what exactly this means, Cyril just nods and smiles.

'Of course, some people call me the Hammer,' Diamond adds menacingly.

Cyril has a pretty good idea what this means. He decides to carefully use his charm to get on Diamond's good side. Hopefully this will get him a better deal.

After viewing five rooms in various buildings, Diamond is getting a little restless. He thinks Cyril is naïve and inexperienced; two things that don't make for good tenants in his opinion. It's a learning experience for Cyril and he tries to make the most of it by asking Diamond lots of questions.

'This is the last one I'm showing you. It's the cheapest of the lot. It's busy with the market from early mornings until four pm, so it's a good place to attract business,' Diamond says.

The property is right in the middle of Berwick Street, in the heart of Soho. Cyril is pleasantly surprised that this place is the cheapest but wonders what the catch is. There's a sign hanging outside the black door offering 'models' for hire. Diamond smirks at Cyril as he leads him inside.

'It's an open-plan studio office with a small kitchen outside the top floor landing, but you share the toilet on the lower floor.'

On the way up the stairs they meet two of the resident prostitutes wearing skimpy nighties and chatting outside their doors. 'Hi girls. Looking lovely today,' Diamond greets them with a smile.

Cyril tries not to stare and follows Diamond. The room on the top floor has a heavily stained red carpet and a double bed with a mattress that looks in a worse state than the carpet. It's stuffy and smells of stale urine. There are two metal chairs; one is broken. Diamond opens a window to let some fresh air in as Cyril stands uneasily with his hands in his pockets. The room is like a petri dish growing mould and God knows what else; Cyril feels like he might catch something if he breathes too much.

'It's only one room, Diamond. And it's bloody freezing,' Cyril says stamping his feet to warm up, immediately regretting the action as a cloud of dust billows from the carpet.

'What, you got staff or something? How much space do you need? You can barely afford a cupboard with your budget, never mind a room. Just get an electric heater and Bob's your uncle.'

Despite the state of it, Cyril actually likes the room and he knows it's in a good location. He bargains with Diamond for a ten percent discount, highlighting the potential health risks of the mould.

'Deal. And I'll throw in the bed for free. Might come in handy if your new business doesn't work out, if you know what I mean?' Diamond says with a smirk. 'You'll have to sign a year's lease with my boss, Mr Soho. Or you can have a rolling lease, but that'll cost you extra. It's up to you.'

'I'll sign the one-year lease.'

'You sure?' Diamond asks. He knows Cyril probably doesn't understand the responsibility of a long-term lease.

The next morning, Cyril puts the small television and VHS machine from his bedroom into the boot of his car. He drives to Diamond's office to pay his deposit and collect the keys. Cyril then buys an electric heater, a writing table and a few brightly coloured fold-up chairs from a nearby second hand junk shop. He just manages to fit everything into his car. Cyril heads to The Star and Garter for lunch and then makes a call to the GPO telephone company, asking for two phone lines for his office in Berwick Street. After his second pint of lager and a sandwich, he goes to the phone again. Cyril places a small ad in two music papers, the *NME* and *Melody Maker*, announcing his new management company and giving his contact details.

Finally, he heads over to his office. He unlocks the door and smiles with satisfaction. It's not much but it's a start. He makes several laboured trips from his car to the office, lumbering up the stairs carrying the TV first. Then comes the VHS player with all his pop video cassettes balanced precariously on top, followed by the chairs, table and, finally, the heater. He spends a while shunting everything about to make the place look as good as it can. Next, the cleaning. This takes the best part of the rest of the day. Cyril has brought a few supplies from the cupboard under the sink at home. He hopes his mum won't notice. Then again, to see the look on her face at the sight of him cleaning would probably be worth it.

He cleans the suspicious mould growing on the windowsill and dusts the cobwebs from the ceiling. The kitchen sink is scrubbed until it shines. The double bed lingers in the corner of the room, a reminder of some of the sordid things the four walls must have seen. *It's never too late for a fresh start*, thinks Cyril as he begins dismantling the bed. He gingerly picks up the used condoms stuck to the bottom of the mattress and flings them into a plastic bag. Under the bed, there's a box of assorted sexual paraphernalia which also finds its way hurriedly into the bin. Just as he is leaving for the night, the red light comes on in the first-floor window. The girls are open for business.

Cyril is back at the room early the next morning. He has another busy day ahead, and Uncle Lew and his wife Sharon are coming over for a Friday night dinner later on. Gina will be furious if he's late home, so Cyril gets straight to work. He puts the kettle on while he jumps into some overalls and flicks the radio on. On his way to the office he had picked up two tins of white emulsion and some paintbrushes. Today he is painting.

Cyril is no Leonardo da Vinci, but his work is passable. The room quickly starts to look much brighter and more office-like; clean and fresh. It's just the carpet that lets the side down. As well as the ominous stains, the carpet is now flecked and spattered with paint where Cyril has been a little over exuberant with his dance moves. He peels up one corner to see what lies underneath. The floorboards seem to be in perfect condition so he manhandles the carpet up and lugs it down the stairs.

He leaves it on the pavement next to the mattress and some fruit and vegetable boxes. At four o'clock, Cyril sees himself in the mirror above the kitchen sink. He's covered in white paint but grins at his reflection and congratulates himself on a good day's work. *Best hurry home and get cleaned up ready for dinner though*, Cyril thinks as he climbs out of his overalls.

Cyril arrives home and has just enough time to run upstairs and shower before dinner is served. He decides that tonight he will tell the family about his new venture. After his shower, he comes downstairs to hear Elvis Presley's 'Suspicious Minds' playing – one of Alf's favourites. His aunt and uncle arrived while he was showering.

'Hello Aunty Sharon – you're looking gorgeous as usual. Younger than ever. Is that a new haircut? It suits you!' Cyril says, playing the charmer. He gives her a hug. 'Lew is one lucky man.'

'Oh, stop it you. Compliments will get you everywhere!' she jokes. Sharon likes a bit of attention and Cyril knows it.

'You know, our Lew used to look like Cyril. When he had a full head of hair, of course,' Sharon exclaims, admiring Cyril from behind as he walks into the kitchen.

Gina laughs. She and Sharon have been friends since their schooldays. Lew is talking with Alf on the opposite side of the room about the Tottenham and Liverpool game, completely oblivious to their wives' conversation. Gina excuses herself to the kitchen to get the food ready for serving. Sharon walks up behind Lew and starts playing with his hair to get his attention.

'Stop messing with my hair – there's not much of it left!' Lew says with mock irritation. He smooths it back.

'Can you two talk about anything other than football for five minutes? You've not even said hello to Cyril yet, Lew!' Sharon says.

Lew obediently walks into the kitchen to find Cyril and Gina crosses him on the way out with a Babycham for Sharon.

'*Shabbat Shalom!*' Lew says to his nephew.

'*Shabbat Shalom*, Uncle Lew,' Cyril replies, and they hug.

'Alf seems to think you've been up to something recently. Apparently you've been acting strange all week. What's it all about?' Lew whispers to Cyril.

'Strictly between us, I have something to tell everyone over dinner tonight and I might need you to back me up,' Cyril admits. The pair have a good understanding of one another and Lew knows not to pry with too many questions at this point.

'I have to say, I'm intrigued,' he admits.

Alf turns off the record player and invites everyone to

stand at the dining table. Gina reminds Cyril to put on his *kippah* before Alf asks Lew to say prayers. Everyone sits down and Gina holds up her Babycham to toast.

'Good health everyone! Tonight we have gefilte fish, chicken soup with matzo balls, followed by roast chicken.'

The men remove their skullcaps and Cyril pours everyone a glass of kosher wine. Alf puts on Gina's favourite record, The Beatles' *Let It Be*. Everyone tucks into their food – there's enough to feed a small army. The family talk over one another, sharing stories and laughing. Cyril struggles to get a word in edgeways, but he finds the rapport between his parents, Sharon and Lew to be very entertaining. It's a typically Jewish affair. Amidst the flowing conversation, Lew suddenly puts a bottle of French wine down on the table with a thump. He grins as everyone looks at him. Cyril's eyes light up when he notices the age of the bottle.

'Wow, 1961!'

'It's a Chateau Lynch Bages Grand Cru. 1961 is a spectacular year for Bordeaux.'

'Must be bloody expensive. Don't tell me, Uncle Lew… Did you get your big television deal?'

Lew nods his head. He'd been working on the deal for quite some time and it had caused him many sleepless nights.

'I just wanted to share my good fortune with you all over this lovely wine. I closed the deal this afternoon.'

There are many congratulations and shouts of *mazel tov*.

'An expensive wine, but is it kosher?' Alf asks, pointedly.

'Well you don't have to partake, Alf. More for the rest of us,' Gina laughs.

'Of course I will. Not every day you have something this exciting to celebrate,' Alf says hurriedly, not wanting to miss out.

The night is illuminated with good natured humour. Alf sings along to 'I've Got You Under My Skin', which makes everyone laugh. Cyril decides now is the perfect time to make his announcement. As the song finishes, Cyril stands up suddenly.

'Sorry for stealing your spotlight, Dad. But I have something to tell you all,' Cyril says confidently. Everyone stops and looks at him smiling. Cyril suddenly begins to have second thoughts.

'I want to make a special toast to Uncle Lew. *Mazel tov!*'

Everyone is slightly puzzled at the toast but they all clap and take a drink. Cyril is still standing so they wait expectantly. *It's now or never*, Cyril thinks.

'Don't tell me you've gone and got engaged,' Gina

asks anxiously.

'No, Mum. This week I left EMI,' he says finally.

'What! Did you get the sack?' Alf snaps, obviously shocked by the news.

'What happened?' Gina exclaims. She is still under the impression that Cyril is up for some kind of promotion.

'I did not get sacked. I quit on my own terms, actually,' Cyril says, trying not to get angry.

'I suppose you think the job fairy will just come along in the night and fix you up with something. Honestly Cyril I…' Alf continues.

'Let Cyril explain himself. I'm sure he has something in mind,' Lew interjects. Cyril is grateful for the interruption.

'Thanks, Uncle Lew. I couldn't take the EMI job anymore; it was killing me. I have dreams and I want to make them a reality. I know I can do it. I'm going into the artist management business – like Uncle Lew. I'm going to find the next big music stars.'

Sharon and Lew look impressed and smile at him proudly, but Alf and Gina aren't so certain.

'Okay, so who are you working for?' Alf asks, folding his arms.

'I'm working for myself, Dad. I've already got an office in Soho and I signed a lease for the year.'

Alf is turning redder by the second. 'Is life some kind of joke to you? How are you going to make money with absolutely no experience? How will you pay the rent? Don't come asking me for money; I'm not pouring my cash down the drain so you can prance about playing silly games.' He throws his napkin down angrily.

No one speaks.

'You could've worked for me,' Alf continues. 'Learnt everything you need to know to take over a successful business and make actual money. The factory is right under your nose but obviously you're too high and mighty for your old man's line of work.' He's exasperated.

'You can stuff your stupid factory,' Cyril says lighting a cigarette with a trembling hand. He doesn't want to come to blows with Alf but feels as though he doesn't have a choice.

Gina snatches the cigarette from Cyril's mouth and drops it in his drink. 'No smoking at the dinner table. And have some respect... Both of you!' she says, casting a warning glance at Alf and Cyril.

'You're not Uncle Brian,' Alf shouts, ignoring Gina.

'Enough!' she commands, and the pair fall into a disgruntled silence.

Lew takes off his glasses. 'I worked with Brian in the early days, when he'd just started out with The Beatles.

He didn't have much experience and he made mistakes – we all do. But he went on to become a wonderful and successful manager. The important thing was that he was passionate. And I see that same passion in Cyril.'

Alf begins to make a counter point but Lew silences him with a raised hand: 'And I would like to wish Cyril all the best of luck with what he's doing. I'm sure he'll make us all proud.' Lew smiles and nods at his nephew.

'Thank you, Uncle Lew. I'm glad you understand.' Cyril turns to Alf: 'I'm not asking you for money. Just your support, that's all. And if you can't manage that then you can sod off,' he concludes, leaving the table quickly before Gina can scutch him around the head for his insolence. He gets a glass of water from the kitchen and stands drinking it at the sink.

In the dining room, Lew and Sharon begin to make their excuses to leave. Cyril walks them to their car as Alf and Gina sit mulling over the events of the evening.

'You know I'll always be there for you if you need any help or advice. Let's have lunch together in Soho sometime; there's a brilliant salt beef restaurant not far from my office,' Lew says kindly. 'And don't be too hard on your dad. I know he's a grump, but he'll come around in time.'

Cyril nods and thanks him.

'I was in pretty much exactly the same position as

you when I was young. I was supposed to take over my family's garment business in Leeds. But I followed my dream and look at me now, thirty years on! The entertainment world led me to meet this beautiful dancer who would eventually become my wife,' Lew says sentimentally. Sharon takes Lew's hand and they smile at Cyril.

'You'll be fine,' he finishes, reassuringly before driving off. 'Call me!'

Cyril goes back inside, prepared for a lecture from his parents. But they're both already up in their room and Cyril is relieved to leave the matter for the night.

Two days later, on Monday morning, Cyril walks into the kitchen, grabs a slice of toast and pours himself a cup of tea. Alf looks at him over the top of his paper but says nothing. They have hardly spoken over the weekend. Cyril took the opportunity to hang out with his friends and play some football. He also worked his shifts at the disco in the evening. Even Gina had been giving him the silent treatment, which was very unusual. Things take a turn for the better that morning though, as the radio plays Love Affairs 'Everlasting Love'; Gina seems to soften and makes an attempt to reconcile with Cyril.

'I love this song. They're from Tottenham you know.'

She pauses. 'You're up early.'

'I've got to get to the office for eight. The man from the GPO is coming to connect my telephone lines.'

Cyril is about to leave when Alf unexpectedly holds out his hand. 'Good luck, son,' he says.

'Thanks, Dad,' Cyril replies, shaking Alf's hand.

Gina calls for him to wait and comes rushing from the kitchen with teary eyes and a plastic container in her hand.

'I'm not leaving home for good; I'm only going to work!'

'Sorry, I can't help it. This reminds me of your first day of school,' she says, handing him a packed lunch.

'Thanks, Mum. You're such a typical Jewish mama but I love you for it!' Cyril kisses her and runs out to his car.

'Good luck, darling,' she shouts after him.

Chapter Four

'Don't you want me?'

The Human League

Journey's 'Don't Stop Believing' is playing on the radio as Cyril pulls up on a side street in Soho. He touches his Spurs logo as usual before getting out of the car. It's just before eight in the morning and Cyril can't believe how quiet the streets are. It's oddly peaceful. However, when he turns into Berwick Street Cyril sees he isn't the only early bird. The boisterous market traders holler to each other, setting up for the day. He walks along the pavement, taking care not to trip over the many fruit and vegetable boxes strewn about. Cyril's attention is drawn to a confrontation between two men who are about to come to blows over something. In his distraction he walks straight into a box of fresh fruit.

'Oi, mate! Watch the boxes,' says one of the rough-looking market men. Cyril apologises profusely.

'You're new here,' he continues. 'Seen you goin' into number thirty-six last week. Some lovely girls in your building – especially that Sam.'

Cyril agrees and tries to appear friendly to towards the man, despite feeling a little bit intimidated.

'I'm Mickey O'Sullivan. You ever need anything… and I mean anything… I'm your man. I know everyone there is to know in Soho.'

'That's good to know! Thank you, Mickey. I'm Cyril.'

'See you around, Cyril,' Mickey says, and goes back to unboxing his fruits.

Cyril goes through number thirty-six's front door and makes his way to his office on the top floor. He can't hear anything from the other rooms. He is greeted by the smell of fresh paint, which is still rather overpowering, so he opens the windows to air the place. Cyril makes himself a cup of tea, not noticing that the milk has gone off until it's too late. He starts again and has black tea instead.

Cyril was expecting the GPO telephone man to arrive at about eight, but as ten o'clock rolls around he's still waiting. He's worked his way through his entire video collection. Mostly it's stuff he's recorded from *Top of the Pops*. Soft Cell's video for 'Bedsitter' is set in sleazy Soho and it makes Cyril smile; it reminds him of his office.

Another hour passes and Cyril is starting to lose patience; there are lots of things he needs to be getting on with. He wants to go and see if the music papers have run his advertisement but he doesn't want to risk running to the shop and missing the telephone man. After watching a couple more music videos he decides to knock on the other doors in the building to see if they will let him use their phone to call the GPO. He works his way down to the ground floor, with no luck. Then a door finally swings open.

'Hello, sorry to bother you but…'

Before Cyril can finish explaining himself, the young blonde girl behind the door pulls him inside. She deftly kicks the door closed and drags Cyril towards her, moving her hands over his crotch.

'Woah steady on,' Cyril says, taking a step back. 'What are you doing?'

'Oh, don't be shy. You've got nothing I haven't seen before,' she smiles. 'Tell me what you want. But cash only, yeah?'

'I think we might have got off on the wrong foot. I've just moved into the top floor; I'm not looking for sex. My name's Cyril Gold,' he says hurriedly.

'Sorry. I thought you were a punter.' She laughs as Cyril reddens. 'I'm Sam. What can I do you for, Mr Gold?'

Cyril laughs too. 'I just wondered if I could use your phone to call the telephone company. They were supposed to come and connect my phone lines today.'

Sam hands him the phone. 'Sure. But only 'cos you're cute,' she says with a wink.

After calling the company and complaining, Cyril asks Sam for another favour: to keep an eye out for the phone man while he runs to the corner shop to get his music papers. He arrives back with the papers and two bottles of milk. He thanks Sam and feels he might have made a friend.

Cyril eagerly turns the pages of the papers, scanning for the tiny advertisement he placed. He misses it on the first run through and has to start again. Finally, he spots it. 'Send your music demos to Cyril Gold Artist Management', it reads, with his phone number and address listed below. Beaming with pride, he leans back in his chair feeling pleased with himself. He drinks a whole bottle of cold milk to celebrate. Just then, someone pokes their head around the door.

'Ey up mate. Not sure if I'm in't right place. Looking for Cyril Gold Artist Management, but I can't see any signs.'

'You must be from the telephone company. Thank God! I was going mad waiting – thought you weren't going to come.'

'Bet those girls downstairs could have kept you busy. Lucky bastard. What they charge in here?' the man asks in a heavy northern accent.

'No idea, mate,' Cyril says impatiently.

After twenty minutes of running up and down the stairs, fixing sockets and wires, the man confirms the lines should be live. He begins to pack up his tools.

'What about the two phones I ordered?' Cyril asks.

'Someone else'll deliver 'em tomorrow or't day after. I only connect the lines,' the man says.

Cyril pulls a few notes out of his trouser pocket.

'Wouldn't happen to have some spare phones in your van, would you? I'll get you a price from the girls downstairs. Might even land you a discount.'

'Alright. I'll have a look,' he says and makes his way to the door. 'Just the price for a blowie, okay? Not got much cash on me,' he adds sheepishly.

Cyril nods. Ten minutes later he's alone in the office with two working phones. He can't wait to make his first call. He dials his home number and Gina picks up.

'Hi Mum! Guess where I'm calling from... my new office! My phone lines finally got connected,' he says excitedly. He chats for a few minutes before saying goodbye.

Cyril feels as though he's been cooped up in the office for ages and so decides to have a cigarette outside. On his way down the stairs Cyril almost collides with the telephone man ducking out of one of the rooms. The man gives Cyril a thumbs up and grins. Cyril nods, amused by the strange antics that the building seems to attract, and heads outside. When hunger starts to get the better of him, he returns to the office and eats the sandwich Gina gave him while watching a recording of Van Halen's 'Jump' on his VHS player.

The phone begins ringing, which makes Cyril jump. He rushes excitedly to answer it. Over the next few hours he receives two phone calls from people enquiring about being represented. He quickly tries to establish if they write their own music and what style it is. Cyril decides to ask them to send demo tapes and a photograph of themselves before meeting, so he knows what he's getting himself into.

There's a knock at the door. Cyril opens it to be confronted by a young man dressed all in black. His appearance is quite striking and Cyril is rendered speechless for a second. The guy's hairstyle and eyeliner catch Cyril off guard – he looks like he belongs in one of the posters on Cyril's bedroom wall.

'Hi, is this Cyril Gold Management?' he asks quietly.

'Yeah – I'm Cyril. What can I do for you?' Cyril replies, trying not to stare at the unusual hairstyle. It's jet black, side parted; short on one side and extra-long on the other. Cyril has never seen anything like it.

'I came down on the train from Sheffield this morning and saw your ad in the music papers. I was passing this way so I thought I'd just drop in,' he says, tripping over his words. He looks mostly at the floor, obviously very nervous.

'I've never been to Sheffield. The only place I've been up North is Liverpool. Can I ask, what kind of hair cut is that; is that the fashion in Sheffield?' Cyril says trying not to laugh.

The young man shuffles his feet and shrugs.

'Is it a wig or something,' he continues unkindly.

'No, it's real. It's unique, like my music,' the guy snaps back, looking up from the floor and straight at Cyril.

Cyril realises he isn't being very professional and immediately changes his tone. 'I guess you're looking for representation. What's your name?'

'My name's Phil. I'm looking for some management advice. Maybe you can help me?' He pauses before continuing. 'I have a small problem though. I was in a hurry to get off the train and in my rush I left my cassettes behind. I have all my lyrics here though and I can sing them,' he says, rifling through papers in a folder. 'Here, this one's my favourite. It's called "Don't You Want Me".' He shows Cyril the lyrics.

As Cyril reads the lyrics, Phil begins to sing:

'You were working as a waitress in a cocktail bar when I met you.

I picked you out, I shook up and turned you around. Turned you into someone new.

Don't, don't you want me…'

'These lyrics are kind of silly,' Cyril interrupts. 'You've got a good voice, and that's great, but I'm just not sure about the lyrics.'

'If you'd let me finish, it'll make sense,' Phil says. Before Cyril can say anything else, he snatches the lyrics back and storms toward the door.

'You're not the right person for managing me. I'm obviously wasting my time so you can get stuffed!' he shouts, slamming the door on his way out.

Cyril thinks that dealing with prima donnas is all part of the business and he finds his encounter with Phil very amusing. He rather likes the new-found power of being his own boss, but gets a little carried away in the moment. Cyril makes himself a cup of tea and settles down to drink it, trying to convince himself that Phil was a waste of time. His hairstyle was completely ridiculous. But Cyril can't get the song out of his mind. The lyrics and the tune are buzzing around his head. Perhaps I shouldn't have written him off so quickly and just taken his telephone number, Cyril wonders.

On his way home, Cyril calls into The Star and Garter for a quick drink. The pub is surprisingly quiet. As Cyril sits with his pint in the public bar, he spots a fresh-faced Asian guy sitting in the corner of the saloon bar. He notices the guy staring at him a couple of times. It's not the first time he's seen him; he's about Cyril's age and is always smartly dressed. As the young guy stands to leave the saloon bar, Cyril catches his eye and gives him a wave goodnight.

'Hey, do you work in the market?' the guy asks with a smile.

'Hi, I'm Cyril. No, I work…'

The young guy cuts Cyril off, turning his attention to an older gentleman who has just stepped into the pub.

'Sorry to be late, Georgie, ready to go?' The young man seems to shift into a different personality, becoming suddenly very businesslike. The two leave together. Cyril is slightly bemused but thinks little of it. He decides to head home, finding himself humming Phil's song as he drives off.

Cyril is listening to Prince's track, '1999' on his new, red Walkman, walking towards his office with a new answering machine for the phone under his arm; both paid for, like everything else, with his credit card. Cyril is expecting to see lots of post today. His advert has been in the paper long enough to have reached some people, he thinks. However, there is nothing waiting for him when he arrives. Over the next few days there is little improvement. He receives a few tapes of people singing cover songs, accompanied by pictures of men and women alike wearing very little clothing. The phones haven't been ringing; Cyril wondered if there was something wrong with the lines. Since Phil with the funny hair, he hasn't had anyone dropping by to see him. He recorded a message for his answer machine but there have been no messages yet. A bit of a slow start, but Cyril is trying to stay positive.

Cyril is expecting Billy to arrive for a chat over lunch. There's a knock at the door, but it isn't Billy.

'Hello, I'm looking for Genevieve,' says a posh, middle-aged man in a smart black suit.

'She's not on this floor. She's downstairs.'

The man apologises and leaves. It seems the only people knocking on his door at the minute are men looking for one of the girls downstairs. Consequently, Cyril has spent the last few days watching MTV and listening to the radio.

Suddenly Billy walks in, rubbing his head.

'Damn! I just hit my head on your doorframe.'

'Why don't you stop growing then, leggie,' Cyril says, glad to finally have someone here to see him. 'Your timekeeping is piss poor as usual.'

'I can be late, Knickerman. Everyone knows the talent never arrives on time.' Billy sits down in one of the chairs and looks around.

'Ha!' Cyril laughs, 'I've got more talent in my left big toe.'

'You call this place an office? It's so small I'm surprised your massive head even fits.'

Cyril tries to tip Billy off his chair and they throw a few fake punches.

'What kind of building is this anyway? I heard some strange noises coming from the other rooms. Can't believe your office is in a hooker joint.'

'Shut up, Billy. What's with the yellow shirt and the pink waistcoat anyway? Always knew you had leanings, you old queer,' Cyril jokes.

'I'm no poof. I'm straight as they come. You're just jealous that I've got some style. The chicks can't get enough. Besides, my manager says I need to look the part.'

The phone rings for the first time in ages, and Cyril answers it before it's finished the second ring. Billy is gazing out of the window, oblivious to Cyril trying to take a business call.

'Some gorgeous women in the market. I could stay looking out this window all day. Getting a semi-on already.'

Cyril waves his hand vigorously at Billy to shut him up.

'Fantastic, you just send me your demo and a photograph and I'll take it from there,' Cyril says to the caller and hangs up.

There's a knock at the door and Cyril answers it. It's another man, this time looking for Sam. He shouts at the man and tells him to piss off. He's the third one today.

'Who was that?' Billy asks.

'Another bloody punter for the girls downstairs. They keep coming to my office for some reason. Let's go for a coffee and a sandwich at Bar Italia.'

On the way out, Cyril waves hello to Mickey O'Sullivan.

'Is he a mate of yours? I got some gear from him before coming up to see you today,' Billy says.

'What are you talking about?'

'He sold me some weed. At a good price too.'

Cyril says nothing. They walk along the bustling streets, saying hi to the girls they meet along the way. The pair take a seat at an outside table; the Pet Shop Boys' 'West End Girls' plays inside the café.

'Did I tell you how good Kevin Cash is?' Billy starts.

'Is he the guy who told you to wear to fairy uniform?'

Cyril laughs.

'He's the best, y'know. He tells the record companies exactly what he wants and that's what he gets. He's a bloody tough manager.' Billy pulls a joint out of his pocket and invites Cyril to join him.

'Don't be stupid; not in public. Put that away,' Cyril says, thoroughly unimpressed, 'You know I don't do that stuff.'

'I think I'll buy a car with the money I'm expecting to get upfront from the record deal. The birds are going to love it,' Billy boasts, changing the subject. He slips the joint back in his pocket.

'I might sell mine. I need cash for the business. Would you be interested?'

'I'm thinking of getting a new one, not an old banger like yours.'

'You don't even have your licence yet,' Cyril reminds him, a little hurt by Billy's remark.

'My manager's golden rule is to never pay for anything. Get the record companies to pay for everything,' he says, making himself the subject of the conversation again. 'I've already told my mum I'm moving out to share a flat with the band. It's in Chelsea – it's the place to be,' he adds.

Cyril stares at him in disbelief. 'Billy, how are you paying for all this?'

'Polydor Records. And guess what? Next week the band are having a photoshoot with a proper photographer and everything.'

'I'm betting your magic manager got the record company to pay for that as well, right?'

'Bang on!'

As he listens to Billy, Cyril is getting a lesson in the art of music business management. He's pleased for his friend, but Cyril wishes that he could have some of the same good fortune that seems to have blessed Billy recently.

They order more coffee and Billy eyes up some of the passing women. 'Now she's hot for an older woman. They do say, with age comes beauty,' he grins, staring at the woman's legs as she stops for a moment to light a cigarette. 'Definitely wouldn't say no to her. I've always liked more mature women. I think it's because I've always been more mature than other people my age,' Billy pontificates. He tries to catch her eye but she doesn't notice him.

Cyril bursts out laughing. Regardless of his taste in women, one thing Billy has never been is mature. Billy scowls for a moment and then becomes very animated as he remembers something funny.

'Kevin told me this great story about someone very famous in the music business and it made me think of you and the knicker factory.'

'Go on then, tell me more.'

'A certain well-known rock star enjoys wearing women's underwear. Apparently, he loves the softness on his body,' he says, 'But he's not gay though,' Billy adds quickly.

'Who is it?' Cyril asks, desperate to know the gossip.

'It's a secret. I can't tell you,' Billy says loftily. Cyril begins to protest and quickly Billy relents. 'Okay, okay. I'll give you a hint. He wears tight leopard print trousers.'

'No! Really? I've heard that story before but I didn't know if it was true.'

'Did you know that Elton John's nickname is Sharon? And Rod Stewart's is Phyllis! They're really close apparently. Do you think there's something going on between them?'

'I think you're reading too many gossip mags,' Cyril says, 'Shall we head over to my second office?'

'You have a second office?'

'No, idiot. The Star and Garter. I need a real drink… and you're buying,' Cyril says, shaking his head.

Billy is getting the drinks at the bar while Cyril puts ABBA's 'Money, Money, Money' on the jukebox.

'Hey Big Billy, this one's for you,' Cyril calls.

'Did I tell you our band already has a few girl groupies?' Billy launches back into telling Cyril every detail about his new adventures, barely pausing for breath. 'I like to get them plastered with that yellow shite, what's it called? Advocaat, or something. They think it's expensive. I have a different bird almost every night and it's fucking great. Think I might have picked something up though – I'm a little itchy round the bollocks. Might be crabs or something.'

'Steady on, Casanova. People will start saying you're a romantic,' Cyril says, laughing.

After an hour of Billy's stories, Cyril is getting somewhat jealous of hearing about how much fun his friend has been having, even if some of that fun is morally questionable. Cyril is happy that things are going well for Billy but is anxious to get back to the office and get some work done. Just as Cyril is about to make his excuses, Billy spots someone looking at them.

'Don't look now but some burnt-rice Paki is checking us out.'

Cyril turns around anyway and sees the same fresh-faced Asian guy from the day before. He gives a friendly wave: 'You alright, mate?'

'Yeah, fine thanks, Cyril,' he replies.

Cyril smiles and turns back around, shooting Billy a glare.

'Oh, you know him then. What's his name? Speaks real posh, doesn't even have an accent. You meet some strange people here in Soho.'

'I've seen him in here a few times – he's just an acquaintance. Come to think of it, I don't even know his name,' Cyril says.

'Well he was definitely staring at us.'

'People have been staring at you all day, what with your bloody outfit and all. I'm surprised it hasn't caused a car accident. Come on let's go.'

Friday comes around and Cyril heads towards the bank in Soho to draw some money with his credit card. He knows he's going to have to keep DJing at the weekends and find more work until he gets the business on its feet. He doesn't know how long this will take; the few enquiries he's received from the adverts haven't shown much promise.

He spends the rest of the day lounging around the office without much to do. He's tired, despite having a largely uneventful week spending most days watching MTV and drifting between various pubs and Bar Italia. Cyril checks his watch; it's just turned four. He decides to give his Uncle Lew a call and ask for some advice. Lew is busy when Cyril calls but arranges to meet him at his house on Saturday, after Synagogue.

As Cyril puts on his jacket to leave for the day, Diamond makes an unannounced visit. He walks in without knocking which gives Cyril a fright.

'Shit, Diamond! You scared me. Haven't you heard of…'

'You never dropped off the rent cheque,' Diamond interrupts, pointing to the cheque book sitting on Cyril's desk.

'Oh, sorry. It's been a really hectic week. I'll write it now.'

As Cyril is writing, there's a knock at the door. Diamond opens it and immediately closes it again while saying 'Downstairs!'

'That keeps happening,' Cyril complains.

'Put a bloody sign on your door then,' Diamond suggests, snatching the cheque from Cyril and walking out.

Cyril looks at his cheque book and closes his eyes. He is beginning to get anxious about the running costs of his business. He seems to have a lot of outgoings with nothing at all coming in yet. Still, he's optimistic.

Chapter Five

'Don't Stop 'til You Get Enough'

Michael Jackson

Cyril arrives on Saturday afternoon at Lew's home in St John's Wood, a posh leafy neighbourhood in north London. Sharon invites him in.

'So lovely to see you again!' she says, pinching Cyril's cheeks. 'Lew is waiting for you in his study. Can I get you something to drink?' The music of 'Anyone Who Had a Heart' by Cilla Black is playing in background.

'Just water please, Sharon' Cyril says and heads into Lew's office.

'Cyril, my boy! Come in, sit down.' Lew greets him warmly, pointing to a chair opposite his large writing table. The walls of the study are covered with photos of famous show business personalities: Des O'Connor, Tommy Cooper and Cilla Black to name a few. The one that got Cyril's eye was Brian

Epstein and the Beatles with Lew at the Variety Club showbiz awards.

'Don't you just love this old song from Cilla? They don't make them like they used to.' Cyril nods in agreement even though he loves the current music scene much more.

'I saw your ad in the papers. I had to look pretty hard to find it, mind you.'

'Yeah, I haven't had much joy with enquiries. I've only had ten this week and one really weird looking guy named Phil who turned up at my office.'

'What do you expect from one tiny ad? And you only ran it for a week, right? Cyril, you need to think bigger! If you're spending money you might as well spend it on something worthwhile. Put in a half page ad in all the weekly music papers to kick off with – for two weeks, not just one. Then after that, run a smaller ad every other week.'

'I guess my little ad was never going to attract much attention.'

'Remember, image is everything in the world of music and entertainment. Brian understood timing and luck played a big part.' He pauses. 'Is money a problem? Do you need a loan?'

'No, I'm alright for now, Uncle Lew,' Cyril says. His pride won't allow him to admit to his uncle how much he's struggling for cash. On top of that, Cyril knows his father would be very cross with him if he went to Lew for money without seeking his help first.

First thing Monday morning, Cyril gets down to serious business and books four weeks of advertisements just in time for this week's papers. He manages to get them on credit. By Wednesday, the papers are out and Cyril's phones finally start to ring with enquiries from singers and bands. They invite him to watch their live gigs, and Cyril is finally busy as he rushes from one venue to the next. While he's out, his answer phone is picking up lots more enquiries. One of the messages is from Alexandra, reminding him not to forget their dinner date that evening. His girlfriends have been feeling neglected recently as Cyril spends most of his time working. He begins to wonder if having two women on the go at once is more trouble than it's worth. Then again, Hannah has been starting to lose interest recently, so Cyril is pleased to have had the foresight to bring Alex into play. In her message Alex said her parents are going away for the weekend, and Cyril knows exactly what this means. He decides to invite Alex over for Friday night dinner to meet Alf and Gina for the first time.

There are several messages from Diamond on Cyril's

answer machine, telling him to return his calls. Instead, Cyril calls Alex to arrange picking her up for their date.

'Hi Alex, sorry I missed you earlier. I'll pick you up on Stanmore High Street in an hour. Oh, and do you want to have dinner with me and my parents tomorrow? Okay, that's great. See you soon. I love you.'

As he puts down the phone Diamond barges into the office, once again without knocking. 'Where do you think you're off to, sunshine?' he says.

'Erm, well, I'm meeting my girlfriend for dinner,' Cyril says, putting on his leather jacket cautiously.

'I've been calling you for days. I've left you a hundred messages. Do I look like someone who likes to be ignored?' Diamond barks. 'Well, do I?'

'No, sir. What seems to be the problem?' Cyril stammers.

'You bounced your fucking cheque on me, you little twerp. And I don't get paid my commission if I don't collect the rents,' he snarls. Tiny flecks of spit fly from his mouth.

'No way. I'm good for the rent. I'll find out what happened to your cheque, don't worry,' Cyril says with more confidence than he really feels.

In one swift movement, Diamond suddenly seizes hold of Cyril with his huge hands and dangles him in the air by his lapels. Their noses are almost touching.

'How much you got on you? You best start turning out your pockets right now if you know what's good for you. Unless you want me to turn you upside down and shake you like a piggy bank.'

'I need this money for tonight,' Cyril says tentatively, remembering his date with Alex.

'You'll have trouble spending it when you've got no fingers,' Diamond replies, cracking his knuckles.

Cyril reluctantly obliges. There is enough money to cover Diamond's commission, but not the rent.

'I'll take all of this, and I'll be back Monday for the rest. In cash,' he snarls.

Diamond swipes the money and Cyril is left staring hopelessly at his empty hand. An anger suddenly grips him: 'That's it! Leave me destitute, you old cunt!'

Before Cyril can draw his next breath, he has become intimately acquainted with Diamond's huge fist and is lying on the floor with blood streaming from his nose.

'You'd better learn some manners, boy. If the rent isn't here on Monday, you'll get to meet my hammer... and I don't mean my cock.' Diamond breezes out the door, slamming it behind him.

Cyril can't turn up to his date with Alex with no money. She'd definitely finish with him after that. But he also can't face calling her to cancel. Cyril cleans himself up a little and heads straight home, thoroughly miserable.

After managing to avoid Alf and Gina on Friday morning, Cyril makes it to the office and attempts to call Alex to explain himself. He hopes she'll still come over for Friday night dinner. He tries calling many times during the day but has no luck. The only thing he brings to dinner that evening is a huge black eye.

'What happened to you?' Gina asks as soon as Cyril walks into the kitchen.

'Nothing. I just fell over; stop making a fuss, Mum.'

Gina gets some ice for Cyril. 'Where's Alex? I thought you were picking her up.'

'She's not feeling well tonight. Don't worry, you'll meet her some other time.'

Cyril works Saturday and Sunday at the disco. He hopes to see Hannah on Saturday night, as this is when she usually goes to the disco. Cyril scans the crowd all night but doesn't see her. On Sunday he does spot Hannah. She is throwing her head back laughing in the arms of a tall, handsome Jewish guy. The man looks quite a bit older than Cyril and he feels a pang of jealousy. Thankfully, he spies Alex on the dancefloor and decides to throw himself into impressing her. Judging by the way she is avoiding his gaze, Cyril can sense Alex isn't particularly pleased to see him. He persists nonetheless.

After playing Alex's favourite Michael Jackson song, 'Don't Stop 'til You Get Enough', Cyril is still getting the cold shoulder. He decides to take a more obvious approach and plays the Jackson 5 hit, 'I Want You Back'. When Cyril finally does manage to catch Alex's eye he gives her a big grin and waves. She shakes her head and turns away. A few minutes later one of her friends appears at the DJ booth, handing Cyril a note.

I'm not into Michael Jackson anymore. You stood me up on Thursday and you didn't even call me. I'm sick of your games and always having to pay for nights out. It's over.

P.S. You need to grow up!!

On Monday morning Cyril very much regrets drowning his sorrows in rum and Coke. Alex has left him; Hannah is seeing someone else. He feels very sorry for himself, even more so when he looks in the bathroom mirror to discover his black eye has only become even worse.

'Morning Cyril. You're late up this morning. Have you heard from Alex? Is she feeling better now?' Gina asks.

'She broke up with me, Mum. I don't want to talk about it,' Cyril replies miserably.

'Oh well. You seemed quite fond of that girl, Hannah, before. I wonder what she's up to.'

Cyril decides not to tell his mother that he knows more or less exactly what Hannah was up to on Saturday night. She was practically all over that guy.

'Your eye's looking worse today, you poor thing. Breakfast is on the table. I've got to run,' adds Gina.

Cyril has begun to realise that running a business is not as easy as he thought it would be. The idea of having to face Diamond later today fills him with dread. He knows it was wrong to bounce the rent cheque – the black eye serves as a reminder of that.

Later that cold morning, after a trip to the bank, Cyril nervously makes his way to see Diamond at his office above a striptease club on Brewer Street. He presses the intercom button and waits. Diamond calls him through and Cyril walks into the office; his eyes are immediately drawn to the plethora of naked woman adorning the walls. The room is hot and stuffy; Diamond leans back on his chair, eyeing Cyril up.

'Got the money?'

'I'm sorry about that, Diamond. It's all here in cash,' Cyril says, putting the money down on the desk.

'Thank you, Cyril. The next time you have a problem with the rent, don't start acting like a little bitch and talking crap. It makes me angry. And sorry about the eye. You really should know better than to call me names, though.'

Cyril nods his head.

'Wanna drink?' Diamond asks amicably.

'Thanks, but I'll have to pass. Got lots to do.'

The next day Cyril walks out of the bank in Soho Square and puts on his headphones, listening to the Bee Gees' 'Stayin' Alive'. He has just had a frustrating meeting with Mr Jones; the honeymoon period is over, and the charm of Cyril's banter has worn off. Mr Jones suggested Cyril sell his car as the bank is refusing to extend his credit card limit any further.

Upon reaching the office, Cyril collects the post. He shuffles through it on his way upstairs, putting bills towards the back and anything that looks interesting to the front. Cyril is suddenly startled by a man running past him, swiftly followed by a scantily clad Sam screaming something about not being paid. They clatter down the stairs and Cyril sighs, bending down to retrieve the letters that are now scattered all over the floor. As he approaches the office, Cyril hears his phone ringing and rushes to answer it. He leaps up the stairs two at a time and almost has another head-on collision, this time with a young woman who is sitting on the top step. Blondie's 'Hanging on the Telephone' permeates through her headphones as she takes them off to speak.

'Hi, are you Cyril Gold?'

'I am. Who might you be?' Cyril replies, wondering at the age of his visitor. She looks like a teenager but has the air of someone older.

'I'm Roxy. Nice to meet you,' she replies with a captivating smile. She is dressed quite plainly in jeans and a denim jacket over a black t-shirt; a slim build and an average height, with a flood of red hair that sets her presence alight.

Cyril is somewhat flustered and drops both his keys and the post trying to edge around Roxy in order to get to the door. He goes for the keys and Roxy for the post. They bang heads.

'Ouch. I'm so sorry. I just need to answer my phone,' Cyril says, cursing his clumsy awkwardness. With one hand rubbing his head and the other unlocking the door, he rushes into the office and grabs the phone.

'Hello? Yes, okay. Well, just post your demos and some photos to me and I'll get back to you, alright? Great, thanks. Bye.' He finishes the call hurriedly and turns to Roxy, who is looking out the window at the bustling market below.

'Sorry, what's your name again? And sorry about your head,' Cyril says.

'Roxy. I'm hoping you might be the first person to hear my demos,' she grins cheekily and perches on the windowsill, crossing her legs.

'Okay. If you want to leave them here I can get back to you.' This has become Cyril's stock line; he must say it ten times a day. But so far nothing has warranted a second glance.

Roxy remains seated on the windowsill and studies Cyril's face for a moment. She seems entirely at ease, like a cat nonchalantly sunning itself in the mid-afternoon.

'I'm dropping my demos off with two other managers in Soho today.'

Cyril is slightly taken aback by her frankness. Roxy clearly means business.

'Which ones?' he asks.

'Kevin Cash and Elton John's manager, John Reid.'

She has Cyril's full attention. He takes the phones off their hooks to stop them ringing.

'I suppose you know them?' she adds.

She holds Cyril's gaze effortlessly and he feels a little overwhelmed by the power of her self-confidence. 'I know of them; never met them,' he says, shaking himself into action. 'I'll listen to your demo now. What's your style of music?'

'I'm more rock oriented, with a mix of Cher and Bonnie Tyler. I write all my songs and I can tell you now, I'm not like anything you'll have seen before.'

Her claims are bold. Discovering someone new and different is something Cyril set out to do when he began the business. Roxy can talk the talk but can she walk the walk? Cyril loads the cassette into the machine and presses play. He turns away from her and closes his eyes, allowing himself to be fully absorbed in the music. When the first song ends, he lets the second play uninterrupted. The song finishes; he stops the cassette machine and turns around.

'That second song, "Waiting for Your Love", has something special. The lyrics are really clever. You've definitely got my interest.'

'So you like my songs?' she asks, her confident façade replaced for a moment by an anxious smile.

Cyril nods. 'Did you work with anyone else on the songs?'

'No, only me. I found a cheap studio to record them.'

'You have a young Chrissie Hynde look about you, except for the red hair.'

'I love The Pretenders! Chrissie Hynde writes amazing songs; I'd love to be a song-writer like her. I couldn't be a vegetarian like her, though. I love my meat too much.'

'How old are you?' Cyril says suddenly.

'I'm nineteen, almost twenty. Most people think I look fifteen; I'm still hoping for a growth spurt. I don't think I'll ever be as tall as you, though. You look like Elvis, but I assume you already know that,' she teases.

Cyril is impressed by Roxy's music and her cheerful, bubbly personality is certainly an added bonus.

'What do you do besides writing music, Roxy?'

'I work on the checkout in a supermarket in south London. That's where I live with my mum.' She pauses before continuing, 'So, are you interested in my songs, Mr Gold?'

'Please, call me Cyril. And, yes, I most definitely am interested. I've been looking for someone exactly like you to join my company.'

'Is that so?' Roxy asks, not completely sure what to make of Cyril and his strange office with the prostitutes downstairs.

'Why don't you join me for a drink down at my local – or, as I call it, my second office. I'd like to get to know more about you and your music.'

'I don't drink, but I'll join you.'

They walk together towards the pub and spot Madame J touting for business outside her venue.

'Hello, MJ. How are you?' Cyril asks.

'Business is bloody slow today, it's terrible. Are you going to introduce me to your friend?'

'MJ this is Roxy. She's going to be the first artist I manage. If she chooses me to represent her, that is. And Roxy, this is MJ. She helped me find my office.'

Roxy casts a glance at Cyril, wondering if he really

means what he says about taking her on.

Madame J looks down at her and exclaims with gusto, 'Well, you lucky girl. You'll be in good hands with Cyril I'm sure.' She flicks her blonde hair theatrically before continuing: 'You do have a pretty face, Miss Roxy, but you look awfully young for the music business.'

Roxy feels slightly intimidated but makes a concerted effort not to show it. She's not unaccustomed to having to prove herself in order to be taken seriously.

'She knows what she's doing, don't worry,' Cyril replies on Roxy's behalf.

'Cyril, those jeans are so tight! They don't leave much to the imagination, but what I am imagining I like very much,' MJ says fluttering her eyelashes and pointing down at the bulge in his trousers with a wicked grin.

'Come on, Roxy. We'd best go before MJ embarrasses me anymore,' he says quickly, waving goodbye to MJ. Cyril doesn't want to give Roxy the impression that he frequents Madame J's on a regular basis.

As they walk away, MJ shouts out: 'The view is even better from this side.'

'I don't think she likes me,' Roxy says when they are out of earshot.

'MJ's alright. She's just a typical drag queen. Probably jealous of your looks and your youth.'

'I don't know why. There's nothing special about me,' Roxy says, laughing.

'I wouldn't be talking to you right now if I thought you were just ordinary,' Cyril says as they walk into the pub.

Cyril takes Roxy into the saloon bar, where they can have a more intimate chat. Over a pint for Cyril and an orange juice for Roxy they discuss how to move forwards. Cyril suggests Roxy records a few more of the songs she has written, and she agrees. The conversation meanders naturally towards more personal subjects as Roxy tells Cyril she had wanted to study music and go to university.

'I got pregnant at seventeen and all my plans went to shit. You've probably heard fifty stories like it. It was an older boy called Struan. We met at a party and it was the first time I'd got drunk. First and last time. One thing led to another; I really had no idea what was going on.' She pauses for a moment before continuing.

'I saw him a few times after that and he seemed really nice. No prizes for guessing what happened next,' she laughs emptily. 'I told him I was pregnant and he disappeared. Not seen him since. Apparently he had a long-term girlfriend living in France and went back to be with her.

'My mum wanted me to terminate but I refused. It's

not been easy to get by but I know I made the right decision. And I know you're probably wondering why I'm telling you all of this, so here it is. I'm a single mother stuck in a job that barely pays the bills. I want to make something of myself but I also have a son and responsibilities and…' she trails off and sighs.

'I need to know that I can trust you and that you aren't going to let me down, or hang me out to dry, or get me pregnant and run off to France, or…'

'Roxy,' Cyril interrupts gently, 'I understand. We'd be in it together, one hundred percent. I'm not going to lie, I'm new to this business. But what I lack in knowledge I make up for in confidence, and I have great confidence in you already.'

Several moments of silence pass as Roxy weighs up Cyril in her mind.

'Music has been a light in my life for as long as I can remember. My mum used to have Helen Reddy and Carole King records playing all the time. I would listen to them for hours, getting completely lost in the lyrics. They were the women who inspired my love for music. My brother bought me a second-hand keyboard when I was young and it's been the one thing that's kept me going throughout everything. If I have a chance to use my music to make a better life for myself and my little Tommy then I know I've got to take it.'

Cyril is rather taken aback by what Roxy has told him but feels his passion for music reinvigorated by her story. He knows the best musicians write songs from the heart and Roxy seems to have plenty of heart to go around.

'Come on, let's put something on the jukebox,' he says.

'I like the lyrics to this one,' Roxy says as she chooses Bonnie Tyler's 'It's a Heartache'. 'Thanks for believing in my songs,' she adds, touching Cyril's arm.

Roxy sways to the rhythm and begins singing, swept along by the melody. When she finishes, claps and whistles erupt from the other people in the pub and Roxy blushes.

'Wow, that was great. Your first fans!'

'Thanks. They're probably just drunk.'

'Roxy, you really should believe in yourself. With your voice and your presence, you've got real talent. You catch people's attention.'

'So, I'm the single mother of a three-year-old and you still want to sign me up?'

'Absolutely!'

'Great. I'm going to have to run now – I have to pick up Tommy,' Roxy says, gathering her coat and bag, 'Oh, and you know I don't want to be some manufactured act, right? I want my music to speak for me.'

Cyril nods and watches her leave the pub. He gets another pint and sits down to contemplate the events of the day so far. He wanders back over to the jukebox and plays The Pretenders' 'Brass in the Pocket', feeling certain that Roxy is going to be the perfect client to get the business going.

The young Asian guy that had caught Cyril's eye the other day strolls into the bar. When he spots Cyril, he heads over.

'Hi, Cyril, how are you?'

'I'm good thanks… Sorry, I don't think I know your name,' Cyril replies. He thinks the man's name is Georgie but doesn't want to embarrass himself by getting it wrong.

'I'm Jerome,' he smiles, taking a seat next to Cyril.

'You're not a Londoner, are you?' Cyril asks.

'No, I was born and grew up in Bradford,' Jerome replies, 'I've seen you in here a lot – don't you have a home to go to?' he asks jokingly.

'As a matter of fact, I do. I run an artist management business and my office is nearby, so I like to call in here for a drink most days. I sign artists up with record companies and stuff like that,' Cyril says, playing it cool to try and impress Jerome.

'Nice to be running your own business at your tender age. You can't be more than twenty-one, right?'

'I'm twenty-three, actually.'

'Same age as me!'

'You look younger,' Cyril retorts.

'It's the Asian genes. We look younger than you Caucasians.'

They laugh.

'So, you must meet some interesting people in your line of work,' Jerome continues.

'It's been a bit of a slow start but it's started to pick up now. In my first week I had this weird guy with the funniest haircut – long on one side and short on the other. His song was silly but the melody was quite catchy. He was from Sheffield, near your neck of the woods.'

'Some great music coming out of Sheffield: Thompson Twins, ABC, Heaven 17,' Jerome adds.

Cyril agrees, but is bluffing; he hasn't heard of any of these bands and makes a mental note to check them out later.

'To be honest, I think I might have missed an opportunity with him. I didn't even take his phone number so I can't get in contact with him again,' Cyril laments, 'You seem to know a lot about music, do you work in the business?'

'No, I'm a student doing business studies.'

'Do you live nearby?'

'Yeah, I live in Chinatown. When I'm not studying I work around here too.'

When Jerome doesn't elaborate on what he does, Cyril becomes very curious but decides not to press any further. Jerome has a charming northern friendliness about him and comes across as both intelligent and streetwise. Cyril is certain there is more to him than meets the eye; the confidence he exudes is far greater than that of your average student.

The pair chat for a while and one drink leads to another. Cyril tells Jerome how excited he is to work with Roxy.

'You seem to really believe in this girl. She must be good. Do you have any cassettes of her music? I may not be in the business but I do have a few music contacts,' says Jerome.

'Hey, that's great! I need all the help I can get. I'll get a copy of her demos made up for you. Thanks,' Cyril says, raising a toast to Jerome.

'Have you found any good venues in Soho yet?'

'I've not seen anything except girlie bars so far. I've not been looking, really.'

'You should check out Ronnie Scott's on Frith Street, Café de Paris… oh, and the Embassy Club.'

'I've never heard of those. Except Ronnie Scott's – that's a jazz club, right? I wouldn't have guessed you were into jazz.'

'Why? Because I'm an Asian boy from Bradford?' They both chuckle loudly.

The drinking continues and the pair are already getting tipsy. They laugh and share stories, relaxing into each other's company.

'My father has a lingerie business. He wants me to work with him but I hate the idea of making and selling underwear!' Cyril exclaims.

'Ha! I was supposed to join my father's business, too. He owns a chain of curry houses in Bradford. I hated the idea of smelling like a poppadom all day,' Jerome shouts excitedly, banging his hand on the table. When the laughter subsides, he continues.

'I had a pretty major disagreement with my family. I don't keep in touch anymore.'

'I'm sorry to hear that. Is that why you came to London?'

'Yeah,' Jerome says sadly. 'Another drink?'

He pulls another large banknote out for the drinks.

'Whatever you do when you're not studying must pay very well,' Cyril says, unable to contain his curiosity any longer.

'A little of this, a little bit of that. You know how it is. A guy's gotta do what he's gotta do to get by,' Jerome replies elusively. 'Cheers.'

They clink glasses and drink. Cyril guesses Jerome is involved in one of two things: drugs or prostitution.

'Cyril, I like your smile.'

'Smile?'

'Are you dating anybody at the minute?' Jerome asks directly, his inhibitions lost with the previous pint.

'Well, I was with Alex. But that didn't end so great.'

'Sorry to hear that. Glad to know you're a friend of Dorothy's, though,' Jerome replies, nudging Cyril and winking.

'Dorothy? Who's Dorothy?'

'You are… gay… aren't you?' Jerome whispers, beginning to feel as though he has misread the situation.

'Gay? No, I'm not gay,' Cyril replies looking puzzled, 'Oh, you thought Alex was a guy.' He laughs heartily.

'My mistake. You Jewish boys do come across camp.'

'I'm guessing you're gay then. I wouldn't have thought it just looking at you,' Cyril says.

'I am, but I'm not camp, am I? I'd describe myself as straight-acting. There are so many gay queens working in the music business, Cyril. You know that don't you?' Jerome says loudly.

'Keep your voice down, Jerome! People are staring. I don't care if you or anyone else is gay – each to their own I say. Cheers!' They drink again.

'My family organised an arranged marriage for me

and an Asian Muslim girl. I couldn't pretend to be someone I wasn't; it wouldn't have been fair on the girl. I wanted to tell my parents, but they couldn't even comprehend the word homosexual!'

Cyril laughs and leans back in his chair. He's laughed so much in the last few hours that his sides ache. The pair sit in silence for a few seconds before Jerome chimes in.

'Well, Cyril, one thing we still have in common is that we're both circumcised!' The pair burst into laughter again.

Later, as Cyril walks back to his car drunk on happiness and beer, he thinks about what an amazing day he's had. Little does Cyril know, he has just met the two most important people of his life.

Chapter Six

'I Can't Get No Satisfaction'

The Rolling Stones

Cyril is at home eating breakfast before he goes to work. It's been two weeks since he first met Roxy and since then he has been sending her demos to the A&R department of every record company. Things with the business are finally starting to move and his imagination is constantly drifting towards the endless possibilities on the horizon.

Collecting his keys from the kitchen side, Cyril sees a letter addressed to him. Inside he finds some money with a handwritten note from Gina. She writes that she is very proud of him for working so hard but knows that some extra cash always makes things easier. She signs off, 'God bless and love you', with three kisses. With a smile, Cyril turns off the radio which is playing Dead or Alive's 'You Spin Me Round (Like a Record)' and heads out the door.

He parks his car in his usual spot in Soho and hurries towards the office, looking forward to seeing Roxy and listening to her new demos. After learning that Roxy doesn't like tea, Cyril had gone out and bought a jar of coffee granules ready for their meeting. He sets it down on the table and tidies the place up a little before Roxy arrives. When she turns up at midday, Cyril greets her with a beaming smile, clutching the granulated coffee enthusiastically.

'Hi Roxy! Coffee?'

'Ha, yeah. Thanks,' she laughs emptily.

Cyril notices Roxy isn't her usual bubbly self. After he makes the drink and sits down opposite, he tentatively enquires whether she's okay. Roxy sighs and stares at her cup for a few moments before replying.

'It's been a difficult few days. My little Tommy was in the hospital with a high fever.'

Cyril does his best to sound sympathetic but is itching to hear the demos. He wonders how he can guide the conversation in that direction without seeming callous.

'Your phones are very quiet today. They were ringing nonstop the last time I was here,' she says.

'Well, you know how it is. Some days are busier than others. Perhaps everyone's gone on holiday,' he replies, more to convince himself than Roxy. Truthfully, the phones have not been ringing much recently but Cyril hopes that throwing all his attention towards Roxy will pay off. He takes this as an opportunity to ask about the demos, but Roxy fires back with questions about the record companies Cyril has already contacted.

'Any news yet?' she asks with a combination of excitement and anxiousness. 'What do they think?'

Cyril can't bring himself to tell Roxy the exact truth; none of them have returned his calls.

'It's only been just over a week since I sent the demos out, Roxy. Things take time – we just have to be patient for now. The people in A&R are always really busy,' Cyril says, hoping he sounds reassuring. He must have made a hundred calls since sending them.

'What's A&R?' Roxy asks.

'Artist and Repertoire. They find new artists for the record labels. There's usually more than one person involved in the decision-making process and that's why it takes so long to hear back from them.'

'Have you really not had any feedback at all? Not even a phone call?' she asks looking anxious.

'Don't worry. We just need to make an extra effort to get you noticed. I thought sending some pictures with your demos might help, so I've brought my camera. It'll be hard for them not to pay attention to that killer smile!' Cyril says, pulling his Polaroid camera out.

'We'll take a few and then I'll listen to your new songs.'

He puts a chair over to a well-lit part of the room and gestures for Roxy to sit.

'Okay, I want to get a few different ones that really capture your personality. Jacket on or off? I think off, what about you?'

Before Roxy can answer, there is a thunderous knock at the door which makes them both jump. Cyril opens the door to find an older man, very red in the face and looking as though he might spill out from the confines of his suit at any moment.

'I'm looking for Mandy. Her pimp told me she's here,' he growls, attempting to barge past Cyril.

'You've got the wrong room. Can't you read the sign?' Cyril says. His attempts to close the door are halted by the man's huge fist.

'Are you Mandy?' the man asks, seeing Roxy over Cyril's shoulder, 'I paid upfront so there's no use hiding.'

'I told you: you've got the wrong room,' Cyril hisses.

'Alright. Well, she'll do. How old are you, love?' he shouts in Roxy's direction.

'Fuck off or I'll call the police, you hear me?' Cyril replies with a final shove, heaving the man back into the corridor and closing the door. His aggressive ranting slowly fades away. Roxy is becoming suspicious of Cyril and stands nervously in the middle of the room.

She feels as though she has put herself in a dangerous situation with a guy she barely knows and is suddenly having second thoughts about her new manager.

'Cyril, I...' she begins.

'I'm really sorry. Ignore that pervert. It's part of the charm of having an office in Soho,' Cyril jokes, unaware of how much the encounter has shaken Roxy.

'When will I get to meet someone from the record companies? she asks. 'I don't want to just wait around for something to happen.'

'Let's just get these photos done, okay? They're more likely to get in touch once they have a face to put with the voice.' Cyril begins snapping pictures.

'You're not using these to pimp me out, are you?' Roxy asks, only half joking.

'What? No, of course not!' Cyril says, 'Unless you count the record companies.'

Roxy doesn't smile at Cyril's joke and instead looks down at her feet.

'Are you okay, Roxy?'

After a few moments she finally replies. 'I didn't record any new demos. I don't have the money to pay for it. And to top it off my stupid younger brother, Jason, has decided to follow in my dad's footsteps and get himself locked up for armed robbery. We grew up on a council estate in Peckham and it's not easy to escape the lure of crime as a way to make a quick buck. I didn't want to tell you,' she says, looking up at Cyril and trying hard not to cry.

Cyril gives her a hug. 'Life hands us all sorts of shit. I don't care what's in your past, only all the amazing things you're going to do in the future.'

He pauses for a second before pulling out the envelope of money Gina left for him that morning and putting it in Roxy's hand. 'Here,' he says. 'Take this and get those demos done.'

'Is this your pimp money?' she asks with a sly smile. 'Are you definitely sure you want me to have this?'

Roxy has never been one for taking handouts but is touched by Cyril's actions and knows this is the only realistic way she's going to move forward with her music.

Cyril laughs. 'No, it's not. But yes, I'm definitely sure.'

She gets up and gives Cyril a small peck on the cheek as she leaves, feeling as though she may have underestimated him.

Alone in the office, Cyril realises he's broken the first rule of artist management: don't pay for demos. But he isn't upset about it. He feels a warm glow creeping up into his soul, which takes him a little by surprise. Shaking himself, he turns his attention to the television. MTV is showing the music video for Foreigner's 'Waiting for a Girl Like You.'

'I've been waiting for a girl like you

To come into my life

I've been waiting for a girl like you (waiting for a girl)

A love that will survive

I've been waiting for someone new (I've been waiting)

To make me feel alive.'

Another few weeks pass and Cyril hears nothing from the record companies. He really thought sending out Roxy's new demos with the photos would generate at least some interest. It seems the A&R people are avoiding his calls.

Cyril wakes up and stares at the empty rum bottle lying on the bedroom carpet. A colossal hangover thumps away inside his head. His constant heavy drinking has become more of a habit than a recreational activity. It's difficult to pinpoint the exact time at which depression rears its ugly head in your life; it occurs more like a gradual deterioration. But Cyril's complete loss of interest in women was certainly an indicating factor for him. With great effort, he rolls over and flicks on the radio. The Rolling Stones' '(I Can't Get No) Satisfaction' plays. Annoyed by the irony, he quickly switches it off again.

With no money to place adverts, he has had few

enquiries from new artists. Although he does fully believe in Roxy's music, getting the record companies to bite is proving nearly impossible and Cyril needs to start making money sooner rather than later. He has no more credit with the music papers and they're chasing him for their money, as are the other creditors he owes. The only payment he is up to date with is the rent, but that's due again in a week.

It feels like his dream is falling apart. Billy helped him out with a modest loan from his record advance but Cyril knows he can't rely on other people to prop him up for much longer – not without any means to pay them back. In a last desperate attempt to get some cash, Cyril has even put his car up for sale. He has a few offers for it, but losing the car is like losing a limb and Cyril is reluctant to follow through with the sale. Asking his father for a loan is out of the question; Alf already expects the business to fail and Cyril is in no hurry to prove him right. His options are fast running out. Cyril knows he only has one more roll of the dice with the business before he must consider the possibility of defeat.

As he walks past the calendar in the kitchen, Cyril scans his eyes over the dates and stops at *Rosh Hashanah*, the Jewish New Year in September. He promises himself this will be the cut-off date. If he hasn't found a way to really get his business going by then, Cyril decides he will switch to plan-B and try to find an artist management company to work for instead. He says a quick prayer, hoping some divine force might take pity on him, and then heads out the door.

To his dismay, the front tyre of his car is completely flat.

'Fuck, fuck, fuck!' Cyril shouts, giving it a good kick and hurting his foot in the process.

He hops about in pain, feeling as though everything in the universe is always working against him. Having checked the boot of the car and finding neither a jack nor a wrench with the spare wheel, he heads to the garage. For a moment Cyril forgets why he came in as he is surprised to see cardboard boxes stacked from floor to ceiling, filling most of the small garage. Wondering what his dad could possibly be storing in here (for Cyril had never seen his mum set foot in the garage) he pulls one down to have a look. Undergarments. Every box is filled with ladies garments; samples from Alf's factory. *He must have started to run out of storage*, Cyril thinks. It seems, in a sort of indirect way, that Cyril's prayers have been answered. Alf won't notice a missing box, but the ladies working in the Soho clubs would certainly notice the appeal of some new, high-quality lingerie. As Cyril schemes, he thanks Alf for unknowingly lending him a hand and promises to make it up to him somehow.

With three boxes of underwear in the boot of his car and the tyre quickly changed, Cyril heads to the office feeling a bit more like his usual self. He cranks up the volume of the radio and sings along to Joan Jett & The Blackhearts' 'I Love Rock N Roll'. Selling the underwear will do as a side-business for making money until the real cash starts coming in with the record deals, Cyril thinks with a satisfied grin.

On his way, he stops off at the bank to withdraw the very last of the money from his credit card. To his surprise, Cyril spots the business manager chatting with George Michael and can hardly contain his excitement. He waits around for them to finish their conversation and then makes a show of coolly strolling past George as he leaves, flashing him a professional smile.

'Hi George. I like your new song,' he says, concentrating more on looking cool than on where he is going – and consequently almost collides head-on with Mr Jones.

'Mr Gold, what brings you here? You seem to be quite acquainted with Mr Michael – do you know him?'

'We met at a record function a few weeks ago. He told me he admires you very much and he's grateful for everything you've done for him,' Cyril says. One of his many skills is being fluent in bullshit.

The manager is obviously glowing with pride but makes an effort to compose himself; 'Well, what can I do for you today? I haven't seen any money coming into your new account yet, which is most unusual.'

'Don't worry about that, Mr Jones. I should have the money coming in very soon, it's just bouncing around a few people at the minute – you know how it is,' Cyril says with confidence, hoping very much that Mr Jones does know how it is and that he isn't making himself sound like an idiot. Mr Jones smiles and nods, so Cyril continues: 'When it does, would you consider giving me a loan?'

'Of course, but you really must prove you can make money first.'

Cyril leaves the bank with a mischievous smile on his face; he has a plan to make some money and it's time to put that plan into action.

On his way to the office, Cyril spots MJ looking her usual exuberant self, wearing a brightly coloured dress.

'Hey MJ! Can I have a quick word?' he calls out.

'Morning, handsome. How can I be of service today?' she replies camply.

'I think I have something you and your girls will love. Come over to my office later and I'll show you.'

'I know you've got something me and my girls would like, but you always seem so reluctant to part with it,' MJ laughs, casting her eyes downwards. ' Anyway, I'm intrigued – I love a good surprise. See ya later alligator.'

At the office, Cyril spends the morning setting up his stall. He lays out an assortment of the ladies' garments in coordinated colours on the table and is quite pleased with the outcome. While he waits for MJ and the girls he watches a music video by The Police.

A while later there is a knock at the door. Cyril throws it open with a flourish, ready to greet MJ and not expecting to be confronted by three spotty teenage boys. He mumbles an apology and tells them to wait there a moment, closing the door in embarrassment. In his rush to scoop the lingerie back into the box he succeeds in scattering some of it onto the floor. Flustered, Cyril returns to the door and invites the boys in, apologising for keeping them waiting.

'What can I do for you?'

'We were in the area, Mr Gold, and we thought we should drop in. We saw your ad in the paper a few weeks ago. We're looking for a manager,' one of them says with a seriousness slightly undermined by the two others who are snickering at the rogue knickers lying just behind Cyril's foot.

'So, you three are Paddies from the Emerald Isle, judging by the sound of you. The Irish are renowned for being excellent musicians and having great voices, so you have a lot to live up to.'

The boys all speak in strong Dublin accents. The talkative one introduces himself as the lead singer.

'You must be the drummer,' Cyril says to the one holding drumsticks.

'How did you know?' he replies with genuine surprise, followed by 'Oh' as Cyril points out the sticks in his hand.

Cyril wants to talk more about their music to discover if they have any talent behind. Listening to their demo, Cyril isn't particularly impressed by their cover of a hit song. All the while they talk, the drummer constantly drums his sticks against his leg, using his thighs as a practice pad and occasionally chiming in to repeat what the lead singer has said. Cyril is struggling to envision what he might do with the group of boys when an idea suddenly comes into his head.

'I want to show you something. Here, watch this video,' he says, loading a recording of The Police's 'Can't Stand Losing You' into the VHS player.

'We're big fans of The Police,' the lead singer says, which is promptly echoed by the drummer and confirmed by the third member nodding vigorously.

'You guys could be Ireland's answer to The Police. You already look a bit like them,' Cyril says enthusiastically, only to be met by puzzled looks.

'Mr Gold, we see ourselves as more of a boyband. We don't want to sound like The Police. Besides, we don't write our own songs or play instruments.'

The drummer opens his mouth, either to remind the lead singer that the drums are in fact an instrument or to simply repeat what he said, but Cyril impatiently interrupts.

'What do you mean a "boyband"?'

'It's all about our voices and looks – our image. We don't need to play instruments to be successful.'

'Well you do have good voices, but you need to write your own songs and forget about cover versions if you want to stand a chance of making it.' Cyril looks at his watch, expecting MJ to arrive any minute.

'We're looking for a manager to finance the demos, work on our style and create our signature image,' the lead singer says confidently.

'Look, I want to help you but you'll need to find your own money to make demos. I can't help you with that.'

The band tumble out of the office in a bit of a daze and bump into MJ on her way up to see Cyril. She's out of breath from climbing the stairs and perspiring heavily. Cyril welcomes her into the office.

'Who are those cuties?' she pants.

'Paddies with big dreams but very few brain cells,' Cyril laughs.

'Oh, shame. We could do with a few more good-looking boys around Soho. Those stairs of yours nearly killed me – any chance of a cup of tea before we start?'

Cyril makes the tea and puts his metaphorical salesman hat on. He holds some of the garments up to himself and turns to MJ.

'So, can I interest you in some very sexy, high-quality underwear for just a fraction of their high street value? Looking this good should be criminal, right?' Cyril says, camping it up for his target audience.

MJ is a sucker for anything lacy and her eyes light up. 'Wow, they're gorgeous.'

'They come in every colour under the sun – you can have a different one for each day of the week! Here, have a look at some of the other designs too,' Cyril adds, ploughing through the other boxes.

MJ holds them up to her body and feels the quality of the material. She looks just like a kid in a sweet shop.

'I love this black and white number; what do you think? Does it come in my size? Extra-large, that is. There's a lot of me to love, right?' MJ rabbits non-stop, almost unable to contain her excitement. 'Jazz and my other girls would look great in these.'

After MJ has finished choosing her favourites over another cup of tea, she puts the cup down slowly on the table and looks at Cyril with exaggerated sternness.

'Now, young man. Be honest with me. Why are you selling these fine-quality goods at a knocked-off price?' she asks. 'I don't want the police banging on my door investigating knicker theft or any such thing. Don't follow in the footsteps of the likes of Mickey Sullivan. He's as crooked as a dog's hind leg that man.'

'Don't worry, MJ, they're legit. They come from my father's factory in east London.'

'Okay then. I'll call my girls and tell them to come over.'

Soon his office is packed with MJ's girls, who are all in varying states of undress as they try on the garments. More of their friends are on the way after hearing about the bargains.

'Ladies, ladies, there's no need to open the other boxes. They're all the same. Let me find the right sizes for you,' Cyril says, his words lost in a sea of giggles and high-pitched squeals. He rushes around trying to keep track of everything, which is rather difficult in the presence of twenty semi-naked women.

After two hours Cyril has sold a whole box of two hundred garments. He's practically rolling in cash.

'Cyril, you certainly know how to sell! You could work

on the market any day of the week,' MJ comments as things start to calm down.

'Thanks for all your help, MJ. I wouldn't have had anywhere near as many customers if it wasn't for you.'

'You can buy me a drink some time to thank me,' she suggests.

'Deal,' Cyril says with a smile.

Suddenly MJ squeals at the top of her voice: 'Girls! Time to get back to work, come on.' She shoos them out the door like a mother hen, winking at Cyril as she leaves: 'Don't forget that drink.'

Cyril takes a deep breath and punches the air. He's made more than enough to cover next month's rent.

With his adrenaline pumping, Cyril heads downstairs to chat with Sam. She also likes the garments and agrees to help Cyril by selling them to her friends. She returns a few hours later with his money and the empty box. Astounded, he sends Sam on her way with some cash to say thanks.

Just before six, Cyril is about to close the office when there is a knock at the door. It's Jazz; she heard about all the excitement she missed out on earlier from the other girls at work.

'I hear you have something for me?' Jazz asks seductively. 'I hope having all the other girls over here earlier hasn't tired you out.'

'I'm never too tired for you,' Cyril answers suggestively, taking a seat on one of his chairs. Laura Branigan's 'Self-Control' is playing in the background and Jazz hums along for a few bars.

'So, this is your office?' she asks, strutting around the room as though she is on stage doing a striptease. 'It's nice, but don't you get distracted by the girls downstairs?'

'No, they don't bother me. I've got good self-control.'

'You think you can resist me?' she asks, putting her hands on Cyril's shoulders and straddling his legs.

Cyril remains silent, holding her gaze. She slides her hands behind his head and plays with his hair.

'From where I'm sitting it looks like you might want to lose that self-control,' she whispers, sliding her hips towards him so that their chests are almost touching.

Cyril blushes. No woman has ever come on to him like this, and he is rather enjoying himself. In the name of professionalism, however, he quickly lifts Jazz off his lap and leads her to the box of garments.

'I think this one will look great on you,' he says, pulling out a frilly red number from the box.

'You have good taste. I love it.'

'It's yours. On the house,' he smiles.

'Generous too! I bet you're popular with the ladies,' Jazz says looking at him intently. 'Come on, though.

There must be something you want.'

'I'd like to take you out.'

'What? Like a date?' she exclaims with a playful smirk.

'Yeah,' Cyril replies confidently.

'Hah, you think you can get me on a date with a pair of knickers?'

'We'll go somewhere posh! You can choose. Anywhere you like.'

Jazz strolls up to Cyril and pulls a card out of her cleavage. 'Okay. Here's my number; call me.' She disappears out of the office, swinging the red lingerie in her hand.

'I will!' Cyril calls after her, slightly stunned by their whole exchange.

Cyril decides a drink is in order to celebrate his successful day and heads off to the pub. On his way he spots Mickey Sullivan closing up his market stall.

'Hi Mickey. How'd you fancy selling some underwear for me? Top-end stuff. Sam and MJ's girls have been buying,' Cyril asks quietly.

'Knocked off? Cheap, right?' Mickey asks.

'No, not knocked off. It's surplus from my father's factory.'

'Well if the price is right I'll see what I can do. I'll

come by your office tomorrow.'

The pair shake hands and Cyril makes his way to the pub. It's surprisingly quiet when he arrives and he heads straight to the jukebox to put on a song. He chooses Whitney Houston's 'I Wanna Dance with Somebody' and finds himself imagining dancing with Jazz. He is torn from his daydream by a tap on the shoulder.

'Hi! I've not seen you in ages. Can I buy you a drink?' Jerome says excitedly.

'Sure! The first one's on me though. Where have you been all this time? I was starting to think you weren't going to come back,' Cyril says as he gets the drinks.

'I've had my exams; all work and no play,' Jerome laments. 'I've got some great news for you though.'

'Me too! Let me go first. I finally found a way to make some money!' Cyril exclaims. He regales Jerome with the events of the day and they both laugh together until Cyril mentions Mickey O'Sullivan's name.

'Cyril, don't get involved with him. He's bad news,' Jerome says, suddenly turning serious. 'O'Sullivan is related to the north London syndicate of Irish gangsters known as the Adams family. Anything to do with money laundering, drugs, clubs and prostitution – they're involved.'

Cyril is surprised and thanks Jerome for the tip. He

knew Mickey was a bit of a con-artist but had no idea he was so heavily involved with organised crime.

'Did you get chance to play Roxy's demos for some of your contacts?' Cyril asks hopefully.

'Well that's my good news! I'm starving though. Come on, I'll tell you about it over a curry,' Jerome says, already pulling Cyril towards the door.

'Oh, tell me now, Jerome. The anticipation is killing me!'

Despite Cyril's complaints, Jerome makes him wait until they've ordered the food and two pints of lager.

'Before I tell you, I need to ask you something,' Jerome says, looking dreamily at Cyril: 'Are you sure you're not just a little bit gay?'

'Jerome! Are you drunk?' Cyril says exasperatedly.

'You just give me such a gay vibe.'

'Maybe it's because of my Jewish upbringing? But I'm definitely not gay. Not even a little bit,' he replies firmly.

'I'll let you into a secret, Cyril. I have a thing for straight guys.'

Jerome pauses and Cyril shifts uncomfortably, unsure what to say. Jerome doesn't seem to sense Cyril's discomfort and continues: 'I've been with a few straight guys. They say after five or six pints any man is up for it.'

'Not me,' Cyril says, shaking his head. 'Anyway, do you have some good news for me or not?'

'Sorry, I was just messing around,' Jerome says, trying to backtrack in order to hide his true feelings for Cyril. 'I played the demo to a client of mine. He's like a god in the A&R department of CBS records. His name's Ashley Goodman and he wants to meet Roxy as soon as possible. Is that amazing or what?'

'That's fantastic! I'll organise a meeting first thing tomorrow,' Cyril says. He's ecstatic and can't wait to tell Roxy the good news. He thinks for a moment before asking: 'What do you mean, your client?'

'From my part time work. It involves… meeting people.'

'What? You set up meetings?'

'My two best paying clients are in the music business? You get the idea, right?'

'No, not really,' Cyril says in confusion.

'Look, I don't get any support from my family, Cyril. How do you think I afford the school fees and the lifestyle here in Soho? Money doesn't grow on trees.

'I know that, but what exactly do you do?'

'My clients are very possessive. They all think they have me exclusively. I give each of them a different name – never my real one. You heard that guy calling me Georgie once, remember?'

'You never fail to surprise me, Jerome. I just hope you don't catch that awful gay disease they say is going round at the minute.'

'It's a risk, but I don't really have a choice. I only have three sugar daddies, so hopefully that'll keep the risk to a minimum. By the way it's not just a gay disease – anyone can catch it.'

'Jerome, I came here for your good news, which is wonderful, but so far you've managed to question my sexuality and depress me with the possibility of catching a dangerous disease too! I definitely need another drink.' Cyril shouts to the Indian waiter for two more pints.

The food finally arrives and the pair demolish the spread as though they haven't eaten for days. Their conversation continues.

'How about going to the Whiskey-A-Go-Go, just a few minutes from here?' says a slightly drunk Cyril. He has money in his pocket and is ready to have some fun.

'That dive? They'll take one look at my brown face and punch my lights out.'

Cyril tries to reason with him.

How many Black or Asian guys have you seen in that club?' Jerome argues.

'Alright, you've made your point.'

'We could go to a gay club? Heaven and Bang are

great – not far from here, too. What do you think?'

'I told you, I'm not gay.'

'You don't have to be gay to go to gay clubs. They're all about the music and having fun no matter who you are – black, white, yellow; everyone's welcome. Everyone there is really friendly,' Jerome promises.

Cyril pays the bill and they make their way to Bang, on the corner of Oxford Street. He's a little hesitant when they arrive but Jerome pulls him inside before he can have second thoughts. They meet an older drag queen taking the entrance fee.

'Ten quid,' she says bluntly.

'Do straight guys get discounts?' Cyril asks jokingly.

'Piss off! Another one here pretending to be straight!' she calls loud enough for everyone in the queue to hear. 'Do yourself a favour and have a look in the mirror, love. You're as bent as they come.'

Embarrassed and slightly annoyed at once again having his sexuality questioned, Cyril pays up.

'What's up with her?' Cyril asks sulkily. 'I was only trying to be friendly.'

'Don't worry about it. She's just got her knickers in a twist about something. The queens can have acid tongues but it's all part of their act to intimidate people. Take off the makeup, wigs and the dresses and they're very different people. Usually quite shy and reserved.'

They continue down the stairs into the main dance area where Donna Summer's 'I Feel Love' is blasting from the speakers. A dense cloud of cigarette smoke hangs in the air, blurring the edges of everything in an atmospheric haze. Cyril is surprised to see how well-dressed everyone is, the spotlights picking out clubbers in all manner of attire, from white t-shirts and blue jeans to leather outfits and tank tops.

The club looks more like a fashion show. Everyone seems to be having a great time. Cyril finds himself slowly trying to absorb the vibrant scene; he's never been anywhere like this before. The patrons are mostly men, with the occasional woman, but Cyril is unsure whether these are 'real' women or not. Guys entirely at ease openly kiss each other; it's a whole different world to the one Cyril is used to. He spots a poster on the wall about catching AIDs. There are six stunningly good-looking Go-Go boys dancing on rostrums in their underwear. Most of them are topless.

Cyril presses himself against the wall as the young clubbers pass him, several of them giving him lascivious looks. There are people with their faces made up in all sorts of different ways: mascara, vibrant eyeshadow, and more glitter than you would expect to find in a glitter factory. He had no idea that so many normal guys wore makeup. Cyril had only ever seen people on the TV or pop stars in magazines looking this extravagant. A group of four pass Cyril, each with an outrageous hair-do in a different colour; *they look like a walking rainbow*, he thinks with amusement.

Jerome returns with the drinks. 'Move away from the wall, Cyril. Don't worry – nobody will touch you unless you want to be touched.'

They move further into the disco and emerge on the first-floor balcony overlooking the dance floor. Cyril looks down at the hundreds of sweaty bodies moving around as if they were all part of one larger being.

'They sure know how to party. Must be a thousand people in here tonight.' Cyril shouts to be heard over the music. 'I had no idea there were so many gay people around.'

'Well now you know! Most gay people can't let their hair down in public. We tone it down – act straight. A lot of people stay in the closet.'

'Are they lesbians?' Cyril asks, pointing in wonder at a group of women. He's heard a lot about them, especially from Billy, but has never seen one in the flesh.

'Some of them are. Those two over there are butch dykes. You do not want to get in a fight with them unless you're happy being reduced to a skid mark on the pavement.' Jerome points Cyril in another direction, 'And those are either lipstick dykes or fag hags.'

Cyril laughs. 'Fag hags?'

'Straight women who love the company of gay guys. I know a few of them,' Jerome explains, as though he is giving Cyril a guided tour.

'Come on, let's dance!' Jerome says when KC and The Sunshine Band's 'That's the Way I Like It' begins to play.

Cyril throws himself head first into dancing like everyone else, enjoying the excellent music choice and the intoxicating atmosphere. After a few numbers, Jerome suggests that they make their way to Heaven nightclub, under the arches in Charing Cross. Cyril agrees without hesitation, swept along on his high of endorphins. They wait in the queue to get in.

'The guys in the queue here are quite different to the last place. Everyone's wearing checked shirts and jeans or leather. They all look so butch and tough.'

'For some of them it's just a façade. A lot of muscle Marys here – they look all big and strong on the outside but a lot of them are bottoms… Most of them want a dick up their arse,' Jerome adds in response to Cyril's look of confusion.

They enter Heaven to the sound of Soft Cell's 'Tainted Love' blasting through the speakers. This nightclub has more of an edge; a darker atmosphere in comparison to the vibrant colours at Bang. The men dancing shirtless with sweat beading on their backs are older and very muscular. The white lights strobe to the music's beat and the bass throbs inside Cyril's chest. There is a strong smell of chemicals lingering in the air and Cyril realises the smell is coming from small bottles that members of the crowd have.

'What are those awful smelling things everyone's sniffing at?' he asks.

'Poppers. Gives them instant highs and the energy to go all night,' Jerome explains, never missing a beat in his elaborate dance moves. 'Tonight is men only; more of a leather clone scene. They like their handlebar moustaches and looking butch. That's just how they look though – I'm probably more butch than any of them, really,' Jerome shouts as he and Cyril laugh.

'What's with the different coloured handkerchiefs? Is it some sort of code?'

'They show what kind of sex the guy prefers; whether he's a top or a bottom,' Jerome laughs, feeling like he's Cyril's tutor. 'Dominant or submissive and other kinds of fetishes. You know what I mean?'

'Who knew there was so much gay lingo to learn,' Cyril says in bewilderment.

Jerome goes to get more drinks and Cyril heads to the toilets.

'Don't get lost in the locker rooms downstairs,' Jerome

shouts after him. Cyril has no idea what he means.

He hurries into the toilets, fearing the many pints in his bladder may burst forth without warning. Cyril keeps his head down to avoid any misguided advances and makes it safely to the urinals. Mid-stream he is accosted by a tall black man who appears suddenly at the side of him.

'Hello, big boy. Looking for some action?' he says grinning down at Cyril.

The guy makes a motion Cyril can only assume means blow-job and he decides to make a hasty exit. Finishing his business as fast as he can, he quickly zips up and turns to leave. It is at this point Cyril becomes aware of the hive of debauchery occurring around him. On his left a skinny young man snorts a line of cocaine from the rim of a sink while his older, much larger, friend fights to coax some pills out of a tiny plastic bag. As Cyril passes the line of cubicles, his peripheral vision is filled by men making creative use of the tight space; the fluorescent light bouncing off bare arses and bellends alike. He averts his gaze and is relieved to stumble back into the main area of the club.

'Damn, Jerome. Some guy just offered me a blow job in the toilet. What the fuck!' Cyril is almost hysterical.

Jerome looks over Cyril's shoulder towards the toilets and spots the man coming out the door.

'You mean him? You're lucky! I'd love to get a good look at his arse,' Jerome laughs. 'I should have warned you about the toilets. Lots of cocaine and sex in the cubicles in this club.'

They dance until the house lights come on. As they are about to leave, Cyril turns to Jerome.

'Jerome, I want to thank you for showing me the gay scene and introducing me to how you guys party. I had a great time.'

Cyril gives his friend a hug before tumbling into the taxi, not in any fit state to drive himself home.

Chapter Seven

'I'm Still Standing'

Elton John

Cyril sleeps until noon the next day and wakes up feeling slightly worse for wear thanks to his heavy partying with Jerome. Despite his aching body parts, sore from the ambitious dance moves he was pulling, Cyril feels better than he has for a long time. He makes his way into Soho with his Walkman playing Katrina and the Waves' 'Walking on Sunshine'. Jerome's connection with Ashley Goodman from CBS records couldn't have come at a better time. Cyril is confident his luck with Roxy is about to change for the better.

As soon as he arrives at the office, Cyril picks up the phone to call Ashley and set up a meeting about Roxy. The call is brief; Goodman's secretary answers and arranges an appointment in Soho Square for next Tuesday at four o'clock. Putting down the receiver,

Cyril leans back in his chair, feeling rather pleased with himself. He finally has the opportunity to get a contract for his first artist. For a few minutes, Cyril disappears into a daydream about all the amazing people he will get to meet when he's a famous manager. He crashes back into reality as the office door bangs open to reveal Billy posing in the doorway, sporting yet another extravagant outfit.

'Hello, Knickerman. What are you looking so pleased about?'

'Look what the cat dragged in,' Cyril jests, leaning back and balancing on the legs of the chair. 'What have you come dressed as today? Some kind of gigolo?'

Billy makes a move to grab Cyril and laughs as he flinches. 'I've gotta look the part today. We're going to sign our record contract at Kevin's this afternoon.' He sits down opposite his friend.

'That's great, Billy. It's all go at the minute isn't it? It's a shame I don't have any champagne to celebrate, but I can offer you a cup of tea.'

'Seems like a fair compromise,' Billy says, lighting a cigarette as Cyril goes to make the tea.

'Since I like you, I'll even open a packet of biscuits,' he calls from the kitchen.

'Jesus Cyril, don't overdo it.'

Billy starts his usual routine, bragging about

anything and everything. He even brags about the toilet paper in his manager's building, but Cyril insists that five-ply toilet roll simply doesn't exist. Billy's favourite topic, though, is money. Although Cyril gets a little tired of hearing the same spiel each time they meet, he gets a good insight into how Kevin Cash runs a successful management company.

'You know, they even built a hidden clause for drugs into the contract. They go down as flowers or singing lessons. To top it off, they lay on extra girls at events to enhance our image. How crazy is that?'

'And this is actually in the contract?' Cyril says in bewilderment.

'Yep, it's true. Here, want some Charlie?' Billy asks, dangling a small plastic bag of white powder in front of Cyril.

'Have they started giving that stuff out already?'

'No. I just picked it up from Mickey before coming up. Really good price.'

'Be careful with that Mickey. He's probably cut it with washing powder or something. Besides, it's way too early for that shit; you shouldn't make a habit of it,' Cyril warns.

'I can handle it thanks, Mum. Kevin takes it all day long. Basically everyone does. It's the only way to get through long recording sessions.'

Cyril makes a disapproving face and decides to change the subject. 'Here's the money back for the loan. You've been a real friend. Thanks for saving my skin.'

'Where did you get all this money from? Did you sign a deal? I knew you had some good news when I came in; saw it on your face!'

'No, not a record deal. It's more of a side business – but that's as much as I'm saying. Only until I get a record deal, which could be any day now. I have a meeting next week with CBS!'

'That's good news! But why can't you tell me about your side business?'

'Because there's more than one reason people call you Big Billy, y'know. You've got a big mouth,' Cyril grins.

Before Billy launches into another story of his antics, Cyril tells him more about Roxy and the meeting with CBS.

'Billy, I can feel it in my gut. This girl is going to make it. Her songs really jump out at you.'

'You fancy her, don't you? I can tell by the way you talk about her. You must've shagged her – go on, tell me,' Billy laughs, banging the table.

'It's strictly business with Roxy. I'm not going to mix

business with pleasure.'

'Oh yeah. And the Pope's not catholic,' Billy retorts.

'How should I know? I'm Jewish.'

They chat for a while longer until Billy announces he has to leave to see a man about a dog, which Cyril knows could mean any number of things.

After Billy leaves, Cyril begins working on a strategy for the CBS meeting. After about fifteen minutes, the office door swings open suddenly for the second time that day. Cyril jumps and looks up. For a brief moment thinks he's seeing double. A pair of mixed-race twins are posed in the doorway, one carrying a massive ghetto blaster, the other with her arms folded. They look about eighteen or nineteen, wearing tight white t-shirts and black shorts that reveal stunningly long legs. Without even speaking, Cyril can tell they are confident and have attitude. He is slightly stunned by their sudden appearance and waits a beat before addressing them.

'Can I help you, girls?' he asks finally.

They girls don't answer, but the one carrying the ghetto blaster places it down on the floor and they assemble together in another pose. Cyril is confused and repeats his question only to be ignored again.

The girls finally seem to have themselves organised and jump into what Cyril realises is a rehearsed routine.

'Hey! Are you Cyril Gold?' one of the twins asks, waving a finger at him. 'I'm Ruby.'

The other twin chimes in: 'I'm Cheryl.'

'Together we are Rub and C,' they both say simultaneously with accompanying hand movements. 'We want your money!' they continue, pointing at Cyril again.

Cyril is happily going along for the ride and grins, finding the display rather amusing. He opens his mouth to speak just as Ruby swiftly hits play on the ghetto blaster and ear-splittingly loud music starts blaring into the room, giving Cyril yet another fright. They begin dancing in sync, shaking everything their mother gave them to the booming beat of the music.

'We want your money; give me, give me your money,' they sing in harmony.

The impromptu performance takes over Cyril's whole office; he's never seen anything like it before. One of the twins suddenly jumps on the table while singing, pointing seductively at Cyril. The other thrusts herself towards Cyril and pulls him out of his chair and, before he knows it, he is part of the routine. The movements become more erotic, and then build towards a frenzied climax at the end of the song, finishing with an elaborate move involving the splits. The pair finish their routine with a pose on the floor and Cyril is left standing in the middle of the room. He claps as they stand up.

'Wow! I didn't see that coming. Did you write that song?' Cyril asks, almost weeping with delight.

Still recovering their breath from the performance, they both nod.

'So, it's Ruby and Cheryl? Did I get it right?' he asks, pointing to each twin.

'Yeah. And together we're Rub and C,' they repeat enthusiastically.

'Well I think you girls are great. What a performance! So, tell me a bit about yourselves.'

'We live with our Irish mother and Jamaican father in Tottenham. Go Spurs!'

Cyril's face lights up at this. 'No way. I'm a big Tottenham fan. Do you have any more songs for me to listen to?'

'We have a few more but this is the only one recorded in a studio. We need money to record some more,' Ruby says as she hands Cyril a cassette.

Cyril listens to the recordings and begins to get even more excited. They are only very rough, but the talent is there.

'We do our own choreography and we design and make our own clothes too,' Cheryl explains.

'We're nineteen and we're both studying fashion at

St Martins College in London. We need a manager who can help us make more demos and get us signed with a record company,' Ruby adds.

Cyril takes the contact details of the twins and does his best to reassure them he's the best person to be their manager. He also offers to pay for more demos on the understanding that he has first refusal on their contract. The new-found cash is coming in really handy, he thinks. The girls make their way out of the office singing 'We're in the money' and Cyril flops down on the chair, hardly able to believe his luck. As he comes down from cloud nine, he puts the radio. 'Just Can't Get Enough' by Depeche Mode is playing. Everything seems to be looking up for Cyril. He decides to call in sick and not do his shift at the disco on Saturday. His good luck has not only brought about the return of his mojo, but also his sex drive.

Cyril calls Jazz to try and arrange the date she promised him. Unfortunately, she is busy this Saturday and they organise to meet the week after instead. Cyril is quite unable to contain himself for another whole week and decides to call up one of his other friends from the disco and meet for a drink. He tries Emma first, who is also not free, and then turns the pages of his address book until he comes to Danielle. A petite blonde physical education teacher, she's twenty-one and newly single. Cyril is certain she'll be up for some fun.

Danielle is more up for it than Cyril had expected, inviting herself round to his house when she hears that his parents are out of town for the weekend visiting Gina's family in Liverpool. She appears at the front door on Saturday afternoon with a bottle of champagne in hand.

'Nice one. French Champagne. You have style! I thought it might have been Babycham.'

Danielle is wearing light blue jeans and an off the shoulder top. She hurries inside and is almost on top of Cyril as soon as he closes the door. As they head upstairs, Cyril slaps her firm bottom and Danielle squeals.

'I've being hoping you can give me some physical education,' Cyril says seductively as he takes off his shirt.

'How long did it take you to come up with that one?' Danielle laughs, putting her hands on his toned abs.

They spend the rest of Saturday and all of Sunday morning in bed. Cyril is in awe of Danielle, who seems to have an even higher sex drive than him. He gives her the nickname 'Mighty Mouse'.

Just before midday on Sunday he thanks her for a great time and hurries her out of the door just as

Tottenham are about to kick off. Cyril is completely drained and falls asleep watching the game.

On Monday morning, Cyril wakes up still feeling exhausted after working late at the disco Sunday evening. Danielle was at the disco too. Every so often she would catch Cyril's eye and give him a knowing grin. He drove her home after the disco and spent another hour kissing and caressing her in his car.

He stumbles out of bed, flicking on the radio which is playing Elton John's 'I'm Still Standing'. Cyril makes for the bathroom, still thinking about his eventful weekend. Only when he looks in the mirror does he see the love bites on his neck. He panics and rifles through Gina's make-up to find something to cover them up. With no idea what any of the various creams are, he gives in and heads to the chemist instead. He buys a neck brace to hide the love bites, thinking he can just tell people he pulled a muscle. He hopes they disappear before his date with Jazz.

Cyril finds his answer machine full of messages. He makes a cup of tea and starts listening to them, skipping the unimportant ones. Roxy has left a message saying she has recorded her new demos; she sounds excited and Cyril hopes she is feeling better after her tough week. She says she's nervous about the meeting and that she's grateful Cyril will be there for support. Cyril smiles and plays the message again just to listen to her voice. In the background, the radio plays Nina Simone's 'My Baby Just Cares For Me'.

He clicks onto the next message and is chilled to hear Diamond's voice. He asks for Cyril to call him back but doesn't give anything else away.

The final message is from Jerome, who was obviously drunk at the time. The message is garbled and difficult to understand. It sounds as though he's in a club as there is music playing. Jerome is wittering on about someone called Mary who apparently wants to put Roxy on TV. Cyril shakes his head and laughs.

Just as Cyril is about to try and call Jerome back to ask about this mysterious Mary person, Diamond breezes into his office. Cyril wonders why he bothers having a door since no one ever knocks.

'Diamond, what brings you here?' Cyril says amicably, hoping he isn't about to get another black eye. Diamond looks quite angry, but Cyril has come to realise he always looks angry.

'What's your game? Have you been avoiding my calls?'

'No, I've only just got to the office. I was just about to call you back,' Cyril explains, gesturing for him to take a seat.

'Don't worry, I'm not here to beat you up today. Looks like someone else already beat me too it,' Diamond says, gesturing to the neck brace. 'I hear you've been doing deals selling ▨▨▨▨▨ and I'm pretty pissed that you haven't given me a look in. My boss, Mr Soho, could move a lot of product for you.'

Cyril is relieved that the issue can be resolved without any physical injury. 'I'm a bit short on stock at the moment. You'll be the first to know when I have more, I promise.'

'My commission is five per cent of the sales, paid in cash, alright?'

Cyril agrees to Diamond's terms and sees him out.

Before Cyril has a chance to call Jerome, he drops by the office sporting a new hairstyle; blonde highlights in his usual jet-black hair. This is the first time Jerome has been to the office and he laughs when Cyril offers to give him a tour.

'I think I can see everything I need to see from here. I was expecting something a bit bigger.'

'Well, I'm just starting out. Anyway, what's with the new hair? You must spend a fortune on your image.'

'What do you expect from a gay boy about town? Are you going to tell me what happened here?' Jerome says, pointing at the neck brace.

'Nothing,' Cyril says hurriedly. He struggles to come

up with a reason on the spot.

'Hiding something, are we?' Jerome asks knowingly.

'What? No!'

'Who's been having a nibble on old Cyril then? Spill the beans.'

'I don't know what you're on about.'

'Come on, Cyril. It's the oldest trick in the book. I know you wouldn't be waltzing around in a neck brace even if you'd actually broken your neck. You look ridiculous. So obviously you're hiding something embarrassing. And that something is a big juicy love bite.'

'Oh shit. I have the meeting with Ashley tomorrow. And Roxy's coming over later. She can't see me like this.' Cyril rips off the neck brace and drops it on the table.

Jerome ignores Cyril's panic as he has important news. 'Cyril, I had dinner with one of the most important director-producers in television last night. I told him about Roxy when I went back to his place for a nightcap.'

'Who on earth is Mary then? The one you were talking about on the phone?'

'He is Mary. That's his nickname in the industry. He has a new live television show, showcasing talent.'

'So Mary is a man?'

'Do try to keep up, Cyril. You're awfully slow sometimes. Yes, Mary is a man and I went back to his house for a nightcap and played him Roxy's demo,' Jerome says.

'What do you mean nightcap? And did he like what he heard?'

'Sex. Have you really not been paying attention to any of our conversations,' Jerome teases. He finds Cyril's naivety wholly endearing. 'More importantly, though – yes! He loved the demos. He was talking about having Roxy on his television show. He wants to meet you Thursday evening for drinks.'

By the end of Jerome's sentence Cyril is practically bouncing up and down with excitement.

'Wow, Jerome! That's amazing – I could kiss you,' he says. Swept away in the moment, Cyril grabs Jerome and plants a kiss firmly on his lips.

At that moment, Roxy comes in and sees Cyril embracing Jerome.

'Am I interrupting something?' she chuckles.

Cyril abruptly removes himself from Jerome and coughs awkwardly. 'Roxy, this is Jerome. He's the one responsible for getting us the meeting with CBS. And he's just told me that a television director wants you in his new talent show.'

'That's awesome! Nice to meet you, Jerome,' Roxy

says, extending her hand to Jerome.

'I was just thanking Jerome for all his help,' Cyril says, looking at the floor in embarrassment. He hopes Roxy hasn't got the wrong idea about him.

'Nice to meet you too, Roxy. I'm your first fan. When Cyril played me your demos I was blown away by your voice. And you have brilliant lyrics, too. You'll be a star someday, I'm sure,' Jerome says with a big smile.

'Oh, you're so sweet. Here, give me a hug,' Roxy exclaims, pulling Jerome into an embrace. 'What is Ashley like; what do I need to do to impress him?'

'Just be yourself. He'll love you.'

'Do you work for Ashley? You must be in the business to have such good contacts,' Roxy asks.

Cyril sniggers until Jerome shoots him a glare, not wanting to disclose the nature of his relationship with Ashley or Mary. The phone rings and Cyril answers; Roxy and Jerome continue to chat. Cyril watches them while he takes the call. It's clear that Roxy has taken a real shine to Jerome; she touches his arm every time he makes her laugh, which is quite often. Jerome compliments her outfit and gushes over her looks. It makes Roxy blush, but Cyril can tell she is enjoying the attention. The pair have immediately developed chemistry and Cyril can feel himself beginning to get jealous.

'Careful, Roxy. Don't get too invested; he's not available,' Cyril says walking up behind Jerome and putting his hands on his shoulders.

'Oh, so you two are an item?' Roxy says, misunderstanding what Cyril means.

Annoyed at this, and still embarrassed by his earlier actions, Cyril tries to set Roxy straight but overcompensates with disastrous consequences.

'God no! I'm as straight as they come. You wouldn't catch me anywhere near those AIDs-riddled bumboys. I mean, except for Jerome – he's a fairy from Bradford, of all places, but he's great,' Cyril laughs as though he's made a funny joke.

'Cyril, you fucking prick,' Jerome snarls, his face falling in dismay and betrayal. He turns and storms out of the office before Cyril even realises what he's said.

Cyril runs after him but Jerome brushes him off. Cyril lets him leave and returns to Roxy.

'How can you be so horrible to Jerome? He's your friend and he's done you a whole heap of favours,' Roxy says, shaking her head in disbelief.

'What? I said he was great! And I was only telling you he's gay and I'm not. What you saw earlier – I was just happy about the news. I didn't want you to get the wrong impression about me.'

'Yeah, you've been quite clear about that,' Roxy says acidly. '"AIDs-ridded bumboys"? Is that really what you think gay people are?'

'I was only joking...' Cyril starts.

'Well it's not funny, is it? It's not even your place to tell me if Jerome is gay. You can't just go around outing people. It can cause them a lot of trouble.'

'I hadn't thought about that,' Cyril admits, starting to realise how terribly he has acted towards Jerome.

'If Jerome wanted to come out to me, that's his decision. Not yours,' Roxy pauses for a few moments, glaring angrily at Cyril. 'My older brother is gay. If you'd have said anything like that to him he'd have flattened you. And outing someone to a stranger? Well, he'd have flattened you twice.'

'You're not a stranger, though. I really didn't mean to upset him,' Cyril says, thinking Roxy is overreacting.

'You don't get it. I only met Jerome today – I'm a stranger to him. And you said all those hurtful things, too. You need to apologise to him before the meeting tomorrow,' she says sternly and walks out of the office.

Cyril hadn't expected her to be so feisty – it was like she suddenly turned into a different person. Cyril is also surprised by how jealous he had felt when the pair were hitting it off and regrets that he took it out on Jerome. He starts to feel sick as he thinks about the awful things he had said. He tries to call Jerome constantly for an hour, but has no luck. After he is just about to give up, the phone suddenly rings and Cyril snatches it up, praying that it's Jerome. It isn't. A woman named Gloria introduces herself. She runs some shops for Mr Soho and wants to come by and check the quality of the garments. Cyril puts the neck brace back on while he waits for Gloria to arrive. He wonders whether Roxy saw the love bites.

The following day, Cyril walks from his car towards Bar Italia. He gets a coffee and thinks about the meeting later that afternoon. Cyril is worried about Jerome; he has been unable to contact him since yesterday to apologise. He hopes it won't affect the meeting with the TV director that Jerome was going to organise. As the day goes by, Cyril gets more and more anxious thinking about the appointment. He is pleased when Billy arrives unannounced and invites him for a drink before his photoshoot.

'Which bird did that to your neck?' Billy asks as soon as they sit down with their drinks in the corner of the pub.

'Her name's Danielle. She's one of the girls from the disco – a PE teacher. Got a weird thing for milk.'

'Milk?'

'Yeah, she took me in the shower and started pouring milk from the fridge over me! What she did after that, I leave to your sordid imagination.' Cyril grins.

'Fucking hell. You're a randy sod – and a lucky one too. Do you think she'd be up for a good time with me? I wouldn't say no to her milk.'

They laugh and Billy continues: 'You're not going to the CBS meeting with all your love bites showing, are you?'

'I had a neck brace but it looks completely ridiculous.'

'Ah, the old neck brace trick.'

Cyril takes a moment to look at Billy's outfit in all its flamboyance. His trousers are striped pink, matching the pink scarf around his neck. The finishing touch is a hat with a feather.

'You look gayer than the gays,' he says shaking his head.

'You've got to look striking to be a famous pop star. Nobody wants you if you're boring. And this is nothing – you should see my underwear,' Billy says, starting to unzip his trousers.

'Pack it in. We already know why everyone calls you Big Billy. You love whipping out that python at every available opportunity.'

'You can't cage this trouser snake,' Billy says and the pair fall about laughing.

When the laughter finally subsides, Billy starts talking about his manager, Kevin Cash, again. Cyril almost rolls his eyes – it's always 'Kevin this, Kevin that.'

'Did you know Kevin worked for Don Arden for six years before he set up on his own?'

'Who's Don Arden?'

'He's an old school Jewish rock and roll manager. He managed ELO and Little Richard. Oh, and Black Sabbath. Kevin calls him "The Intimidator" because he used to terrorise the staff at the record companies. Kevin learned a lot from him. He also terrorises people, but in a calm and collected way. His nickname is The Silent Assassin.'

'Sounds like a really great guy,' Cyril interrupts sarcastically.

'That's how he got us the three-album deal and money in advance for the contract. We haven't sold a single record and yet we have all this money. Fucking amazing!' Billy continues, ignoring Cyril's remark.

After a drink, Cyril is starting to feel more relaxed about the meeting. Over more drinks, he tells Billy about his latest discovery: Rub and C.

'Rub and C?' Billy starts to laugh. 'Sounds like a porn act.'

'Shit you're right. We'll have to change the name.'

'They sound interesting, though. You must be pulling

lots of birds on the casting couch.'

'I said before – I don't want to mix business and pleasure. Uncle Lew told me that.'

'You should lighten up and have some fun,' Billy says. 'This is the music business after all.'

Over Billy's shoulder, Cyril sees MJ and Jazz walk into the pub. They head straight to the bar but Cyril knows he will inevitably be spotted when they go to sit down.

'Shit,' Cyril says and yanks the pink scarf from Billy, winding it around his own neck to hide the pesky love bites.

Confused, Billy turns around to see what spooked Cyril and spies Jazz. He looks back with a knowing grin. 'I wouldn't want to ruin my chances with her either. She's smoking hot.'

'I didn't know you were into transvestites,' Cyril sniggers.

'Not her! The brown sugar!'

'Her name is Jazz, you idiot. Now shut up and behave; they're coming over.'

'Hey boys,' MJ greets them. 'Your stuff is really popular with my girls. They want more. Can you bring me another box later?'

'Sure, MJ. Drinks are on me – I owe you one, remember? What do you ladies like?' Cyril asks, adjusting his scarf self-consciously.

'A gin and tonic for me, and a snowball for Jazz,' MJ replies, taking a seat beside Billy.

Cyril heads to the bar to get the drinks, leaving Billy gawping at MJ. She looks him up and down.

'Are you in the fashion business?' she asks sarcastically.

'No! I'm the drummer in a band.'

'Could've fooled me. You look like you got dressed from the lost and found bin,' MJ says, laughing at her own joke.

Billy falls silent and MJ turns her attention to Cyril who has returned with the drinks. 'What's with the scarf, Cyril? You've only been in Soho a couple of months and it's already turning you into a poof.'

Jazz laughs at this, placing her hand on Cyril's knee under the table and gives him a wink.

'Why do people keep saying I'm gay? Can a man not be stylish and still be straight?' Cyril exclaims with mock outrage.

'Sweety, they can. But that scarf is not stylish,' MJ replies camply, at which everyone bursts out laughing.

After they have a drink and a catch up, MJ announces that she and, by implication, Jazz, must get back to work as there is money to be made. As the pair leave, Billy and Cyril get another round.

'Can't help but notice the way Jazz looks at you.

Have you got something going on with her or can I call first dibs.'

'She's a woman, Billy, you can't just call dibs on her. But no, she's not my type,' Cyril lies. He wants to disclose as little as possible of his love life to Billy as Cyril knows telling him will only lead to endless questions.

'Fuck off – she's every mans' type! Is it because she's black and you're Jewish? You can only marry Jewish girls, right?'

'I can marry whoever I want.'

'Yeah, tell me that after you've invited her over for one of your Friday night dinners. I'm sure Alf and Gina would be thrilled.'

Cyril throws a beer mat at Billy's head in opposition to his accusation. He sighs, thinking for a moment.

'I'm still feeling nervous for later. Do you have any advice?' Cyril asks reluctantly. As annoying as Billy can be, Cyril knows he has more experience with things like this.

'Just go in all guns blazing so they know you mean business. You want something to help you get in the zone? I always find speed works best. Everyone does it,' Billy replies unhelpfully.

'No, thanks. You know I don't go for that stuff. I'll go and order us some food.'

Cyril gets up to order at the bar and Billy has an idea. He thinks Cyril is too pure to piss and could do with letting loose – it'll help him in the long run. Billy decides his friend needs a little push in the right direction if he's ever going to be successful and so slips a bag of speed out of his pocket and knocks some into Cyril's pint.

'There you go, mate. That'll get you going,' Billy says under his breath.

Cyril returns and a few minutes later their food arrives. The pair continue chatting while they eat. As Billy bursts into fits of laughter at one of Cyril's jokes, Mickey stalks into the pub and spots them.

'Hi you two. The knickers are going down a treat, Cyril. I'll be needing another box before long, yeah? Gotta run – only popped in for some fags. See you soon.'

Billy nearly chokes on his pint of lager when he realises what Cyril has been up to. 'So this is your secret multi-million business – selling pants! You really are living up to your nickname, Knickerman.'

'Alf and Gina don't know anything about this, okay? So keep your big mouth shut,' Cyril says glancing at his watch. 'Shit! My watch has stopped. What time is it?'

'Quarter to four.'

'Shit. Shit. Shit. I'm going to be late for the meeting,'

Cyril yelps, draining the last of his pint and throwing on his jacket.

Cyril runs out of the pub towards CBS, his scarf flailing frantically in the wind in a way that is comically majestic. He doesn't stop until he arrives in Soho Square and sees Roxy waiting outside the building. He ushers her inside and tries to catch his breath. As Cyril informs the receptionist they're here to see Ashley Goodman, Roxy looks disapprovingly at her manager.

'You're very late and you smell of drink, Cyril,' she hisses quietly. 'I was so nervous; I didn't think you'd come.'

'My watch stopped,' Cyril says, trying to wipe the sweat from his face and make himself presentable.

'Where's Jerome? Did you apologise to him?'

'No. I couldn't find him. He's disappeared and he wouldn't answer my calls.'

'Aren't you worried about him,' Roxy asks, shaking her head in disbelief.

'Trust me, he can look after himself,' Cyril replies, straightening his tie.

A few minutes later, the receptionist sends them through to Ashley Goodman's office. At this point, the effects of Billy's speed start to kick in and Cyril begins to feel very strange. At first, he attributes the sensation to being nervous and a little drunk and hopes the feeling will go away once the meeting begins. Ashley Goodman is an older Jewish man and Cyril hopes their shared faith will work in his favour. He's a no-nonsense, experienced music executive; the head of the A&R department and well respected for his many successful signings. He is not impressed with Cyril's lateness, or the garbled story about his car breaking down.

'Do you always drink and drive?' Goodman asks pointedly as Cyril tries frantically to make himself look more presentable. 'Tea? Coffee?' he continues.

'Coffee, please,' Roxy replies quietly.

'Champagne is in order, don't you think, Ashley?' Cyril says loudly, plonking himself down heavily in one of the chairs. His heart is beating almost out of his chest.

'Don't get ahead of yourself, Mr Gold. We have a lot to discuss.'

Roxy is beginning to feel more and more nervous. She's angry at Cyril for turning up in this state but works hard to hide it as she knows showing her annoyance would seem unprofessional. Cyril is also aware of his unfortunate first impression and decides to dial back his cocky banter and instead go for a more amiable approach.

'You might know my uncle, Lew Cohen of Variety

Management Soho? You remind me of him.'

'You're related to Tight Fisted Cohen?'

'Ah, so you know him?'

'Who doesn't? And I hope you don't mean I look like him. He's almost bald and a good twenty years older than me.'

Cyril laughs nervously. 'Of course not! I mean you have the same boldness. The same powerful presence.' Cyril rambles on for a good few minutes about his uncle, saying anything that comes into his head. Roxy wonders what on earth has gotten into him. He seems totally off his trolley, she thinks.

At last she steps in simply to shut Cyril up. 'I recorded the two other songs last week, Mr Goodman.' She hands him the tapes.

They chat for a while about music while Cyril is quiet and concentrates on not throwing up. The room feels like it is spinning. Goodman puts the tape into the machine and presses play. Within seconds, Cyril has returned from his brief silence and is talking on and on about how great the opening riff is.

'Stop talking, goddamnit!' Goodman booms.

Roxy is so embarrassed she can hardly keep herself together as Cyril fidgets excessively and bobs along to the music in the most unusual way, playing with the scarf and mumbling incoherent rubbish. As the tape finishes, Goodman takes out the cassette and hands it to Roxy with a grin.

'Not bad…' he begins.

'Not bad? They're amazing songs with great lyrics. You have a star here with Roxy!' Cyril butts in.

Ignoring Cyril, Goodman continues talking directly to Roxy: 'I like that the songs come first with you – it really comes across in the music. We can work on developing you a signature image…'

Cyril interrupts again, raising his voice: 'Roxy already has a great style. She doesn't need a makeover. She wants to be her true self, not some manufactured act!'

At this point, Roxy decides she has to intervene to stop the whole meeting going down the plughole. 'Cyril, sit down and shut up,' she says in a clipped tone.

Stunned, he does so.

Goodman starts talking about recording some songs and organising studio time and Cyril is suddenly up out of the chair again.

'Slow down, cowboy. I'm not interested in a Mickey Mouse deal,' he shouts, remembering what Billy said about Kevin Cash driving a hard bargain. 'I want a real record deal for my artist; three albums and cash up front.'

This is the last straw. 'Who do you think you are?

You're a nobody. You think you can walk in off the street with no experience and try to intimidate me? Well you've got another think coming. Get the fuck out of my office, you schmuck,' he yells, pointing at the door.

'I'm no schmuck, you homo!' Cyril retorts, as Roxy steers him towards the door and apologises profusely.

'Do yourself a favour and get yourself a proper manager, love. Not an idiot like him,' Goodman adds as Roxy closes the door.

Roxy drags Cyril down the stairs, ignoring his incessant rambling about how Ashley Goodman is a prick and there are hundreds of record companies to choose from. She is crushingly disappointed in Cyril; he has let her down. When they finally tumble out into the street Roxy turns to Cyril and glares, expecting some sort of explanation. He sits down shakily on the pavement with his head between his knees. Everything feels in hyper focus.

'Roxy, I really don't feel well. I don't know what's wrong with me.'

'How much have you had to drink, Cyril? What the hell? Chances like that are once in a lifetime and you just threw it away like it was nothing. Do you think this is all just a game or something?' she shouts, visibly distraught. 'Who are you trying to impress, pulling all that hardened manager crap? Did you really think Ashley Goodman was going to buy it? He's right – you are a nobody.'

Roxy shakes her head and turns on her heel to walk away. She puts on her headphones and listens to Phil Collins' 'In the Air Tonight' as she makes her way home.

Chapter Eight

'Let's Get Physical'

Olivia Newton-John

Cyril arrives at the office just before twelve o'clock. After a night wandering alone around the clubs in Soho and drinking away his sorrows, he would much rather still be in bed. Although Cyril has no recollection of how he got home, unfortunately the memory of the meeting with Ashley Goodman is still crystal clear in his mind. The opportunity with CBS is most definitely blown and Cyril is doubtful that Roxy will forgive him. He isn't quite sure why he acted the way he did; something came over him all of a sudden, but it wasn't like being drunk.

I hadn't had that much to drink before, had I? Cyril thinks, doubting himself.

He is filled with regret about Roxy. Jerome is also on his mind; Cyril is ashamed of the things he said to

158

Jerome and reflects on the names the children at school used to call him because he is Jewish. He hopes he can apologise soon.

Despite already knowing what is in his diary, Cyril takes a look anyway: *Drinks with TV director, Edwards, 7pm.* Jerome was supposed to get in touch about going to the studio together but he hasn't called. A prickle of worry starts to irritate the back of Cyril's mind. Jerome avoiding him is one thing, but something happening to him is another. What if Roxy was right – should he be worried? Ignoring the throbbing in his head, Cyril grabs his coat and heads out of the office. He decides to visit all the places Jerome usually frequents.

Before long, two hours have passed and Cyril has had no luck. He finally has to admit defeat and heads over to the studio by himself, praying that the director will still see him. Despite passing several pubs, Cyril ignores the desire to have a drink to calm his nerves. He is anxious to make up for his mistakes of the previous day.

Arriving at the television studio, Cyril strides up to the reception desk with much more confidence than he really feels. A familiar voice calls out from behind him.

'Good to see you're not late.'

'Jerome,' Cyril cries, turning around and rushing

towards him.

'I heard about your car crash meeting with Ashley. You crazy bastard. Insulting me is one thing, but insulting Ashley Goodman... in his very own office? I'm not sure "sorry" will cut it for him,' Jerome says shaking his head, but smiling.

This isn't the response Cyril had expected; 'Forget Ashley – it's you I need to apologise to. I'm so sorry for everything I said the other day. I don't know what came over me – and I know it's no excuse. I hope you can forgive me.'

'You'd better be sorry. I know I'm a drama queen but what you said really hurt me. I'll forgive you this time, but what you did to Roxy's chance of a big break is pretty terrible. She turned up at The Star and Garter crying – it's a good job I was there. She told me everything, Cyril. Turning up late? And drunk! Roxy said it seemed like you were on something but I told her you don't do that stuff.'

'I don't,' Cyril cut in. 'Billy offered me something to get me going for the meeting but I said no.'

'And you don't think Billy might have given it to you anyway?'

'What? Of course not,' Cyril says hurriedly, coming to his friend's defence. Then he takes a second to consider. 'Shit.'

'Did he spike you?'

'I don't know; it doesn't even matter. I fucked it up big time. But I have to fix it for Roxy. She trusted me and I absolutely can't let her down,' Cyril says desperately.

'You have another chance tonight. Just don't mess it up. If Mary wants to go out for dinner, you pick up the bill, okay? If you think Ashley is bad, you should try getting on the wrong side of Mary. She will annihilate you.'

'Message received, loud and clear. I won't fuck it up.'

'I won't be able to join you and Mary tonight. I agreed to have dinner and a nightcap with Ashley to make up for your stupidity.'

'I'm sorry about that, Jerome. I didn't mean to put you in this position. But please come with me tonight – I need you there! I obviously don't know how to deal with these show business people.'

'Man up, Cyril. You can do it! Just lay on the charm to get what you want; nothing too outlandish. No shouting or demanding. And no getting drunk.' Jerome leans into Cyril and whispers: 'Remember: play the game with Mary. Camp it up, be flirtatious. He'll love it.'

'I swear on my mum's life I won't let you down.'

'Don't say that – nothing is worth your mother's life,' Jerome says, pulling Cyril into the staff bar area.

They see Mary having a drink with two younger guys who look like they are about to leave. Cyril walks over and greets them; they're Simon and Nick from Duran Duran. They signed Cyril's autograph book one time when they were at the EMI factory.

'Hi Simon. Hi Nick,' Cyril says, putting his hand out for them to shake. Neither remembers him.

'You both signed my autograph book at the EMI factory,' Cyril tries, hoping to jog their memory.

'Oh, I see,' Simon says. 'We were just leaving.'

'Cyril, this is Mr Michael Edwards,' Jerome says hastily, hoping to snap Cyril out of his star-stricken state.

'Hello Mr Edwards. Nice to meet you.'

'Just call me Michael. Everyone does,' he says, flicking his long white hair away from his eyes. He is a failed actor turned successful director, early fifties but dresses younger. He wears blue jeans and a white long-sleeved shirt with the top three buttons undone.

'I thought everyone calls you Mar…'

Jerome stamps on Cyril's foot.

'Mar…ichael?' he says, saving himself.

'Michael. Yes, that's what I said. I see you know Simon and Nick. They've agreed to be the first special guests on my new live talent show.'

'That's fantastic. Jerome told me about your new

show and that you'd like to feature Roxy.'

'I loved that song, "Waiting for Your Love". That's the one I would feature if she comes on the show. Do you have a photo of Roxy, Cyril?'

Cyril pulls out some of the Polaroids he took at the office. Jerome sees the pictures and reacts quickly.

'Did you not bring the professional headshots?' he asks, knowing full well that Cyril doesn't have any. 'That bloody photographer should've got back to you with the prints by now.'

'These are fine. She looks adorable. The camera loves her face,' Michael says, striking a camp pose. He laughs; Jerome and Cyril join in.

'I know it's short notice, but would Roxy be free for the first live show next week? Someone has just dropped out,' Michael continues.

'That would be brilliant, Michael. But how much will it cost me?'

'Oh Cyril, you're so funny. Let's have dinner tonight to celebrate getting Roxy on board.'

'Yes, let's do that! You choose any restaurant you like,' Cyril says excitedly.

'My favourite restaurant, Le Gavroche, in Mayfair.' Michael begins speaking in French, none of which Cyril understands.

At this point, Jerome makes his apologies, saying

he has to go home and do some last-minute studying for an exam. Michael is visibly upset, as he had been expecting Jerome to join them for dinner.

'Don't worry. Cyril will be excellent company tonight. He'll look after you. Isn't that right Cyril?' Jerome says, shooting him a look.

'Will I see you later tonight, perhaps? For a nightcap?' Michael grins.

'Another night. I want to be fresh for my exam tomorrow morning.'

'It's just you and me tonight then, Cyril.'

Cyril is shocked when he sees Michael's dark blue, open-top convertible Rolls-Royce parked in the studio's underground car park.

'Wow, this is some car. What a beauty!'

'Ah, just one of my little toys,' Michael exclaims, gliding into the driver's seat. He starts the engine and turns on the radio, which plays 'Steppin' Out' by Joe Jackson.

Cyril notices people turn to stare at the car as it passes. When they arrive at La Gavroche, the maître d' greets Michael like an old friend, exchanging words in French and then taking them to his usual corner table. Cyril can't believe the number of famous faces in the restaurant.

From the corner table, Cyril can see everyone in the

room and surveys the scene in awe. Michael and the maître d' continue to talk in French and suddenly a bottle of champagne appears, sent over by the head of Virgin Records, Dan Evans. Michael waves and mimes a thank you. He clinks glasses with Cyril and takes a sip.

'Dan wants his new signing on my show,' Michael explains, waving and nodding to several other people in the room.

'You know so many people here.'

'La Gavroche isn't just my favourite restaurant, it's also where lots of prominent people in the music and entertainment world come to make contacts and do business.'

Cyril nods his head, hanging onto Michael's every word. Michael adores the attention.

'Look over there, at that table of three. The older woman, in her fifties – she's one of the most influential managers in the music world.' Michael hails the waiter and asks him to send three glasses of champagne over.

'She seems nice. Is that Tom Cruise she's sitting with,' Cyril asks in disbelief.

'Yes, that's Tom. With another new girlfriend no doubt. Don't be fooled by the Mumsie, sweet-looking exterior. She's ruthless, pushy, and I dare say unstable. But you didn't hear that from me. I've heard she threatens record companies if they don't accept her demands.'

'What's her name?'

'She goes by a few names, actually. Depends on who you ask. Lady Muck, Queen Bea. But her real name is Bea Solomon. I bet she's trying to get Tom to allow her artist's song to feature in one of his films. She'd love to go to bed with Tom. But he's too powerful for her to make that demand of him. She can only get the more vulnerable ones into bed – like a fox amongst the chickens. You'd be surprised how many people are willing to sleep with her to get a record deal. It's a tragic story, really; her late husband left her for a younger woman after their only son overdosed. Turned her into a monster. Her ex died in suspicious circumstances…'

As interesting as Michael's story is, Cyril spots something even more exciting: 'Shit! Is that Olivia Newton-John having dinner with Tina Turner? Who'd have thought it?'

'They have the same manager,' Michael explains.

'You know everything and everyone – it's amazing.'

On another table, Barry Manilow is having dinner with a few male friends. Cyril has never been so starstruck and is struggling to hide it. Michael loves it.

'My mum, Gina, loves Barry. She has all his records. I'd love to get his autograph for her.'

To Cyril's amazement, Michael gives Barry a wave

and the singer heads straight over to their table.

'Barry, this is Cyril. His mother is a big fan of yours.'

'To say she loves you would be an understatement,' Cyril says, his jaw almost dropping to the floor. 'Would you mind signing an autograph for her?'

'How sweet! Of course – I always carry a few autographed photos around with me.'

Cyril thanks Barry and thinks about how excited Gina will be when he shows her the photograph. Barry takes his leave, giving Cyril a flirtatious wink as he goes.

When the menu arrives, Cyril is left wishing he'd paid more attention in French class at school.

'I don't speak any French,' he admits. 'Would you mind ordering for me? And don't forget the wine. It's my treat tonight, Michael.'

Michael smiles and nods. Cyril roots through his pockets and pulls some receipts out of his jacket while Michael is ordering.

'Do you like to gamble? I see betting slips,' he asks as the waiter leaves.

'Sometimes. I like a little flutter on the horses. It's the risk-taking side of me,' Cyril replies.

Dan Evans breezes up to the table and says goodnight to Michael. He asks about the new television show starting next week.

'It's all going very well – all very exciting.'

'I'm looking forward to seeing it. Maybe we'll see some Virgin artists on there at some point.'

'I'm sure we can make that happen. By the way, this is Cyril. He has an incredible artist by the name of Roxy. She's appearing on the first show. A star in the making... and unsigned,' Michael says, giving Dan a knowing nod.

'Well, with such a high recommendation from you, I'd best check her out. Can you send me her demos please, Cyril,' Dan says, handing over his business card.

Cyril can't believe his luck; Virgin A&R never retuned his calls but now he's got a ticket in.

'Thank you for that, Michael. I owe you one. How can I repay you?' Cyril says when Dan has left the restaurant.

'Oh, I'll think of something,' Michael says with a grin.

As the drinks and conversation flow, Michael becomes more and more flirtatious with Cyril.

The wine sommelier arrives next to them with a small table. On it, he has a candle, a decanter and the bottle of wine that Michael ordered. The sommelier lights the candle and starts to pour the wine into the decanter, keeping the candle's flame just below the bottle's neck to examine its contents for sediment. After he has finished, he pours a little into his glass to taste, in case the wine is corked. He then proceeds to pour some wine into Michael's glass so he can approve it. Michael takes a sip and nods; the sommelier pours the wine for Cyril and tops up Michael's glass. Cyril watches the performance in wonderment. A lager drinker, he had no idea that choosing a wine was such an involved task. He usually just chooses the cheapest bottle, but something tells him this isn't Michael's approach.

'Lovely wine. Full bodied, like you,' Michael says, taking another sip of the wine and looking at Cyril. He puts his hand on Cyril's thigh. Cyril just smiles, remembering what Jerome told him.

The first course arrives and Michael says 'Bon appétit', raising his glass. Frogs legs for Michael and escargot cooked in garlic butter, served in puff pastry, for Cyril. Cyril doesn't know what escargot is, but thinks it tastes pretty good.

'You must like it – you devoured it quickly,' Michael comments.

'It was lovely. I'm looking forward to the main course though; I'm starving. What is escargot, anyway?'

'Snails,' Michael replies casually.

Cyril takes a long sip of wine and swills it around his

mouth, trying to get rid of the mental picture of snails rather than the taste.

The main course arrives and Cyril is relieved to see it looks a little more familiar; meat and vegetables. He dives in eagerly.

'This beef is delicious; it's tastes so different to my mum's cooking. The best I've ever had.'

'It's pork, Cyril.'

'And so it is!' Cyril exclaims taking another gulp of wine. He has never eaten pork in his life, but he's so hungry he doesn't care. He also doesn't want to offend Michael.

The waiter asks if they would like a second bottle of wine; Cyril is drinking faster than Michael.

Later in the evening, Cyril brings up his other artists, the twins. He tells Michael how wonderful they are and how great they would be on his TV show.

'A pair of mixed-race twins who sing, dance and write their own songs? Sounds interesting. Send me the demo and I'll have a listen. What are they called?'

'Erm. Rub and C…'

'I'm not sure about the name. It is a family show after all.'

'I know, I've been trying to come up with a new name for them. Do you have any ideas?'

Another one of Michael's friends comes over to say hello and Cyril excuses himself to the toilet for a quick cigarette. He knows Michael doesn't approve of smoking. While Cyril is washing his hands, he is surprised as someone pats him on the back.

'Hello, Cyril. Didn't expect to see you here.'

'Uncle Lew! Small world, right?'

'I saw you sitting with Mary and thought I'd best not disturb you. Things must be looking up for you.'

'You know Michael's nickname?'

'I've been in the entertainment world for donkey's years, my boy.'

'Mary just confirmed that one of my artists, Roxy, is going to be on his new show. I'm buying him dinner to say thank you.'

'That's great, Cyril. I hope you're good for the cash – it'll be an expensive affair eating here. It's worth it for the exposure your artist will get. The food is great, though. What did you have?'

'Beef,' Cyril replies quickly.

Cyril arrives back at the table and dessert has already been served.

'My favourite; peach melba. Aren't you having any?'

'I'm sweet enough,' Michael says, looking a little coy.

After hearing the remark, Cyril starts to become nervous, and Michael moves closer.

'Oh, you smoke?' he says disapprovingly.

'Yeah, I just had a fag in the toilet.'

'Fag? It's a disgusting, smelly habit.'

'Well, I'm not kissing anyone tonight,' Cyril says jokingly, draining another glass of wine. Jerome told him not to get drunk, but Cyril could only relax into the evening after a few glasses, and Michael keeps topping up his glass.

'Is that so?' Michael says with a glint in his eye.

Cyril tries to ignore the implication in Michael's voice and decides this is a good time to ask for the bill.

'Cyril, do you have a girlfriend or a boyfriend?'

'I had a girlfriend, but not anymore. Are you seeing anyone?' Cyril asks, feeling uncomfortable.

'No. Like you, I'm alone and looking for the right person. Have you ever had a boyfriend?' he asks, touching Cyril under the table again.

'It's not really my scene. I hope you understand,' Cyril says, gently removing Michael's hand.

'I love straight men like you,' he whispers, and Cyril nearly chokes on his wine.

He wonders why on earth gay men seem to like straight guys so much. He's struggling to deal with Michael's advances.

'You'd be amazed how many straight guys enjoy the experience. You just lay back and I'll do all the work,'

Michael says with a wink.

Cyril can only smile. 'Thank you for an incredible amazing evening. But I really have to go. I've got a very early start tomorrow.'

The bill arrives. It's more expensive than Cyril could ever have imagined. The two bottles of wine are twice as much as the food, which is expensive to start with. Swallowing the dry lump in his throat, Cyril gives the waiter his card. The card doesn't go through. The waiter tries a few more times and Cyril begins to panic. Michael looks annoyed and pulls out his own card and tosses it to the waiter.

'I'm sorry Michael. I'm not sure what happened. There's definitely enough credit on there.'

'Cyril, don't worry about it. So, how about a nightcap to finish the night?' he asks, looking Cyril straight in the face.

A million thoughts buzz around his head. Cyril wants to leave as fast as his legs can carry him, but Jerome's words ring in his head; Don't mess with Mary. She has a mean streak and she hates to pay.

He hesitates. 'Er, Michael I…'

'You want Roxy to be successful, don't you?' Michael butts in.

He can't let Roxy down again; 'Sure. Just one drink then.'

Michael drives his car wildly, singing along to Olivia Newton-John's 'Let's Get Physical'. Cyril feels sick and uncomfortable.

The next morning, Cyril heads straight to the office. He would've liked to have gone home and showered first but his busy schedule doesn't leave him time. He has a hectic morning ahead. First the twins are coming by with their new demo and to organise a photoshoot. Cyril also has to meet with Mr Jones to sign the paperwork for a new loan. The bank manager believes Cyril's business is doing well, seeing regular payments coming in, and so was happy to give him the loan. Finally, Cyril has a date with Jazz in the evening. He doesn't feel particularly up to it but doesn't want to cancel. Before the twins arrive, Jerome turns up unannounced.

'I wasn't expecting to see you. How did it go with Ashley last night? Has he forgiven me?'

'What do you think? I had to work doubly hard last night – on his ego and his dick. More importantly though, how did you get on with Mary?'

'Mary was amazing. He's excited to showcase Roxy on his show. He even introduced me to the head of Virgin Records. And Barry Manilow – he gave me his autograph for my mum,' Cyril says, pulling out the picture.

'How come you are in the same clothes as last night? Didn't you go home?'

'I had a problem with my credit card. It was okay though, Michael picked up the bill.'

'Cyril, what the fuck? I told you Mary hates paying for anything.'

'Yeah, well you didn't tell me he'd take us to the most expensive restaurant in London. I made it up to him anyway,' Cyril says quietly.

'What do you mean?'

'He took me back to his for a nightcap.'

'What? You keep telling me you're straight.'

'I am straight. Even more so after last night. I couldn't let Roxy down again, alright? It's not her fault I didn't have enough money to pay. I just laid there thinking of England and he did all the work. I'm not proud of it and I don't want to talk about it.'

Jerome is jealous. He had always hoped Cyril might show him some affection, but he didn't want his friend to be put in a situation like that. The phone rings and Cyril indicates to Jerome that he is busy, so he leaves, closing the door behind him.

Cyril makes his way to the bank to sign the paperwork for the loan. He then withdraws money for his night out with Jazz. He also decides to pay Alf back for his various loans. By the time Cyril arrives back at his office, the twins are waiting outside with a suitcase.

'I hope you're not wanting to move in here,' Cyril jokes as he sees the suitcase.

'They're our costumes. We have an amazing student photographer friend called James. He goes to our college and he's agreed to take our photos for free,' Ruby says excitedly.

'He's going to be famous one day,' Cheryl adds, pulling out his portfolio to show Cyril.

The quality of the work is impressive.

'Girls, can you tell James to do something that'll surprise me? I want something really different to show off your attitude. I want to shock the record companies into noticing you so we can get a deal.'

The twins are full of enthusiasm and open the suitcase to show Cyril all the clothes they will be wearing for the shoot. He had expected them to be bright and colourful, but instead they have a hard, edgy look. Cyril isn't convinced.

'This is our look,' Ruby says firmly.

'We call it "street clothes" because the kids will able to relate to what we wear,' Cheryl adds.

'Why do you only have black and white shades — don't you want some colour so you stand out?'

'We'll stand out for different, better reasons. No glitter or bright colours. We're hoping we might even get a fashion deal with the record deal.'

Before Cyril has a chance to object, the girls have stripped down to their underwear and are getting ready to try on the clothes to put on a fashion show. He doesn't know where to look. Someone knocks on the door, but walks straight in rather than waiting for an answer. It's Diamond.

'Auditioning, are we? I thought you were in the music business.'

'They're here to plan a photoshoot.'

'Whatever floats your boat. I'm here for my commission.'

As Cyril goes to fetch the money, Diamond eyes up the girls.

'I can see you girls going far. Here's my business card. If you ever need any extra work, give me a call,' he says dropping his card on the table.

Cyril is not impressed. 'They're only young Diamond. They don't need anything from you.'

'Well, you never know.'

'Here's your money,' Cyril says and waits until the door closes after Diamond to add 'sleazebag' under his breath. He snatches the card from the table and throws it into the bin.

As the girls get dressed, Cyril listens to their new demos.

'Your ideas for your image might be great, but you need to work on the song writing. These two songs aren't good enough – there's no catchy melody grabbing my attention,' Cyril says.

The phone rings and he turns to take the call. The girls are deflated by Cyril's comments. While he is looking away, Ruby takes Diamond's business card out of the bin. Cyril finishes the call and turns back to the twins.

'I need a few more hit songs from you before I can approach the record companies. Here's some money – go back to the studio. Don't look so disheartened; you'll get there. My other artist, Roxy, is going to be on TV soon, and I want to capitalise on that for you two.'

The girls collect their things and leave feeling slightly more optimistic at the mention of being on television.

Chapter Nine

'Karma Chameleon'

Culture Club

After the twins leave, Cyril rushes home to get ready for his date with Jazz. He is thankful that Alf and Gina aren't back from work yet and immediately jumps in the shower. Alone with the memories from the night at Michael's, Cyril attempts to scrub them from his body. As he steps out of the bathroom, he forces the matter from his mind and concentrates on choosing his outfit. He lays out various options on his bed and ponders which one Jazz will like best. The radio plays Madonna's 'Into the Groove'. He sprays Brut aftershave into his underwear and Old Spice on his freshly shaven face. After dressing, he wonders how much cash to take. Cyril looks at the money he took out of the bank to pay Alf back and puts it in his pocket just in case he needs extra. He runs down the stairs and almost collides with Gina as she comes through the front door.

'You smell like a chemist shop, Cyril. What are you up to now? And where were you last night? I was worried sick.'

'Sorry, Mum. I was working.'

'Hmm. With one of your female friends I bet. What's her name?'

'Mary,' Cyril says with a small laugh. 'Anyway, never mind that. Close your eyes.'

Cyril puts the signed Barry Manilow photo into Gina's hands and smiles. She opens her eyes and screams.

'Cyril! Is this real? How on earth did you get it?'

'I met him last night at the restaurant. And Roxy is going to be on TV!'

Gina throws her arms around Cyril and kisses him. The doorbell rings and Gina answers it, despite Cyril shouting that he'd get it. A chauffer stands smartly in his black suit.

'Looks like your ride is here, Cyril,' Gina shouts. 'Who is paying for all this?' she adds as Cyril appears.

'The television people.'

'Are you coming home later?'

'I hope not,' Cyril grins as he kisses Gina goodbye. The limo glides into Soho while Culture Club's

'Karma Chameleon' plays on the radio. The limo parks just around the corner from MJ's club. MJ notices Cyril walking over to collect Jazz and calls out to him.

'You're looking good tonight. You've really pushed the boat out it seems!' she says before turning towards the club and shouting: 'Jazz! Your Prince Charming has arrived.'

Jazz walks out of the club looking stunning. Her hair is done up in a magnificent afro and she is wearing a tight black dress that shows all her curves. Cyril picks his jaw up from the ground and greets Jazz. She is almost as tall as he is in her red high heels, complete with matching earrings.

As they walk towards the limo, MJ calls out: 'Don't do anything I wouldn't do.'

'So, where are we going tonight?' Jazz asks, fanning herself. The evening is hot and very close.

'It's a surprise.'

'It better be a good one. It took me hours to get ready.'

'I promised you a good time, didn't I?' Cyril replies, opening a bottle of champagne.

Jazz feels like a film star as she watches everyone else from behind the tinted windows. Lots of people turn and stare at the limo, thinking someone famous is inside. Thirty minutes later, the limo arrives at the VIP entrance of a stadium in east London.

'What the hell is this place, Cyril?'

'It's Walthamstow Stadium. World famous for greyhound racing,' Cyril says with enthusiasm.

'I knew you were soft in the head. Now you've just confirmed it.'

'I thought you'd like something a bit different. The restaurant is beautiful inside. We can have a romantic dinner. You'll love the dogs.'

'Mangy dogs running around a track isn't my idea of romantic, Cyril.'

'Come on, Jazz. Trust me, you'll have a good time.'

Still not convinced, but willing to go along with it, Jazz steps out of the limo. They head into a lift which takes them to the top floor VIP restaurant. They find their table, overlooking the track, and Cyril pulls out a chair for Jazz, acting the perfect gentleman. He orders some more champagne hoping this will get Jazz in the mood.

'Beautiful, isn't it?' he asks.

Jazz gives a non-committal reply. She hasn't forgiven him for making her come to watch dog racing on her only day off.

'Here. Put this on your favourite,' Cyril says, handing Jazz a stack of money.

'Really?' Jazz says, cautiously. She wants to get

annoyed at Cyril and call him a cliché but she finds herself smiling.

'Yeah! I like a gamble on the dogs and the horses. You're my lucky charm tonight.'

She leans over and kisses Cyril, whispering in his ear, 'Normally men expect something from me when they give me a wad of cash.'

Cyril begins to apologise and say it wasn't what he meant but then realises Jazz is looking at him seductively and smirking.

Over dinner, Jazz talks about her family in Liverpool and how they think she's working as a beautician. When she first arrived in London she hadn't been able to find work and quickly ran into money problems. She had part-time work in a pub, but this didn't pay enough to cover the bills and the money she needed to send home to her single mother and younger siblings.

'With your looks, you could be a model,' Cyril suggests, topping up their glasses.

'Yeah, I tried that. Someone who said they could get me into the business gained my trust. He promised me all sorts of things. But all he did was get me hooked on drugs and pimp me out to horrible men. If it hadn't been for MJ, I'd probably still be stuck with that bastard. Or dead.'

Cyril reaches out and touches Jazz's hand. 'I'm sorry,' he says.

They stare into each other's eyes for a while before Cyril catches site of his dog almost winning.

'Come on number four!' he shouts, suddenly jumping up.

Jazz turns towards the track and laughs as her dog pips Cyril's to the finish line.

'Damn! Second again. That's the third time tonight.'

'It'll be nice to be with a man who doesn't come first for a change,' she says with a mischievous grin.

Cyril is confused for a few moments before he realises what she means. Unfortunately, Jazz's sexual advances are slightly marred by the fact he has lost almost all his money betting on the dogs. He was so desperate to make back his losses that he bet on every race, each bigger than the last.

'Talk about beginner's luck. I should've followed your bets,' Cyril says, trying extra hard to mask his disappointment.

'Can you collect my money on that last race, please? I just need to nip to the ladies before we go.'

Cyril collects the winnings for Jazz and removes just enough money to get him by for the rest of the evening. He hands the rest to Jazz as she comes out of the toilet and she stuffs it in her handbag. She pulls Cyril in for a long kiss.

'Come on, let's go. It's too warm in here,' Jazz says.

They walk to the limo holding hands and Cyril thinks his luck is in.

'Thank you for a wonderful evening. Turns out the dogs can be fun. Especially when you win,' Jazz says, snuggling into Cyril in the limo.

'I was thinking of buying a horse as an investment. If I do, I'll name it Lucky Jazz.'

Jazz laughs and kisses him again. When Cyril begins to pull away, Jazz pulls him closer and they remain in a passionate embrace.

'I'll tell the driver to take us back to your place. Where do you live?'

'Sorry, charmer. I have to pack when I get home. I'm going to Liverpool on the train tomorrow morning to see my mum and my sisters. Next time you can come over for dinner and stay the night,' Jazz says with sincerity.

'Sure, next time then,' Cyril replies, pretending he doesn't care. He was so looking forward to spending the night with Jazz. But good things come to those who wait, he hopes.

The driver drops Jazz off at home, and Cyril gives her a heartfelt kiss goodbye in the hope that she might change her mind and invite him in. She waves as the limo pulls away. 'Long Hot Summer' by Style Council plays on the radio.

It's Saturday morning; Alf is about to go and fetch his newspaper and some cigarettes when Gina calls out to him from the kitchen.

'Alf! Can you stop off at the Paki shop and get some milk? Cyril drank the whole bottle again.'

Cyril apologises as he comes down the stairs. He grandly tells them both he wants to take them to dinner with Uncle Lew and Sharon. Alf starts talking about how long it's been since he went to his favourite Jewish restaurant, Reubens.

'Dad, we're going to Soho for an upmarket dinner. Don't worry, it's not too far and it has some of the best kosher food,' Cyril reassures his dad, knowing he doesn't like going too far out of his comfort zone.

'Do you remember the old days when we were courting? You used to take me out to Isow's in Soho,' Gina says.

'Oh yes. All those famous stars used to visit. Danny Kaye, Frank Sinatra, Judy Garland.'

'We stopped going out as much after we got married,' Gina butts in sadly.

'That restaurant is closed now, Mum. But we're going to have your favourite – fish and chips.'

'Fish and chips?' Alf remarks irritably. 'That's not upmarket.'

'Uncle Lew recommended Graham's fish restaurant on Poland Street. Apparently, lots of famous people go there. I want to celebrate Roxy's TV appearance.'

'How come you have the money to take us out but you've not made any attempt to pay me back. Don't think I've forgotten.'

Cyril bites his tongue, knowing it's unfair to call his dad a pain in the arse but wanting to say it anyway. 'I've not forgotten about the money. I think about it every bleeding day. I just wanted to do something nice for us all.'

Gina gives Alf a glare and he quickly changes his tune. 'Fine. What time do we leave? I'll drive.'

Lew and Sharon are already waiting at the restaurant when Cyril and his parents arrive. Before they've even sat down, Sharon is asking Cyril about his love life.

'So, I'm guessing you'll only be dating famous people now you're in the entertainment business? Are you seeing anyone?'

'I don't know about that. And no, not yet. But I'm working on it.'

'Cyril, I have to take my hat off to you. You pulled a masterstroke in getting Roxy on that new live TV show. I'm convinced you'll get a record deal from that,' Lew says.

'Oh, I hope so! My Cyril needs a bit of luck. He's been doing all that DJ work at the weekend while trying to get his business off the ground,' Gina says, holding Cyril's hand and smiling.

Alf rolls his eyes. 'Shall we order? I'm bloody starving.' He tries desperately to catch the attention of one of the waiters.

After dinner, Gina and Sharon go to the downstairs toilet to have a quick cigarette.

'Alf hates me smoking. I only secretly started again because of our Cyril. Keeping me up all night with worry, the sod. You see this grey in my hair? That's Cyril,' Gina says shaking her head.

'He's a good-looking boy. He just needs to get a steady girlfriend to settle down with. That'll sort him out,' Sharon replies, putting out her cigarette.

'Don't tell him, but the other day I was cleaning his room and I found a load of condoms by accident. Hundreds of them, there were! He had some saucy Polaroids of girls too. I didn't know what to do, so I just dusted around them.'

Sharon bursts out laughing and they head back upstairs. The men are deep in a conversation about the only thing that matters to them: the upcoming

Tottenham game with Manchester United.

'Football again,' Sharon sighs.

'It's a big game tomorrow. It's crucial we beat those Mancunians,' Lew explains.

'Do you have this all the time at home, Gina?'

'Of course. We're football widows!' she exclaims.

In the midst of the conversation, Lew mentions bumping into Cyril at Le Gavroche earlier in the week.

'Le Gavroche! That's my favourite restaurant,' Sharon squeals.

'Have you done something new with your hair, Sharon?' Cyril tries, hoping to prevent a further line of inquiry.

'No, same as usual,' she replies. 'So, who were you with? Must have been someone important.'

'I can only afford to take Sharon for special occasions or I'd be broke,' Lew laughs.

Cyril stays quiet, hoping that Lew will talk about his evening there instead. Alf cuts him off.

'Where did you get the money from to go to such an expensive restaurant?'

'Do you always have to question me like it's the Spanish Inquisition? The television director picked up the bill,' Cyril says in a rush to defend himself.

Lew looks panicked. 'What? You mean you didn't pick up the bill?'

Cyril tries to give Lew a wink to stop him asking any more questions, but Gina is quick off the mark in noticing that things don't line up.

'I thought you said you were out with Mary? Don't tell me you made her pay and she still took you home?'

'Mary is the television director,' Cyril says, unsure how to proceed in the matter without catching himself out.

'What does she look like?'

It dawns on Lew that Cyril has talked himself into some kind of predicament and decides he'd best help him out.

'Mary is a beautiful young woman. And a gifted director. She's instrumental in getting Roxy on TV.'

Alf can sense there is something going on, but, as usual, has absolutely no idea what that might be. Lew takes the lull in conversation as an opportunity to completely change the subject, bringing up his next holiday to the south of France. Cyril gives him a smile to say thanks.

The bill arrives and Cyril reaches into his pocket only to realise he has left his credit card at home and panics. Gina reads all of this on Cyril's face and turns to Alf.

'This is your son's big moment. Don't you think we should treat him?'

Noticing the look in Gina's eye that warns him not to make a scene, Alf reluctantly pulls out his money clip.

Cyril protests, but not too much, and is relieved when Alf insists on paying.

Over the weekend, Cyril works out his last-minute plan to get the record companies interested in signing Roxy up after the Friday television show. He has decided to invest in some black and white photographs of her and goes about organising a professional photographer for Wednesday. Later on, Roxy arrives with Tommy holding her hand. They haven't discussed the meeting with Ashley Goodman, and Cyril is glad. He'd rather forget it and move on to better things.

'Hi Cyril. Sorry, I couldn't find anyone to look after Tommy today. Tommy, meet Cyril.'

'Don't worry about it. Hi, Tommy. I've heard a lot about you,' Cyril replies, crouching down to greet him.

Tommy darts behind his mother and Roxy laughs. 'He's shy. He'll be chatting away soon enough.'

'I love kids. I always wished I'd got some brothers and sisters,' Cyril says, rubbing Tommy's hair as he peeks around the side of Roxy.

'Let's talk about the hectic week we've got. I want it all to go as smoothly as possible for you,' Cyril shouts from the kitchen. He returns with a coffee for Roxy, a glass of milk for Tommy and a packet of biscuits.

'How old are you Tommy' Cyril asks.

'I'm nearly four,' he replies quietly.

'Well here's four biscuits for you Mr Nearly-Four-Years-Old.' He turns to Roxy: 'Right where to begin. The television studios are expecting you for a costume fitting tomorrow morning.'

'Okay. Shall I meet you here or at the studio?'

'I won't be able to come with you, sorry. I've got a lot of other things to organise. They just want to see what you look good in and embellish you a bit. You have an idea of your image, right?'

'I do. Oh! I just realised I don't have anyone to look after Tommy tomorrow morning.'

'You can leave him here with me. Just drop him off before you go. We can have lots of biscuits. You'd like that, wouldn't you Tommy?'

Tommy nods excitedly.

'Thanks, Cyril. That's a great help,' Roxy says.

'Next, the photoshoot. I have a talented student photographer coming from St Martins College of Art on Wednesday. I've booked a studio for you and told him to take as many pictures as he wants. Here's some money to go and buy clothes to create the image you have in your mind.'

'Isn't this going to be a bit expensive?'

'Don't worry about it. You need to look the part.'

He re-reads the letter from the television studio which outlines the schedule for the day: sound checks in the morning at 11am, lunch at 1pm, camera rehearsals at 3pm and full dress run-through at 5pm. The show goes live at eight in the evening.

'You'll have a dressing room to yourself, just like a real star. And your own personal make-up lady!'

'What time should I get there?'

'Drop Tommy off here at 10 and you can jump in a cab and be there by half past.'

Tommy is occupying himself rooting through a box in the corner of the room.

'Stop messing about with Cyril's things, Tommy,' Roxy says when she notices.

Tommy turns around with a bra in his hand and Cyril cracks up laughing. 'Looks like he's a breast man.'

Roxy laughs too.

'It's stock from my father's business. I've been selling it on the market as a side business and they're proving quite popular.'

'You make me laugh with all the stuff you get up to. Even the meeting with Ashley Goodman was pretty funny after I'd had time to calm down,' Roxy admits with a shy smile.

'I've got to make money somehow until we get a deal done. I have a feeling lots of offers will come our way soon. I'm going to call Ashley Goodman and apologise, too. I was out of line.'

'I'm glad. He seemed quite nice – I liked him.'

'I think that's everything for today. Now you go shopping with Tommy,' Cyril says, taking the bra from Tommy and tossing it in the box.

'Can we go to the zoo? I want to see the animals,' Tommy asks, staring up at Cyril.

'One day, little man. I'd love to take you. Now be a good boy for your mummy.'

Tommy and Roxy leave hand in hand and Cyril smiles.

The next day, Cyril is up early. Over tea in the kitchen, he makes notes for the next few days. Money is still a problem; the bills keep arriving. He grabs the car keys and walks towards his car. After quickly scanning around to make sure no one can see, he nips into the garage and grabs three more boxes of garments, hurriedly dumping them in the back of his car.

Roxy arrives with Tommy at the office.

'Wow, Roxy! Is this the new look you've been telling me about?'

'Yeah, do you like it?' She says, doing a twirl. Her red t-shirt matched with her Kicker shoes stands out from her distressed and frayed black denim jeans and heavily-studded short black leather jacket.

'You always look lovely but the short haircut with highlights is just amazing! You look hot! Madonna meets Chrissie Hynde.'

'Don't flatter me. You're too kind!'

'I love it!' Cyril exclaims, grabbing her with both hands. In the heat of the moment, Roxy thinks he might kiss her. Cyril wants to but thinks better of it. He hugs her instead.

'Be a good boy for Cyril while I'm at the TV studios. I'll only be a few hours,' Roxy says to Tommy, awkwardly waving goodbye.

Cyril feels awkward too as he closes the door.

'My mummy likes you,' Tommy says. 'And I don't have a daddy.'

Cyril isn't quite sure what to make of this, so laughs and offers Tommy a biscuit. Before Cyril can do anything else, Billy shuffles into the office looking unhappy. He isn't dressed in one of his usual outlandish outfits, just jeans and a blue t-shirt. Cyril hasn't spoken to him since the disastrous CBS meeting. He's almost certain Billy spiked his drink but doesn't want to start an argument in front of Tommy.

'Just seen this lovely bit of skirt going down the stairs. Who is she?' Billy asks, with less enthusiasm than would be typically expected.

'That's Roxy,' Cyril replies coolly.

'And whose child is this? Or have you been busier than you were letting on?'

'It's Roxy's son.'

'Cyril's my new daddy,' Tommy says excitedly.

Billy laughs for a short while but then drops down into a chair with his head in his hands. Despite being angry with him, Cyril is suddenly worried.

'What's up, Billy?'

'I got sacked by that fucking nasty bastard Kevin. He told me drummers are ten a penny and that I talk too much. Someone has to speak for the group...'

'Hey, there's a kid here, don't swear. And he can't just sack you because you talk too much. There must be a good reason.'

'Our first record was doing well in the charts and everything. But my so-called bandmates deserted me. Didn't even put up a fight for me to stay. Bunch of yellow bellied, cock sucking, good-for-nothing pricks with no balls,' Billy shouts, kicking the table leg.

'Billy!' Cyril replies, as Tommy stares open mouthed. 'What was the actual reason?' He is quickly losing patience with Billy's dramatics.

'Fine. I told this bitch that I was shagging that Kevin was supplying drugs for his artistes. I was pissed, alright, and I just wanted to get laid. Turns out she's a fucking journalist. Well, she printed the bloody story, didn't she? Lying whore. I spent good money on her...'

'Jesus Christ, Billy. My heart bleeds for you. Maybe you should've slowed down a bit instead of acting like the prize knob head that you are. Sex and drugs only get you so far. And don't think I didn't notice the shit you put in my drink the other day...'

'Did it help?' Billy says with a huge grin plastered across his face.

Cyril stares in disbelief and shouts: 'No, Billy. It didn't!'

The phone starts to ring and Billy stands dumbfounded in the middle of the room.

'I'm not finished with you yet but you need to go. My phones are ringing and I've got loads to get on with,' Cyril says picking up the phone and leaving Billy to see himself out.

'Hi, Cyril. It's Mark Jones from EMI records. I hear on the grapevine that Roxy will be on the new television show on Friday night. I just listened to the demos that you sent me a while back. Are you available to meet up for a chat now?'

'Sure. See you in thirty minutes.'

'I'm hungry,' Tommy complains.

'We'll go and get some food soon. I just need to make one more phone call.'

'Can we go to the zoo after?'

'Maybe,' Cyril replies, wondering how Roxy puts up with this all day. He dials Ashley Goodman's number, wondering if the possibility of a deal with EMI might get him interested again. His secretary answers and she tells him that Mr Goodman is busy all day.

He takes Tommy to the sweet shop around the corner and lets him choose his favourites. He hopes they will keep him quiet for a few hours. They walk together to MJ's club. Cyril approaches her with a big smile.

'MJ, I need a massive favour. Roxy has left Tommy with me but I've got to run to a meeting to discuss a record deal for her, and I have to go there now. Could you watch Tommy for an hour?'

MJ reluctantly agrees. Tommy seems quite content to be handed off to a stranger. His main focus is the large liquorice stick in his hand.

'You're the youngest man I've ever had in my club, Tommy. You can run around in the basement but upstairs is for adults only, okay?'

She leads him inside, mumbling something about children always being sticky. Cyril hears the girls squealing with delight and fussing over him. He knows Tommy will be well looked after.

Cyril catches a taxi to EMI's office in Manchester Square. He remembers the front cover of the Beatles 1963 album, *Please Please Me*, that features the Fab Four looking down from the stairs in the EMI building. Cyril is kept waiting for twenty minutes, and glances anxiously at his watch. Eventually Mark invites him in and apologises for the delay. He gives a brief tour of the building on the way to the A&R department. Cyril is grinning; he has always wanted to go inside the building that has played host to the likes of Queen, the Sex Pistols, Kate Bush, Pink Floyd and Bowie.

'Take a seat,' Mark says, waving a hand in front of his desk. 'Can I offer you a drink?'

'Just water, please.'

Mark calls his secretary and asks for two glasses of water.

'I'll cut straight to the chase. I love Roxy's demos. She has a few good songs on the tape, but "Waiting for Your Love" is the big one. That's a mega hit.'

Cyril stays quiet, taking a moment to think. He's eager not to repeat the same mistakes as last time.

Mark continues: 'I'm recommending that we sign Roxy up to be part of EMI.'

Cyril tries to contain his excitement, acting as professionally as he can. 'That would be great. She has enough material to complete her first album.'

'I love Roxy's working-class lyrics. So genuine and soulful. Songwriters aren't usually compelled to write about the state of the world, but she's different. How about calling the album *The Working Class*. It would be in line with the current mood politically. Thatcher's government not doing its bit for the poor and all that.'

'You can suggest that to Roxy when you meet her on Friday after the television show. There's been quite a bit of interest in her.'

'Sure. The head of A&R has the final say, but he'll definitely be on board. We must have a night out at the Embassy Club on Bond Street and get Roxy to join us.'

Cyril smiles and nods, trying to look cool. He excuses himself, saying he must go to another meeting. As soon as he is out of view of the EMI building, he hails a taxi and heads back to MJ's.

She isn't in her usual spot outside, so Cyril heads in and is concerned to hear the sound of women squawking at one another. To Cyril's horror, MJ is stood in front of Roxy, who looks as though she is about to swing a punch. They both turn towards him to launch an attack. Roxy makes the first move.

'How could you leave Tommy with this horrid Welsh tart? In a brothel of all places.'

'Roxy, I…' Cyril starts.

'This is the last time I do you a favour, Cyril. Bringing this screaming banshee to my door,' MJ cuts in, glaring at Roxy.

Roxy storms out and Cyril runs after her, making an apologetic gesture to MJ as he leaves. Cyril knows leaving Tommy with MJ wasn't the best thing to do, but the EMI opportunity was too important to pass over. He is desperate to tell Roxy the good news, but decides to wait until she has calmed down first.

In the meantime, Cyril decides to try and call Ashley Goodman again to make amends. The secretary tells Cyril once again he is busy and hangs up. Cyril decides to try a different tactic. He picks up the phone.

'Hello, can I speak to Ashley please. It's Jerome,' Cyril says in a slightly higher pitched voice. The secretary puts the call straight through.

'Hello Jerome. I'm looking forward to seeing you tonight. Can you be a little gentler this time? You know what I like, you bad boy,' Goodman says before Cyril has a chance to say anything.

'I want to apologise for last week,' he says, ignoring

what Goodman has said.

'Who the fuck is this?'

'Jerome's friend, Cyril. Roxy's manager.'

'You bloody freak, coming at me pretending to be Jerome. What's your problem,' Goodman screams down the phone. Cyril can tell he is incensed and is starting to have second thoughts about his plan.

'I have some important news for you,' Cyril tries.

'I don't care if you have the schedule for the second coming of Christ, you self-important cretin. You don't know shit about management. It's honestly embarrassing. I wouldn't work with you if you had the last artist in the world with working vocal cords.'

Cyril starts to rip into Goodman in retaliation but realises he has already hung up. He calls Jerome, but has no luck. The same for Roxy.

The next day, Cyril turns up at the hired studio where James, the photography student, is snapping away at Roxy. Ace's 'How Long (Has This Been Going On)' plays in the background.

'You look lovely, Roxy. Give the camera lots of attitude,' Cyril says with enthusiasm. Hoping Roxy has forgiven him. She completely blanks him.

'Okay Roxy, we're all done with this one. Ready for the next set,' James calls out. 'You must be Cyril,' he says, turning around.

'Hi, yeah. I need these photos printed ASAP for the record companies. Can you come by the office later so I can choose the ones for printing? You'll have them ready for Thursday, right?' Cyril says, watching Roxy walk off to the dressing room without even acknowledging him.

'Yeah, no problem.'

Roxy returns fifteen minutes later looking completely transformed; a rather boyish look. She is wearing white jeans, cut off just below the knee, and a black t-shirt with her name in silver glitter on it. Her hair is gelled back, emphasising her heavily made up, striking eyes. Cyril can't believe how sexy she looks.

'Wow Roxy! You look the business!' Cyril shouts.

'I need to concentrate on this, Cyril. I think it's best if you go.'

'Okay! I'll pick you up on Friday at ten, from your house. It's your big day. Just call me if you need anything,' Cyril says with a big smile, trying to help the situation. He considers cheering her up with the news from EMI, but he can't gauge how she will take it. Cyril walks away hoping Roxy will stop him. She doesn't.

Back in his office Cyril is frantically scheming, trying to think how he can make things up to Roxy and show her that he cares. After a few minutes he calls a lawyer recommended to him by Uncle Lew.

'Hello, I'd like to speak to Maurice Cohen, please. I'm Cyril Gold.'

'I've been expecting your phone call. Lew told me you might want to form a publishing company. That's a great idea if you have a good songwriter.'

'Yes, but in this case I want it in the artist's name.'

'What? Why? You paid for her demos; you took the commercial risk. If I'm your lawyer and I have your best interests at heart, I'd advise you to do differently. Put the songs into your publishing company.'

'Thanks, I know where you're coming from. But, just this once, put everything in Roxy's name.'

'Do you have a formal written management contract with Roxy?'

'Not a written one. We have an understanding. I trust her and she trusts me.'

'This is very peculiar. You know you don't have a leg to stand on if she decides to walk away?'

'I know,' Cyril replies.

James arrives in the afternoon with the photo contact sheet. Cyril is astounded by how much the camera loves Roxy. He gives James the go ahead on the photos he likes, insisting the photos must be with him early tomorrow. He has reserved all of Thursday for hand delivering demo tapes and photo packs to twenty-five record companies. As James leaves, the phone rings. It's Roxy.

'Hi Cyril.'

'Hi Roxy! How are you?'

'Look, I'm sorry for not talking to you at the shoot. I was pretty upset with you about Tommy. What were you doing anyway?'

'I'm so sorry Roxy. It was for a good cause. I have some really exciting news for you, but I'll tell you in person on Friday.'

'Well, okay. You always manage to get yourself off the hook somehow, Cyril. Looking forward to seeing you. Bye.'

Cyril goes down to the shop to buy some more cigarettes, listening to Tina Turner's 'What's Love Got to do With It' on his Walkman. He returns to find he has missed a call from Jerome, who has left a very angry message.

'Cyril! What the fuck are you playing at? Using my name to get Ashley on the phone? He's a powerful man, Cyril. I should never have introduced you to him.'

Cyril deletes the message, feeling he has made yet another bad decision.

Chapter Ten

'Make It Easy on Yourself'

The Walker Brothers

Alf and Gina are discussing Cyril over breakfast. The radio plays 'A Little Respect' by Erasure. Cyril is about to enter the kitchen but stops for a moment when he overhears them.

'Never in my wildest dreams did I think Cyril would make a success of his business. I think I'm being proved wrong, I'm happy to say,' Alf remarks.

'You should've had more confidence. He has good ideas and works hard when it's for something he really cares about.'

'I don't know about hard-working. Have you seen how much time he spends in the pub?'

'Well, just lay off him about the money for a while, will you? You've got to trust him,' Gina replies sternly. She turns to the door, smiling as Cyril decides to make an entrance. 'There you are!' she says. 'You look smart. Not that I can see too well – my eyes are watering from the smell of all that Brut.'

Cyril smooths his light grey mohair suit, tucking his white shirt into his trousers.

'This is the most important day of my life, Mum. Getting Roxy on TV means offers from record companies. And then I'll never have to look back,' Cyril says with a mix of excitement and anxiousness.

'I'm sure they'll be queuing up to meet you, darling. Don't you think you need a tie?' Gina asks, beginning to fuss over Cyril.

'Your mum's right; you can't be an important businessman without a tie,' Alf agrees.

'I'm in the music business. We don't have a uniform,' Cyril replies, reaching into his jacket pocket, 'Here's the money I owe you. I'm sorry it took me so long but we're all up to date now.'

'This is unexpected. Where did the money come from?'

'Billy owed me some and he finally paid up.'

Alf looks deep in thought for a moment before replying: 'Keep it for now. You'll need it. Pay me when you've got your deal.' Gina smiles at Alf.

'I'm fine, Dad. I want to pay you back,' Cyril replies hastily pushing the money into Alf's hand and making for the door.

Gina makes a motion at Alf to suggest he give it back, but Cyril is already gone. She runs out the door and catches him just before he gets in the car.

'*Mazel Tov*! Make it happen tonight, son. God bless.' She throws her arms around him and gives him a kiss. '*Rosh Hashanah* is just around the corner; your good fortune will come. God is looking down on you. What a celebration we'll have!' she adds, wiping a tear from her eye.

'Thanks, Mum. Love you,' Cyril says as Gina waves goodbye.

Cyril does his usual routine of touching the Spurs logo before he starts the car. He drives towards Roxy's council estate listening to 'My Sharona' by The Knack. He is making good time but the traffic gets busy after crossing Waterloo Bridge to South London. Cyril looks at his watch; it's ten o'clock, and Roxy's house is only a few miles away. He is a little nervous still after the incident with Tommy, but Cyril's excitement is building. However, before he can get too excited his car starts to splutter. He struggles to change gear, cursing loudly, and the engine gives out. With excitement replaced by panic, Cyril coasts to the side of the road and jumps out of the car. He gives the rear bumper a good kick and makes for the nearest telephone box.

'Hi. Can you send someone to fix my Ford Escort? It's urgent.'

'What's your membership number?'

'I'm not a member.'

'Before I can send the recovery vehicle I'll have to make you a member. I'll need your credit card for payment. It should take about ten minutes to complete the paperwork. Is that okay?'

Cyril is about to start tearing his hair out when the woman tells him the recovery vehicle will arrive in an hour. He doesn't have enough time to wait. With a sigh, he dials Roxy's number.

'Hi Roxy. My car's broken down – I think the clutch has gone. Just my bloody luck. Of all the days this had to…'

'How long will it take to fix?' Roxy interrupts Cyril's rant. She was already feeling nervous and this has only made things worse.

'I don't know; I'm sorry. You're going to have to get a taxi to the studio while I wait for them to fix it.'

'Why do you have to stay with the car? You should've known it was going to break down. It's in the garage more than it's on the road.'

'Look, I'll see you as soon as I can. Don't worry, you

can trust me – I'll be there. I'll just nip into the office and then I'll be straight there.'

'Whatever, Cyril. You better not let me down.'

Roxy gets a taxi to the South Bank television studios, heaving her small suitcase of outfits into the back of the cab. When she arrives, a young female production assistant comes to reception to meet her.

'Hello, Roxy. I'm Jules, Mr Edwards' production assistant. You must be thrilled to be on the show tonight. It's an amazing opportunity.'

'I know, I'm just really nervous. This is all so new to me.'

'You'll be fine; don't worry. Let me run you through the schedule for the day on the way to your dressing room.'

Jules explain that there are six singing contestants on tonight's show, and that Roxy will be last to perform. Roxy is also the youngest contestant.

'I'll come back for you to do your sound recording test. After lunch, the costume and makeup people will be here to get you ready.'

Roxy looks around her dressing room wishing Cyril was there to calm her nerves. She feels out of place and uneasy in the chaos around her. Roxy decides to call Cyril and finds a phone outside the room. He doesn't answer so she leaves a message asking him to hurry up.

An hour later, Roxy is led to a small studio to do a sound test, followed by lunch in the canteen. She feels very self-conscious sitting alone in the corner of the room, looking out the window at the River Thames. Jules spots Roxy and makes her way over to chat.

'I didn't realise you were here on your own. Isn't your manager here looking after you?'

'My manager's car broke down this morning and…'

She stops mid-sentence and starts to cry. Jules sits down and puts her arm around Roxy. 'He'll be here soon. You have nothing to worry about – you sounded terrific in the sound check and Mr Edwards loves you. He's looking forward to meeting you.'

Roxy thanks Jules and heads back to her dressing room to pull herself together. She tries Cyril again but this time the phones are engaged. Wondering what on earth he could be doing wasting time on the phone, she calls and calls until he finally answers.

'Cyril Gold Artist Management. This is Cyril speaking.'

'Don't you Cyril Gold Artist Management me, Cyril! What are you doing at the office? I need you here,' Roxy says angrily.

'It's gone mad here. I've had so many messages from record companies wanting to talk about you. I thought I should call them back now to make sure we stay fresh in their minds.'

'They'll still be interested tomorrow, won't they? This is the scariest thing I've ever done and I don't want to be doing it on my own. I feel sick with nerves.'

'I'm trying to get a record deal for you, Roxy. This is good, honestly. I'll see you soon, and try not to worry – you're doing great.'

Roxy hangs up feeling frustrated that Cyril doesn't understand how she is feeling. He's always so calm and confident; she wishes she knew how to be more like him. Jules catches Roxy on the way back to her dressing room and tells her to come to the studio for camera rehearsals. The studio is enormous, filled with people who all seem to be looking at her. Roxy has never felt so small.

'Lovely to meet you at last, Roxy! I'm a big fan. Where is dear Cyril?' Michael asks, looking around for him.

'He's on his way. He had a problem with his car this morning,' Roxy says.

'Car, credit card; what next?' Michael replies, dramatically flicking his hair. 'I hope he isn't avoiding me,' he adds.

Roxy looks down at the floor, not exactly sure what Michael is talking about.

'To be honest, Mr Edwards, I'm feeling a bit nervous. I'm more used to singing to a bar full of drunks who aren't really listening. This is a totally different kettle of fish.'

'Firstly, Roxy darling, call me Michael. Mr Edwards makes me sound old. Secondly, don't be worried. I just want you to sing your beautiful song, "Waiting for Your Love", as you normally do, and I'll do the rest. The cameras will love your steely blue eyes. Come on, let's do the rehearsal.'

Roxy stands in the centre of the darkened studio floor. She feels as though the silence might swallow her up; only the sound of her own shallow breathing reaches her ears. A spotlight shines down on Roxy's face; the first camera moves forwards for a close up of her eyes as she starts to sing. The second camera moves in for a close up of Roxy's black t-shirt with her name sequined on it before pulling out to reveal her short, white mini skirt and red kicker shoes. When she finishes the song, Roxy receives and unexpected round of applause from the television crew. She blushes and smiles.

'Roxy! Congratulations. You held my attention every second you were on camera. Your live vocals are exceptional. I've got a nickname for you – Bette Davis!' Michael is very impressed and gushes over Roxy as she stands in disbelief. A very well-dressed woman floats into the studio. Roxy feels her presence before seeing her.

'Ah, Roxy. Meet Bea Solomon. The most successful agent in the business.'

'You flatter me, Michael. We go back years, isn't that right?' she says languidly.

'Yes, I suppose we do, but I still feel like a teenager most times,' Michael laughs.

'All my stars appear on Michael's show, so it's nice to see someone different around here. I hear you write all your own songs. And what a voice you have.'

Roxy beams and feels immediately at ease with Bea; her tone is friendly and her motherly face is very reassuring.

'I'm going to make a prediction,' Solomon continues. 'You will have a number one hit very soon. Let's go get a coffee and chat.'

She leads Roxy towards the canteen and they take a seat at the table. Roxy feels as though she's caught in a whirlwind.

'Is it Ms or Mrs Solomon,' Roxy asks anxiously.

'Most people just call me Solomon,' she laughs, 'but my friends call me Queen Bea. And by friends, I don't really mean friends.' She accents 'friends' with air quotes. 'No one is your friend in this business. It's a dog eat dog world and there are some very jealous people who aren't pleased to see a woman doing well for herself.'

Roxy finds Solomon's honesty refreshing.

'Where's your manager?' she asks suddenly, after a brief pause. Her voice is filled with concern, but her mind sees only an opportunity.

'Cyril was supposed to be here hours ago but he's always late or having problems with something,' Roxy admits, fed up with defending him.

'That's not good, just leaving you on your own like this.'

Roxy mumbles something in agreement.

'So, I hear you have a little boy. Michael told me,' Solomon says.

Roxy tries to hide her surprise.

'Don't worry. I won't tell anyone. I've had it tough too. My husband left me for a younger woman and took all my money. It hasn't been easy being a single mother, but I don't have to tell you that.'

Roxy finds it difficult to picture Solomon having a difficult past as she sits across the table in her expensive tailored suit, with perfectly manicured nails and hair. She chastises herself for judging by appearances and is glad they have something in common.

'It really is a man's world, like the James Brown song

215

says. The entertainment business is full of men. Most of them I wouldn't piss on if they were on fire,' Solomon adds, with a perfectly manicured laugh to top off her perfectly manicured appearance.

'Us women have got to stick together, I guess,' Roxy suggests with a hopeful smile.

'Absolutely, darling,' Solomon replies, touching Roxy's arm. She slips a hand into her Chanel handbag, pulling out cigarettes and her diary. One of her business cards fall out onto the floor. Roxy picks it up and holds it out to Solomon.

'Keep it. Like you said, we women need to stick together. Call me if you need anything,' Solomon says, squeezing Roxy's hand. 'Some lovely young studio camera men here tonight.' She smiles as two guys walk past. 'Pity they're queer. What a waste.'

Meanwhile, Cyril is still in his office answering the calls from various record companies. For the first time since he started the business, people are interested in talking to him. It seems like everyone wants to be his new best friend. Cyril enjoys finally being in the driving seat of negotiations; feeling the slight anxiety in the voice of the A&R department heads as he plays hardball with them. Cyril is having such a good time basking in the attention that he has quite forgotten about Roxy at the studio. The potential for a record deal is the only thing occupying his mind, and he knows he's coming close to getting it in the bag. Queen and Bowie's 'Under Pressure' plays on MTV in the background.

At the studio, Roxy sits alone in her dressing room. There is a knock at the door and Jules walks in.

'Michael thought you might need some company.'

Roxy's face lights up as Jerome appears in the doorway. She immediately throws her arms around him.

'Please tell me you're here to watch the show tonight. You'll stay, won't you?' she asks hurriedly.

'I'm staying. Of course I'm staying!'

'Michael nicknamed me Bette Davis. Can you believe that?' Roxy says, beaming.

Jerome laughs and starts to sing the Kim Carnes song, 'Bette Davis Eyes'.

'I have news for you. The word is out in the music industry – they're all talking about you. The guest list tonight is full of record company executives. You'll meet them all in the green room after the show,' Jerome says.

'The green room? What's that?'

'Where everybody goes after the show to get pissed! If you win the viewers' vote tonight, the world's your oyster!'

They both jump up and down in excitement.

'Now, tell me who put that outfit together. You're smokin' hot! All the men will go wild.'

'Are you going straight?' Roxy jests and they both laugh.

Cyril looks at his watch; it's almost six in the evening. He should have left for the studio hours ago. He rushes to collect his things, puts on the answer machine and makes for the door. The phone rings and Cyril can't help but listen to the message being left: 'Hi Cyril. It's Dan from Virgin Records. My head of A&R says you aren't returning his calls and your lines are always busy. Pick up the phone if you want a three-album deal with a generous cash payment up front…'

Cyril almost trips over trying to grab the phone before Dan hangs up.

'Dan! Hi. How are you? I was just on my way to meet Roxy at the television studio. It's been non-stop with the phone calls today.'

'Cyril, I'll get straight to the point. Why not come over to my office now and close this deal for Roxy? Our band Simple Minds is on *Top of the Pops* tonight so I'm in a particularly good mood.'

'I'll come over on my way to the studio. But we'll have to make it quick,' Cyril says, glancing anxiously at his watch.

He dashes out and hails a taxi to take him to the Virgin Records office. A woman called Esther meets him at the entrance and introduces herself as head of press and publicity. Cyril can't help but stare at her perfectly formed bottom as he follows her up the stairs. When Esther opens the boardroom door, Cyril is surprised to see Dan, the head of A&R, the director of Virgin Music Publishing and some other key staff. The group of important people make Cyril almost lose his nerve, but he maintains a confident appearance.

'Cyril, meet the team. We all love Roxy. She's something else – every song on her demo is a hit. Let me get you a drink.'

'Rum and Coke, please.'

The Virgin staff talk about their marketing ideas and how they would like to promote Roxy. Esther's hand lingers as she gives Cyril his drink. He grins and looks around the room, realising Virgin is desperate to sign Roxy. Someone turns on the TV to watch the live *Top of the Pops*. The presenter, David 'Kid' Jensen, opens the show by announcing Heaven 17.

'We made Simple Minds and Culture Club happen. Roxy could be next,' Dan says, trying to impress Cyril.

Cyril isn't really listening to Dan. His eyes keep wandering to Esther. However, when Dan asks about Roxy's background he pulls himself back to planet Earth.

'Erm, Roxy lives with her mother in Peckham. She's intelligent but life hasn't been kind to her; she's had many setbacks. And she has a lovely little boy.'

'Single mother? Let's downplay that one. It could affect her image if people know she is a single mother. That would affect record sales. People want a sexy, young, carefree girl. Not a single mother from Peckham. Same principle if she was a lesbian. It'd be a problem for record sales. Image is everything.'

'I thought it was all about the music?' Cyril asks with a nervous laugh. Dan laughs loudly and claps him on the back.

Esther returns with a bottle of Cristal champagne.

'I feel like this warrants a proper drink,' she says, pouring Cyril a glass.

Everyone chats and clinks glasses until David Jensen starts his rundown of the top ten singles. The number one song is announced, followed by shouts of excitement and more champagne popping.

Dan stands up and grins. 'Virgin has the number one record this week. Thanks to you all for making The Human League an unexpected chart-topping success.' The song begins to play.

'You were working as a waitress in a cocktail bar.

When I met you,

I picked you out. I shook you up and turned you around.

It turned you into someone new,

Now five years later on, you've got the world at your feet.

Success has been so easy for you.'

The music video features a close up of a young man with strangely familiar face and voice, even though his distinctive hairstyle is all slicked back. Cyril recognises him as the guy he laughed out of the office in his first week. A sick feeling forms in Cyril's stomach when he realises he could've been his manager.

'Cyril, you must meet Phil, the lead singer of The Human League. He's from Sheffield. He'll be coming over to celebrate soon,' Dan shouts.

Cyril puts his glass down on the table and begins to make his excuses to leave. 'I'm so sorry, but I must be getting to the studios now or I'll miss Roxy's performance.' The shock of seeing Phil brings him to his senses.

On the street, Cyril dashes about trying to get a cab, but he has no luck. And then it starts to rain. Heavily. He is drenched in seconds and it seems as though the taxis are actively avoiding him. He walks out into the road in an attempt to catch a driver's attention, only to be splashed with rainwater, covering him in grey sludge. As Cyril steps backwards onto the curb, he catches his heel and falls straight into a puddle, tearing his suit.

By the time Cyril arrives at the studio, it's already past eight and the show has started. He runs into reception and asks to be let in so he can find Roxy before she goes on. The guards look him up and down and shake their heads. He looks like a deranged madman.

'I'm sorry. Your name isn't on the VIP guest list. You'll have to leave.'

'Please, check again. My act, Roxy, is on the show tonight. I'm her manager.'

The receptionist and the guards exchange smirks and Cyril gets angry. He bangs his fists on the desk.

'I know Michael and he isn't going to be happy if I'm not there to sort my act out for the show.'

'Think you need to get your act together first, son. You need to leave,' the guard says sternly.

'I'm not your fucking son. Just get someone on the phone so I can explain.'

The security guard makes a quick gesture and, before Cyril can protest any further, two more guards have hoisted him off the ground and are carting him towards the door. They dump him on the pavement and walk smugly back into the building.

'Another washed up wannabe,' one of them

comments, and they all laugh.

Inside the studio, Roxy is the last of the six acts to sing after a commercial break. Michael comes over to give her some words of reassurance.

'Remember, look down until your vocals come in. Only then do you look up at the camera and smile. I'll have a spotlight on you like we did this afternoon. Good luck!'

Jerome gives her a thumbs up from the side of the stage and winks. 'You'll be great,' he says, followed by a chorus of disgruntled shushing from the stagehands. Roxy takes her position and tries to stop her hands from trembling.

Outside, Cyril sits on the curb for an hour in the cold wind and pouring rain. He jumps up as the studio audience begins to stream out of the exits. He hears several of them talking about how good Roxy was.

'Excuse me, can you tell me who won tonight?' Cyril asks a couple as they get into a taxi.

'Roxy! She was terrific,' the woman replies.

Cyril makes a move to slip past the security guards but they've been keeping an eye on him.

'Oi. You. I thought I told you to bugger off,' the tall one shouts.

'I'm not looking for trouble. I just want to see Roxy and Michael.'

'You are trouble. The stars leave through the exit in the underground car park. Now bugger off and don't come back.'

Cyril walks to the car park entrance and tries to loiter without looking too suspicious. The parking attendant seems more interested in his magazine and singing along to the radio, which is playing The Walker Brothers' 'Make it Easy on Yourself'.

The green room is full of guests from the entertainment world. When Roxy walks in, she receives a standing ovation and cheers from everyone. She thanks them and blushes, trying to hide behind Jerome as much as possible. Everyone in the room wants to talk to Roxy and they keep addressing Jerome as though he is her manager, trying to make deals left and right. Michael pulls Jerome aside.

'How about a nightcap later?'

'I don't think so. I need to look after Roxy tonight since Cyril isn't around.'

'Where is he anyway?'

'I have no idea. The record company executives keep trying to get me to make a record deal with them for Roxy. I just can't believe he'd be missing this opportunity.'

'You might as well be her manager. You're more reliable than him by a mile.'

Roxy wanders away from Jerome, trying to take everything in. She is suddenly approached by a tall, handsome man wearing a light grey suit and an open-neck shirt.

'Here, toast with me,' he says, holding a glass of champagne out to Roxy.

'Thanks, but I don't drink.'

'All the more for me,' he says. 'So, I hope you let little Tommy stay up to watch your big performance.'

Roxy is startled for a moment and wonders how everyone and their grandmother seems to know about Tommy.

'Who are you?' she asks cagily.

'My apologies. So rude of me not to introduce myself. I'm Kevin Cash.'

'You're Kevin Cash?' Roxy replies in disbelief. 'I was going to drop my demos off at your office until I found Cyril.'

'And how are you finding Cyril? I must admit I haven't seen him tonight, which is most unusual. Especially on such a momentous occasion.'

'Something unexpected came up,' Roxy says vaguely, mostly to protect herself but also partly to protect

Cyril's dignity.

'He should be here cutting you a deal with these people,' Kevin probes, hoping to elicit some sort of response.

'How did you hear of me?' Roxy asks in an attempt to change the subject.

'Ashley Goodman sent me your demos. He's a fan of your music and he thought you deserved a better manager. Someone professional and experienced,' Kevin says with a shrug.

'Cyril is a great guy,' Roxy says, reflexively coming to his defence.

'You don't have to keep defending him. He's done you no favours by not being here. You don't owe him anything.'

Roxy stares at him, holding his gaze boldly.

'Business is business. You can't be too personal about these things. My artists expect certain things from me and I always deliver. And I only work with the best artists. Artists like you, Roxy. You're too concerned about hurting Cyril's feelings. But if you change your mind, it might be the best decision you ever make.' Kevin hands Roxy his card and walks away.

Roxy looks around for Jerome and walks over to him.

'Kevin Cash just offered to be my manager,' she says, half confused and half excited.

'What? Really? What did you say? Are you going to just ditch Cyril?'

'No. I didn't say anything. He just left me his card.'

Before they can discuss the matter any further, Michael flounces up to them and announces that they are invited to dinner in order to celebrate the show.

'How exciting! Where are we going?' Jerome asks.

'The Elephant on the River,' Michael announces. 'And Kevin is paying!'

'I've always wanted to go there. It's one of the most talked about places to eat in London,' Jerome says excitedly. Roxy doesn't look so sure.

'I should get home for Tommy.'

'Come on, Roxy. Tommy will be in bed by now. This is your special night.'

'I know. It just doesn't feel the same without Cyril. I want him to explain himself. Also, I don't know what to say to all these record executives.'

'Just play it cool. Cyril can deal with them tomorrow.'

Michael calls for silence and then gives a toast to Roxy. Everyone lifts their glasses. Kevin walks up to Bea Solomon and the two vultures look at Roxy across the room.

'Look what the cat's dragged in,' Solomon begins.

'Save it, Bea,' Kevin replies under his breath.

'I know your game. You want Roxy. I saw you talking

with her earlier.'

Kevin simply smiles and walks away.

Cyril is just about to give up and walk back to his car when a convoy of expensive vehicles begin to emerge from the car park. Cyril sees Michael's car among them, with Roxy and Jerome laughing and enjoying themselves in the back seat. He can hear them singing along to Cyndi Lauper's 'Girls Just Want to Have Fun.' He throws himself towards the car, trying to catch their attention by shouting and waving his arms. But they drive off without seeing him. Once again, Cyril finds himself left alone on the pavement.

He walks dejectedly back to the office, stopping to get a bottle of rum on the way. His mind is all over the place, going from the highs of a deal with Virgin Records, to the low of letting Roxy down. The light on his answer machine is flashing.

'Cyril, where are you? I'm so pissed off at you. You'd better turn up.'

The next message: 'I have twenty minutes before I go down to the studio. I can't believe you've just left me here to do this on my own.'

Angry and frustrated, Cyril knows he can't go home to face a thousand questions from Alf and Gina. He puts two chairs together to make a bed but it's so uncomfortable he chooses to sleep on the floor instead.

Jerome and Roxy leave the restaurant and go on to Monkberry's nightclub in the West End. They are introduced to Freddie Mercury and Elton John by some of the music executives hoping to impress Roxy into signing a deal with them. Jerome is even more excited than Roxy; he's always wanted to meet Freddie.

They end the evening in Tramps nightclub, and by this time it's actually the early hours of the morning. Neither Roxy nor Jerome had any idea who was paying for the bar tabs, but the drinks kept coming so they didn't ask questions. Just after four in the morning, they stumble out of a taxi absolutely legless.

'Where are we Jerome? Are we getting more food?' Roxy asks, taking another swig from the bottle of champagne she is holding.

'This is where I live. The flat over the Chinese restaurant.'

They stumble up the stairs, followed by the smell of grease and cooking until they close the door of Jerome's flat behind them.

'I didn't expect it to be so clean and tidy,' Roxy exclaims, flopping down on Jerome's bed. Jerome kicks off his shoes and joins her.

'What did you expect from a gay boy from Bradford? I have my standards,' Jerome exclaims with mock offence.

'Wow. What a night. Did you hear Elton when he said he liked my song? He's so lovely.'

'I know. And Freddie was amazing. I think he took a shine to me.'

'You wish!'

'No, really! He invited me to a leather club in Earl's Court but I had to tell him I was looking after you. For someone who doesn't drink, you're certainly very drunk.'

They laugh together. Until Jerome adds, 'So, are you going to call Cyril?'

'I'm not ringing him. He can call me and apologise,' Roxy says, suddenly serious.

'Sorry for ruining the mood,' Jerome replies quietly.

'No, you didn't.' She looks at him for a few seconds and then leans forwards to kiss him.

'What are you doing?' Jerome says, pulling away.

'You kiss men for money, why can't you kiss me? I just need some love tonight.' She puts her hands on Jerome and tries to undo his trousers.

'Roxy…'

'You have a cute smile, you know that? You're very handsome. I bet people are always telling you. Wow, it's really warm in here.' As Roxy says this, she undresses. She takes off her knickers and Jerome turns away.

'Roxy! Put your knickers back on! You're embarrassing me. Look, I'll find you a nice straight guy, I promise.'

Roxy throws her knickers at Jerome and bursts out laughing, and he laughs back.

'I'm sorry, Jerome. I think I'm going to be sick.'

'Not in the bed. The bathroom – go!'

She just makes it to the toilet in time and Jerome tries not to listen to the sound of her heaving. She returns to the bed and curls up next to Jerome.

Chapter Eleven

'Love Is the Drug'

Roxy Music

Roxy, tired and very hungover, leaves Jerome's flat the next morning and crawls into a black taxi. She smiles down at the television award sitting in her lap.

'Where would you like to go, young lady?' the friendly taxi driver asks.

'Home, please,' Roxy replies distractedly before adding, 'Peckham, south London.'

The driver turns up the radio which is playing Fleetwood Mac's 'Go Your Own Way.' Roxy leans back and closes her eyes, wondering if last night was just a dream. She hopes Cyril will call and explain himself so that they can just move on; it seems like everything is looking up and Roxy wants to share her excitement with Cyril. As the taxi turns onto her estate she wonders whether Tommy has missed her.

'Looks like there's something going off near your house, love,' the taxi driver comments.

Just as Roxy is about to say she has no idea who they are, the crowd appears to notice the taxi at once and swarm towards it. They all seem to know her name, cheering and calling out. Some are waving pens and paper, asking for autographs.

'Are you famous, Miss? Should I know who you are?' the driver asks with a grin.

'Perhaps,' Roxy replies with a laugh.

As the taxi stops, the real frenzy begins, with the press pushing forwards to get the best shots; cameras flash constantly and they shout questions at Roxy before she even gets out of the vehicle. They begin to surround the taxi and Roxy realises she must make her escape now or she will be trapped. She politely thanks the taxi driver and takes a deep breath before opening the door and making a run for it.

She makes it safely behind the front door of the ground floor flat and locks it quickly. Roxy's mother appears holding Tommy and looking anxious.

'I'm so glad you're back, sweetheart. They've been here for hours, knocking on the door. They wouldn't believe me when I said you weren't here. I said you'd be back soon. I was going to ask if they wanted a cup of tea but I don't think we have enough mugs!'

'Sorry, Mum. I had no idea this would happen.'

Tommy takes an interest in Roxy's award and she bends down to show it him. 'Your Mummy's a winner, Tommy!'

He takes the award, more excited by how shiny it is than what it means, and runs into the kitchen.

'Tommy! You be careful with that,' Roxy's mother shouts as Roxy just laughs. 'You we're brilliant last night. I couldn't stop screaming at the telly when they announced you the winner.'

Roxy beams with pride but her attention is drawn to a strange banging noise. She throws open the curtains only to find a group of people gathered right outside the window. They cheer and a flurry of flashes follow. Closing them quickly, Roxy grabs the phone and dials Cyril's number.

But Cyril isn't home, and he isn't at the office. He is making his way across London to Roxy's house. After waking up, he knew exactly what he needed to do: explain everything to Roxy and hope she forgives him when he tells her the excellent news about Virgin Records. Cyril also wants to surprise Roxy with the publishing rights to her songs. He has the document drawn up by Maurice to show her.

When Cyril doesn't answer his office phone and Gina informs her that he hasn't been home since yesterday, Roxy can't help but feel this is the last straw. She needs him now even more than she did last night. The mob outside feel very threatening and Roxy has both her mother and Tommy to worry about. After a few moments thought, she roots through her bag and pulls out the business cards she was given last night. Kevin Cash and Bea Solomon. She picks up the phone and dials.

'Hello, this is Roxy. Can I speak to Ms Solomon? She told me to call if I ever needed any help.'

'She's on a call at the moment. Can I take a message?' asks Solomon's long-time assistant, Rose.

'Can I hold please? It's urgent.'

'She's just finished the call now. I'll put you through.'

'Hello, Roxy, my lovely. How are you?' Solomon asks, taking a long drag on a cigarette.

'I've got a hundred people outside my mum's flat in Peckham. Journalists, TV crews and fans. I don't know what to do with them. My boy's crying and my mum's gone mad trying to give them all tea! What should I do?'

'You shouldn't have to do anything, darling,' Solomon replies slowly.

'What?' Roxy asks, in no mood to play guessing games.

'Where's your manager? This is his domain.'

By now, Roxy is sick to death of people asking her this. 'I don't know,' she says flatly.

'Well I have eyes everywhere,' Solomon begins mysteriously. 'A little birdie told me they saw him outside Peter Stringfellow's strip club with some girl. She must have been quite a looker. Why else would Cyril miss your big night?' Solomon pauses for dramatic effect. 'You don't want a manager who puts his cock before his clients,' she adds, turning around to Rose with a sly smirk so that her assistant can watch as she plays out her deceitful game of chess. Bea Solomon's lies have exactly the devastating effect she desired.

Roxy is stunned and hurt for more reasons than one. A weighty pause hangs between them. Eventually, Roxy speaks: 'Please, I just need your help.'

It might not sound like an outright victory, but Solomon knows she has essentially won Roxy over. It's not like Cyril was a worthy opponent anyway. *Like taking candy from a baby*, she thinks with a wry smile.

'Pack a suitcase. I'll take you somewhere until it quietens down. Don't worry, darling; Queen Bea is on her way.'

'Thank you, Ms Solomon,' Roxy replies, and gives her address.

Solomon hangs up the phone and starts to laugh.

'Rose, my plan worked better than I'd hoped. If only

I could see Cyril's face when he finds out he's handed me his chart-topping artist. It's obvious that Roxy has feelings for Cyril, otherwise she'd have left him the first time he let her down. Better to rip that plaster off quickly, I'd say. I've done her a huge favour.'

Rose agrees vehemently.

'Get me a taxi to Peckham. And you can call off the media circus in about half an hour. I want to swoop in and play the hero first,' Solomon continues, touching up her makeup in a compact mirror.

'I have to hand it to you; they don't call you Queen Bea for nothing. You played that one superbly,' Rose says, helping Solomon into her long, black fur coat.

Cyril hears the crowd of people before he sees them. They are all chanting Roxy's name. He pulls the car over to the side of the road and gets out. At first, he is excited to see the mass of press coverage – it feels like real fame. But then he realises how scared Roxy and her mother must be inside. And, of course, little Tommy. Cyril breaks into a sprint, heading down the pavement towards the gathering. A dark figure steps in front of him and he comes skidding to a halt.

'Hello.'

Cyril looks up at the woman in front of him and recognises her from the restaurant where he met

Michael. Bea Solomon. He opens his mouth to speak but she gets there first.

'Ah, the famous Cyril. So good of you to finally make an appearance.'

'Why are you here?' Cyril replies with more confidence than he feels.

'Roxy asked me to call you,' Solomon begins, revelling in Cyril's confusion. 'You let her down one too many times.'

'I can only be in one place at a time,' Cyril says defensively, immediately regretting letting his guard down.

'That's the difference between you and me. You bring excuses and I bring results.'

'What are you saying?' Cyril snarls.

'You're through. She doesn't want you anymore.'

'No. I don't believe you. I want to talk to her,' Cyril says, making a move to go past Solomon. She puts a hand on his shoulder.

'The deal is already done, Cyril. She made me her manager last night,' Solomon lies, with a devilish grin.

'You stole her from me,' Cyril protests.

'You can't steal something from someone who isn't even there,' she laughs derisively.

Cyril barges past her, a fire ignited in his chest. And then Solomon plays her final hand.

'She doesn't love you.'

He stops in his tracks and turns around. Solomon laughs inwardly at how marvellously predictable young people are. Always falling in love. Always letting it ruin everything.

'You don't know what you're talking about,' Cyril tries, but Solomon's parasitic words have already eaten through to his core.

'Roxy said she was worried you'd let your feelings get in the way of business. But then you went and let her down anyway. You can't play with a girl's heart like that, Cyril. If you want to spare her any more pain, you'll leave her alone. You know I can do everything for her and make her the star she deserves to be – the kind you can only dream of. You'd only hold Roxy back.'

Cyril remains silent because he knows what she says is true. Solomon recognises the face of someone who has been completely defeated and congratulates herself on a magnificent performance. She steps past him deftly and glides through the crowd towards Roxy's front door. The final injury is the look of relief on Roxy's face when she opens the door to let Solomon in. Cyril feels himself becoming just another face in the crowd.

Having never felt so alone, all Cyril wants to do is disappear. He phones his parents and tells them he's gone to America for a few weeks to follow a new opportunity. He doesn't care whether or not they believe it, he just can't face explaining everything to them. Each newspaper article covering Roxy and her new deal with CBS feels like a punch in the gut. He falls further and further into a dark hole. At the loneliest times, drink feels like a good friend. And a close friend of alcohol is drugs.

After the fourth day of sleeping in the office, Mandy, a girl from downstairs, invited herself into Cyril's office for a drink. She offered Cyril lines of cocaine and, believing he had nothing left to lose, finally gave in and joined her. Mandy was nice enough; she let Cyril shower at her place and they spent most the time, when she wasn't working, drinking, having sex and doing coke. Cyril would have done anything to feel something other than the pain in his heart. While Mandy works, servicing men from her apartment, Cyril stares blindly at the TV in his office. He watches MTV recordings over and over again until he dreams about the music videos in his drug-induced sleep. He is haunted by Solomon's words.

Billy wanders down the street, not in any particular hurry, and spots Mickey Sullivan on his market stall.

'Hey, Mickey. Business slow today?'

'Yeah, something like that,' Mickey grumbles.

Sensing he isn't in the mood to chat, Billy smiles and walks on.

'Oi,' Mickey calls, 'if you see that mate of yours, Cyril, tell him he still owes me for the blow I gave him last week. He seems to think it grows on trees.'

'Wait a minute... Cyril's in town?' Billy asks, quickly retracing his steps.

'Yep. Hanging round here like a bad smell that one is. Don't know what's got into him. Well, except a shit tonne of coke.'

The Cyril that Billy knows would never touch drugs. He knows something is wrong and decides to find him. Billy scouts out all their usual spots but it is by pure chance that he finds Cyril. He almost doesn't recognise him; pale skin, grey smudges under his eyes and dirty, unwashed clothes. Cyril is sitting on a bench reading a newspaper and Billy watches as he uses the newspaper to disguise taking a swig from a hipflask.

''Ello, 'ello, 'ello. What do we have here?' Billy says, impersonating a police officer as he strolls up to Cyril.

Cyril almost falls off the bench with shock and then realises it is Billy looking down at him, not a copper. 'What do you want?' he asks aggressively.

'Woah, alright. Your mother told me you were in America,' Billy says, sitting down. He notices Cyril smells of alcohol.

'What's going on? You were closing a record deal for Roxy, right?'

'Haven't you read the papers?' Cyril asks wearily. 'Roxy signed a huge deal with CBS.'

'Yeah, but I thought it was your deal.'

Cyril starts to laugh and shake his head before looking up desperately at Billy. 'I fucking blew it. I lost my star.'

'Okay. Start at the beginning and tell me what happened.'

After twenty minutes of explaining, Cyril finishes the story by telling Billy how he has spent the last week; drunk and alone. He starts to cry and Billy tries to console him.

'Can you get me a drink, Billy? I could do with a stiff one but I've run out of money.'

'I think you need to give the drinking a rest. Let's go and get some food.'

They walk to St Anne's Gardens, the public park on Wardour Street, after getting some fish and chips. They sit on a bench to eat. Billy tries to say all the right things, telling Cyril there will be other acts to make into stars.

'Don't you get it? It's not just about the record deal; I wanted Roxy to be my girl,' Cyril says exasperatedly.

'Believe me, I get it. In fact, I got it before you, remember? I said you had a thing for her the first time I saw you both together.'

'I was being professional...' Cyril mumbles with regret.

'Does Roxy know you fancy her? Maybe losing her as an artist was a good thing because now you don't have to worry about being professional.'

Solomon's words ring in Cyril's ears, sending a shiver down his spine.

'I don't think so,' he replies. 'She wouldn't want a loser like me anyway.'

'Shut up! You know you can pull any bird you want. At least you can when you've had a shower,' Billy says, giving Cyril a good-natured punch.

Cyril laughs and Billy suggests they walk back to his office.

'I had to pick myself up after that shit Kevin Cash sacked me; you can do the same. You just need to get your mojo back. Get back on the horse, and all that.'

Cyril opens the door to his office and Billy does his best not to convulse at the miasma of aromas that immediately assault his senses. The most prominent ones being piss and stale food. Billy casually wanders over to the window and opens it wide.

'Did I tell you I'm living at home with my mum again? It's great. She cooks, washes my clothes and irons them. Can't remember why I ever left.'

Cyril sits down heavily in a chair and sighs.

'I'm joining a new rock band called Diamonds. I'm replacing their drummer; a real tosser. The best part is, they've already got a record deal.'

Billy realises that Cyril is completely ignoring him and busying himself doing lines of cocaine from the grimy table. This stuns him into silence. Billy is more than familiar with drug use; there aren't many things he hasn't snorted or smoked. But seeing Cyril in this state makes him realise just how much of a mess his friend is really in. Billy had often wished Cyril would get down off his high horse about drugs; it was one of the reasons he had slipped him the speed before the meeting with Ashley Goodman at CBS. A pang of guilt works its way through Billy's body. If Cyril had gone to that meeting with a clear head, perhaps he would have got the deal with CBS, before Roxy was poached by some vulture of a manager.

Cyril lays down on the floor and closes his eyes. Billy doesn't want to leave him but a glance at his watch sends a jolt of panic through him as he realises he is going to be late for a meeting with the band. He explains to Cyril that he will be back soon but gets no reply.

As Billy walks down Berwick Street, wondering how he could help Cyril, an idea pops into his head and he makes a detour.

'Madame J, can we have a chat?' Billy asks, trying not to get distracted by the attractive hostesses flitting around.

'I can do you one better than a chat. We have some luxury rooms upstairs,' MJ replies with a grin.

'Any other day and I'd say yes, but I'm here for Cyril. I'm worried about him; he's in a bad way.'

'Hm. I've been wanting to see him actually. The last batch of lingerie he sold me was full of rejects; everything falling apart at the seams,' MJ begins.

'Go easy on him,' Billy interrupts, 'he's not in a good place. I think he needs help.'

'Drugs, is it?' MJ asks.

'How did you know?'

'It always is with these show business types. I'll see what I can do.'

Up in the office, Cyril has been joined by Mandy and they start doing more lines together. Then, just like old times, Diamond barges into the office.

'What the fuck are you playing at, Gold?' He stops in his tracks, looking around the room. 'This place looks like a fucking crack den.'

'Diamond! Come join us. It's on me.'

'You shut the fuck up. The last lot of underwear you gave Gloria was a load of shite. I want my money back.'

'It's all here,' Cyril giggles, holding up the cocaine.

'Don't play funny with me. You want to piss off Mr Soho? You useless toe rag.'

Cyril falls about laughing, getting more hysterical, which makes Diamond angrier. Cyril turns up the radio playing 10cc's 'I'm Mandy Fly Me'. Diamond turns around and removes a wooden mallet from his huge coat pocket. As Cyril and Mandy both start singing, he wheels back around and smashes the hammer into the table. Cocaine flies up in a cloud of white. Mandy screams and runs out of the office. Diamond pushes Cyril around the room, demanding to know where he keeps the money. Eventually Cyril gives him the cash box and Diamond counts it.

'You're short. Empty your pockets'.

Cyril just laughs and he turns his pockets inside out. 'That's it! No more money. Bank is closed. Bye, bye.'

In a blind rage, Diamond lifts the hammer and swings it at Cyril's leg. Cyril yells in pain and falls to the floor.

'I'll give you something to laugh about,' he shouts,

raising his hammer again. Mercifully, MJ appears behind Diamond and grabs his arm. She whispers in his ear: 'Stop, or I'll tell everyone you like cock.'

'You fucking bitch. He sold me seconds.'

'How much are you short. Or do you want a blow job for old times' sake,' MJ asks, pulling a wad of cash out of her cleavage.

'Trannie slag. Don't you go telling lies about me or you won't have a pot to piss in by the time I've finished with you,' Diamond growls, grabbing the cash and storming out.

MJ rushes to Cyril on the floor as he holds his leg.

'I'm taking you home.'

'No, I can't go home. My mum thinks I'm in America. I can't face them yet.'

'Billy told me everything. Come on, get up. We'll go back to my place in Camden Town. It's not as posh as Stanmore, but it's home to me.'

As he hobbles along, Cyril explains that he didn't mean to sell Diamond seconds, it was a genuine mistake.

'I must have picked up the wrong boxes.'

MJ believes Cyril; an intoxicated mind often tells the truth. In the taxi on the way to her house, all Cyril talks about is Roxy and it doesn't take long for MJ to work out that Cyril has had his heart broken.

When they arrive, Cyril stumbles around admiring

everything in the basement flat. 'What a lovely place you have! It has your personality stamped all over it. I love the chandeliers, and you could fit three in that bed.'

'Believe me when I say I know,' MJ laughs. 'But you'll have your own room.'

Cyril follows MJ down a small corridor that looks somewhat out of place in the flat. He limps along, feeling lucky his leg isn't broken, and digs his hand into his pocket to find the plastic bag of cocaine. He drops it to the floor. MJ turns around and scoops it up swiftly.

'Why have you started doing this shit?'

'I just need it to feel better. I have all these awful feelings. And now my leg hurts like hell.'

'You just need to sleep it off,' MJ replies, pocketing the bag.

She opens a door and reveals what Cyril assumes to be his bedroom for the night. The room before him, however, is more of a sex dungeon than a bedroom. There are no windows and the walls are quilted in red and black. A bed sits in the centre with a record player and stacks of records next to it.

'What kind of room is this? Cyril asks. 'Actually, I don't care. It'll make a change to sleep in a proper bed.'

He flings himself onto the sheets and picks up a record. 'I love music! I'm a DJ, y' know.'

'Well enjoy listening to the records and I'll see you tomorrow,' MJ replies, closing the door. She opens the little hatch in the door and adds: 'Don't worry about making too much noise, the room is soundproofed. Sleep tight.'

Cyril looks through the albums on the floor, oblivious to the fact he is locked in the room. When he starts to feel hungry, he tries the door to go in search of some food.

'Very funny, MJ. Now let me out.' There is no response.

He shouts and shouts until she eventually returns and opens the hatch. Cyril presses up against it so that their faces are only inches apart.

'It's for your own good, Cyril. The drink and the drugs – it's all too much. You need to go cold turkey for a while.' And without another word, she shuts the hatch.

Cyril sinks to the floor and the terrible feelings he has been trying so hard to keep away come crawling from the shadows of his mind.

Later that evening, MJ returns and holds some beans on toast through the hatch. He grabs the plate and throws it back at her.

'Let me out of your fucking cell, you freak. And I hate baked beans.'

'Love you too, darling. You'll eat anything when you get hungry enough,' she replies nonchalantly and closes the hatch.

Chapter Twelve

'Reflections'

Diana Ross & The Supremes

Six days on, and Cyril is still inside MJ's cell. He has played every album in her extensive collection of Motown and Soul records many times over. Cyril has stopped cursing and eats whatever food is passed to him through the hatch. It's been a rough few days, but he's sober and his mind feels clearer than it has in a long time. Cyril plays 'Reflections' by Diana Ross, and sings along:

'Through the mirror of my mind
Time after time
I see reflections of you and me
Reflections of
The way life used to be
Reflections of
The love you took from me

Oh, I'm all alone now
No love to shield me
Trapped in a world
That's a distorted reality
The happiness you took from me
And left me alone.'

With nothing to distract him, Cyril has had plenty of time to reflect on everything; he knows he must move on with his life and forget about Roxy. He's been putting it off for days, but eventually Cyril works up the courage to call his parents.

'Mum?'

'Oh Cyril! Are you okay? I was so worried. How's America?'

'It's great,' Cyril replies. 'How's Dad?'

'He's fine. We're so excited about Roxy. She's all over the papers and the TV. We're surprised you're not here to enjoy all the attention.'

'She's being well looked after,' Cyril replies, struggling to keep the tone of regret from his voice. 'I'm going to have to go. This call is costing a fortune.'

'Alright, Love. But *Rosh Hashanah* is just around the corner. You'll be home for that, won't you?'

'I haven't forgotten, Mum. I'll be there.' Cyril hands the phone to MJ through the hatch and she hangs up. The phone call has left Cyril feeling homesick.

'Are they alright?' MJ asks.

'They're fine. I just can't tell them the truth, not yet anyway.'

'How about a cup of tea?' MJ smiles.

'That would be great,' Cyril replies, his face lighting up. 'It'd be nice to see the sun at some point, MJ. I don't know whether it's day or night. How long have I been here now?'

'This is the sixth day,' MJ says as she unlocks the door, holding out a cup of tea to Cyril.

Cyril jumps up and rushes towards the open door. MJ flinches, almost expecting Cyril to hit her. But he just takes the cup of tea and scurries out the door.

'I thought you'd never let me out,' he complains, sitting down on MJ's sofa.

'To celebrate your release, I've got us a Chinky takeaway,' she puts her hands together in an oriental greeting. 'You've suffered my cooking long enough.'

Cyril looks hungrily at the takeaway. 'Chinese – my favourite.' He begins eating as though he hasn't been fed for weeks.

'Those few days were just what I needed to get my head straight. I feel like I'm ready for the world again.' He pauses. 'I'm really sorry about the horrible things I shouted at you. I know it's no excuse, but I really wasn't myself. You definitely aren't a freak; you're a great friend.'

'I know, Cyril. It's okay. Jerome was asking about you yesterday. We had coffee.'

'What did you tell him?' Cyril asks.

'The truth, of course, darling. He found it most amusing that I had you locked up in my little room eating beans on toast. He nearly fell off his chair laughing. Don't worry, he promised not to say anything to anyone else.'

They continue to eat; Cyril savours every bite.

Through a mouthful of Chicken Chow Mein, MJ tells Cyril about her day.

'I saw a fortune teller today. He told me I will meet a tall American, we will fall in love and he would help me become a star. He also said I would get back together with my ex, too. What do you think about that?'

'You're already a star in Soho!' Cyril replies dutifully.

'You're right. I am,' MJ replies, striking a pose.

After they have eaten, MJ lights a cigarette and suddenly becomes more serious.

'I know you can see the funny side of the situation, and that's good, but I didn't do this just for a laugh. I'm dramatic, but not crazy – getting you to go cold turkey was the best way I could think of to help you.' She takes a long drag on the cigarette and looks thoughtfully at Cyril. 'I lost an older brother to drugs.

He had an addictive personality, and I see the same trait in you. Once you start something, you can't leave it alone. If you don't keep the drink and drugs in check, it'll eventually destroy you.'

Cyril is quiet.

'Can you go and see someone for help? If you thought the withdrawal was bad this time round, try kicking a ten-year-long habit.'

Cyril nods his head in agreement.

'MJ, can I ask you a personal question? You don't have to answer if you don't want.'

'Ask away.'

'Can you explain your sexuality to me? Are you a man dressed as a woman? Or have you had your bits chopped off,' Cyril asks with a cheeky grin.

'Oi, I'll chop your bits off if you're not careful! Cheeky sod,' she laughs and then pauses to take a deep breath. 'Okay. I was born a man, yes. But I knew it felt wrong from quite a young age. I was brought up to be a good Catholic boy. God knows I tried to fight it. I prayed for help, but none came. I was in a very dark place; I had to choose whether to kill myself or accept the person that I am. I've reached a happy place now. I've almost saved up enough for the operation to become a complete woman,' she smiles. Cyril reaches out and gives MJ a tight hug.

'Now, moving on: how are you fixed for money?' she asks.

'I'm broke. And I can't keep borrowing underwear from my dad to sell – he'll find out eventually.'

'Borrowed?' MJ exclaims. 'You mean I've been wearing stolen goods?!'

Cyril looks sheepish, shifting uneasily.

'This must stop right now. No more stealing; no more substance abuse. You can come and work for me in the evenings until you get back on your feet. I have to visit my elderly mother this week. She lives in a small village in Gwynedd.'

'Gwynedd – that's Wales, right?'

'Jazz has taken quite a shine to you. She's not an easy woman to charm, so you should have no trouble attracting business for the club with your charisma. I'll show you the ropes, but then I'll be off to Wales for a week. You can make good commission if you work hard.'

Cyril agrees with amusement, imagining himself drumming up attention for MJ's club as he had seen her do many times in the past.

The following morning, Cyril arrives in Soho listening to 'Give Me Just A Little More Time' by Chairmen of the Board on his Walkman. He picks up a bottle of milk from the corner shop and makes his way towards the office. As he looks around at the people passing by, Cyril realises it's been a long while since he has taken the time to even notice his surroundings. This becomes painfully evident as he opens the door to his office. It looks as though a bomb has gone off. Empty takeaway containers litter the floor; to say the room smelt stale would be an understatement. One of the chairs is broken and Cyril can't even recall how it happened. He wonders how on earth he spent so much time rotting in this dump as he throws open all three windows. After making a cup of tea, he sets to work.

He opens the mountain of post that was waiting for him; mostly invoices. The messages on his answer machine are painful reminders of everything Cyril wanted to be. He listens to them anyway. As he starts cleaning, Cyril keeps finding black and white pictures of Roxy around the office. He starts putting them all in a folder, but something makes him change his mind and he stuffs them all into the bin, except for one, which he puts in his pocket. One of his mum's favourite phrases comes to mind: 'It's better to have loved and lost than to never have loved at all.' The distant ache in Cyril's heart makes him think otherwise.

He collects the empty rum bottles and the cans of lager, throwing them into black bin liners. The phones don't ring anymore. Cyril vaguely remembers drunkenly telling several people to piss off when they called asking about Roxy. The nostalgia of being back in the office makes Cyril want to head straight to the pub; all of his ambitions and dreams once lived in this room. But MJ's warning rings in his head and he doesn't want to let her down. Instead he drinks the cold milk from the fridge.

With the office looking much better than when he started, Cyril heads to get some dinner. On the way back, he finds Jerome waiting on the landing. They look at each other for a moment before Jerome scrambles up and rushes to give him a hug.

'MJ told me I'd find you here.'

'I'm so sorry for everything that happened. I'm sorry about calling Ashley Goodman and pretending to be you, and blowing the TV show with Michael. And I'm sorry I didn't apologise sooner and explain everything to you.'

'Cyril, stop. It's okay; water under the bridge. I don't know if you remember, but I came to see you a few times after Roxy signed the new deal. But you were always either drunk or off your head on something, and me being there just seemed to upset you more.'

Cyril hangs his head in shame; he doesn't remember at all, but can imagine he was pretty horrible to Jerome.

'Sorry for that, I really am. But I'm feeling more like myself now. No more drink and drugs.'

'I'm glad to hear it,' Jerome replies, giving Cyril a hug. Those old feelings for Cyril make him an easy person to forgive.

They catch up over tea, laughing like old times. When there is a lull in the conversation, Jerome looks at him carefully. 'So, what did happen that day? Where were you?' he asks gently.

Cyril sighs. 'Oh, I don't know. I got too caught up chasing the deals and I forgot that Roxy needed me to be with her more than I needed to call back every single person who left a message about a record deal. I only ever wanted the best for Roxy – I'd landed her a deal with Virgin Records. That's why I was so late. And then they wouldn't let me into the studios. I waited all night until I saw the both of you come out in Michael's car. I knew I'd lost her then. And I thought I might have lost you, too.'

Jerome can see Cyril is getting emotional delving into his past mistakes.

'Can you explain everything to Roxy for me? I don't want her to think I abandoned her on purpose. She's better off now, anyway, but I want her to know how much I cared,' Cyril continues.

'You should just call her!' Jerome exclaims.

'I can't. She doesn't want to speak to me.'

'How do you know?'

'Let's just say I have a pretty strong feeling,' Cyril replies, recalling all the things Solomon told him.

'I think you're wrong. Roxy will forgive you if you just explain. I've hardly spoken to her recently – she's so busy promoting her new single.'

'How's the delightful Mary? Have you seen her recently?' Cyril asks to steer the conversation away from Roxy.

'Oh, she's fine. We're having dinner tonight at La Poule au Pot in Belgravia.'

'What kind of place is that?'

'It's a famous rustic French restaurant with bare floorboards, big windows draped in lace, close-packed tables, and fantastic food. I love the coq au vin and Tarte Tatin.'

'Cock o'what?' Cyril asks with bemusement.

'Chicken in wine, you fool. Come on, let's go to The Star and Garter for a quick one.'

'I'm on the wagon, Jerome. I promised MJ I'd stay completely dry for at least a month.'

Jerome laughs. 'No problem mate. By the way, MJ told me about the cell.'

'That stays between us, okay? No one must know.'

'Scout's honour,' Jerome replies, holding three

fingers up, trying not to laugh.

'Sorry, Jerome, but I've got to make a few phone calls to start sorting out the mess I've made.' He picks up the phone, and Jerome takes his leave.

Later that evening, Cyril makes his way to MJ's club listening to Van McCoy's 'The Hustle'. The Soho streets are becoming busy with people going out for the evening to the theatre, restaurants and clubs. There is a mild chill in the air, and the slightest touch of autumn colours the leaves. As Cyril approaches the red-light area in Tilbury Court, the streets become crowded with men looking for something. The neon lights signpost exactly what that something is and where it can be found. Scantily clad women entice passers-by into sex shops and clubs; male pimps offer customers pleasure of every kind. MJ's drinking club has Earth Wind and Fire's 'Boogie Wonderland' blasting onto the street. Cyril approaches MJ who is out front hustling for business.

'I wasn't sure you'd come,' MJ says, turning to Cyril.

'Wasn't it part of the terms of my release?' Cyril jokes. 'I need the money and something to occupy my brain.'

'Lose the cigarette. And tomorrow, wear a shirt and jacket. You're representing my business now, okay?'

MJ explains that the first rule is to be nice to every

single customer; they are where the money comes from.

'Never judge a book by its cover. We have many different types of people visiting us; all ages, shapes and sizes. But they all have something in common. They want company. Whether that's sex or a chat over a drink, we provide it.' Cyril nods and MJ continues: 'I have six girls working tonight, but not Jazz. It's her night off. Let me show you around. The ground floor bar with seating around the stage is to watch pole dancing. Many of the girls get extra for private performances around the back of the bar. We also have a dance floor and a small stage for singing. I do most of the singing – I love the applause.'

'I didn't know you can sing!' Cyril says with surprise.

'There aren't many things I can't do,' MJ says with a wink.

MJ continues the tour upstairs where the naughty rooms are. 'We have three rooms and we charge by the hour,' she says.

Cyril peeks with wonder into each one. All three follow a red and black colour scheme, similar to the room in MJ's home, and are kitted out with all sorts of sex-related paraphernalia. One room even has some kind of swing. Cyril is about to ask MJ how it works but has second thoughts. The room is called The Dungeon. An assortment of whips and masks are hung from the wall. A length of rope lies on a bench and Cyril picks it up inquisitively. MJ takes it from him and demonstrates by putting it over his head and tightening it around his neck. His eyebrow twitches.

'This room is all about treading the line between pleasure and pain,' MJ says, leaving Cyril to untangle himself. 'Each room has a different cost,' she adds, thrusting a glossy pamphlet with photos into Cyril's hand. It reminds him of a travel brochure and he tries not to chuckle.

'As it says there, we cater for every taste, from Vanilla to S&M, as well as an assortment of special interests, like voyeurism. You get ten percent of the profit from hiring out the rooms. You have to promote them as they're where we make the big bucks. The regulars know about them, but new customers need a gentle push. Oh, and we charge them more because they don't know any better.'

Cyril wishes he had brought a notepad and pencil to write all this down.

'We aren't supposed to provide sexual services in the venue. So we have to be careful when we promote the extras. We get visits from the council and sometimes the police, but I have my informants.'

'Got it,' Cyril replies a little uneasily. He could really do without getting involved with the police.

'Although we make a lot of money from upstairs, the bar and the dancers are the main attraction. Everyone pays an entrance fee; the drinks and the girls are on top. My girls get a cut of the bar profits for promoting drinks,' MJ takes a breath and looks at Cyril. 'Right, just one more thing. Sometimes we do get a bit of trouble.'

Cyril is about to ask what MJ means when she reaches behind the bar and pulls out a baseball bat. 'If we're in real trouble, and this doesn't scare them off, call for one of the pimps in the street or go next door for help. We're all a family here; we look out for one another.'

Later, Cyril watches how MJ catches her punters and gets them interested. She has a plethora of different tactics as there are all kinds of customers to attract. Two older Orthodox Jews walk straight in and ask for their regular room. MJ tells Cyril to sort them out with what they want. He waits as they look at the girls and decide which ones they want to take upstairs.

Cyril is easily distracted inside the club; he watches the two girls on the poles in admiration. The pair are a double act. Honey, a beautiful Japanese girl, and Dana, a blonde Eastern European. MJ is quick to notice Cyril staring.

'Honey and Dana are a couple,' she points out. 'A lot of the girls who work here are lovers; some are lesbians but most are bisexual.'

'So how does it work with them having sex with men in the club then?'

'Some of them don't. Take Honey: she mostly stays on the pole and attracts punters for Dana. Dana doesn't mind having sex with men – we call her The Dominatrix. She knows her way around all the whips and restraints. But it's just work to the girls – no emotional involvement whatsoever.'

MJ knows how to keep her customers entertained, telling saucy jokes to the patrons in her strong Welsh accent. Cyril soon has all the naughty rooms booked out for the night and MJ is impressed.

'Good job, Cyril. I can see the regulars feel at ease with you. Keep it up and you'll make great commission tonight,' MJ says with a smile as she prepares for her main act.

Cyril watches as MJ takes the stage and Sylvester's 'You Make Me Feel (Mighty Real)' begins to play. He almost falls off his stool when MJ starts to sing. He hadn't expected her to be so good. She gives a tremendous performance, reaching all the high notes with gusto and some of the other girls join in with dancing. MJ exits the stage to rapturous applause and wolf whistles.

The next day, Cyril sits in his office all morning working on a plan to salvage his business. He has a nap in the afternoon before heading straight to MJ's club in the evening. He enjoys the atmosphere in the bar and has picked up the tricks of the trade very quickly.

'Lots of pervs in tonight; must be their annual outing or something. It's absolutely full downstairs.'

'Cyril! Don't ever use that kind of language to describe our clients,' MJ warns him. 'You shouldn't be so judgemental; everyone deserves to have their sexual fantasies fulfilled. Just because they go about it in a different way to you doesn't make them pervs.'

Cyril apologises and gets back to work. He notices a man disappearing off upstairs with Dana.

'MJ, who was that man going upstairs just now? I think I know him.'

'You might do. But people don't tend to use their real names in here. He's a regular – goes by the name of Dave. He's a real gentleman and always tips well.'

An hour later, the man comes down and is paying when Cyril's voice pipes up from behind him, making the man jump.

'Uncle Lew, fancy meeting you here!'

Lew immediately reddens but tries to maintain his

composure.

'What are you doing here, Cyril? I thought you were in America? And please, can you keep this between us. No one else must know. I can explain…'

'Don't worry about it,' Cyril interrupts. 'I'm working here part time. But don't tell my parents you saw me here.'

'Of course not, but we should talk. Not here, though. Bar Italia, eleven o'clock tomorrow?'

Cyril agrees and Lew hurriedly leaves.

The following day, Cyril arrives at Bar Italia to find Lew sitting outside and looking very cold.

'Morning, Lew. Shall we sit inside? It's freezing.'

'I'd prefer to sit outside, if that's okay. I couldn't sleep last night,' Lew begins. The waitress brings them two cappuccinos and Lew continues as she walks away: 'But first, tell me about you. How long have you been back from America?'

Cyril sighs. 'I never went to America. I lost Roxy. I've got no record deal, no clients and no money. I'm working for MJ until I get back on my feet.'

'You're working as a pimp? Or a sex worker?' Lew asks anxiously.

Cyril laughs and sets him straight.

'Alf and Gina both think you've hit the jackpot with a big deal. They've been collecting every newspaper clipping with Roxy in it and wondering why your name hasn't been mentioned.'

'I didn't know how to tell them,' Cyril replies. He falls silent.

'Let me explain why you saw me last night,' Lew says.

'Oh, that's not necessary,' Cyril tries, hoping to save his uncle from embarrassment.

'I need to tell someone. It's eating me alive. I'm a successful businessman with a wonderful wife, and three lovely grown-up kids. I need Dana. She…'

'I don't need to know the details, Uncle Lew.'

Lew takes no notice and continues: 'I don't have physical sex with Dana. We don't even kiss. But she does things to me that I could never ask Sharon to do. Yes, Sharon and I still have sex. But only ever in the dark. Of course, I love her as much as I did when we got married, but it's different now we're older.'

Cyril shifts uncomfortably in his seat but listens attentively. It's clear Lew needs to get it off his chest.

'Dana punishes me, you see. That's what I really want… I always feel so much better after a session with her. It feels cathartic.'

Since they are on the subject of personal matters, Cyril decides to share something with Lew.

'I've been in love with Roxy since she first walked

through my door. I tried hard to keep it professional so that I wouldn't screw our relationship up, but I ruined it anyway. I wish I'd just told her how I felt when I had the chance.'

'Is she Jewish?'

'No, but I don't care,' Cyril replies.

'You remind me of myself when I met Sharon. She isn't Jewish, you know.'

'I had no idea.'

'So, when are you going to come clean with your mum and dad? You can't pretend to be in America forever. It's *Rosh Hashanah* tomorrow, and I know Gina thinks you'll be coming home. Just tell them the truth; they'll be understanding.'

After spending another night at MJ's, Cyril goes home to Stanmore listening to The Cars' 'Drive'. He pulls into the drive and sits in the car until the song finishes. Then Cyril waits an extra twenty minutes while trying to plan what he will say. Eventually, he takes a deep breath and walks up to the front door. He lets himself in.

The house is quiet. For a brief moment, he thinks they aren't home. But then Cyril spots them sitting in the garden and reading from the Hebrew bible. He pops his head round the back door.

'Say a prayer for me,' he says with a smile.

'You're back, Cyril! You should have called us. I was so worried,' Gina says giving Cyril the biggest hug and not letting go.

'I told you, Gina, he's a man now. My prodigal son returns! Congratulations, Cyril. I'm so proud of you.'

His parents' excitement makes breaking the news even more difficult. He steps away from Gina.

'Mum, Dad: I have something I need to tell you…' Before Cyril can begin, he starts to cry and turns his back to hide.

'What's wrong? Tell us,' Gina says, holding him and guiding him to a chair. She sits beside him stroking his hair.

Cyril shakily recounts the events of the last few weeks, telling them about Roxy, Bea Solomon, the stolen lingerie, the drink and the drugs. When he finishes he looks Alf in the face.

'I am so sorry. And I understand if you can't forgive me. I lied to you and I messed everything up, exactly like you knew I would. I should have listened to you.'

Gina speaks first. 'You worked so hard for Roxy, though. Surely you must get something from the deal. She can't just leave you with nothing.'

'I didn't have a signed contract, Mum. I don't have a leg to stand on. I was so stupid.'

'I'm just glad you're okay, Cyril. You didn't have to go through all this on your own.'

Cyril smiles weakly and gives Gina a hug. Alf is yet to give his verdict. Then he does something Cyril wasn't expecting. Alf puts his arms around Cyril and hugs him tightly.

'I'm still very proud of you. It can't have been easy to come here. You showed us that you can work hard and you'll learn from this. Today is a special day, and we must find forgiveness in our hearts for those who need it.'

The family come together in a group hug. Alf says a prayer in Hebrew asking for a family blessing.

Chapter Thirteen

'Please Please Me'

The Beatles

After the Jewish holiday, Cyril is ready to begin picking up the pieces of his business and start again. Alf doesn't want Cyril to struggle and has offered him a loan to help out.

'Thanks, Dad, but I have a plan. With a bit of luck, I won't have to borrow any money from anyone,' Cyril replies, graciously turning down Alf's proposition.

He heads out the door and gets in the car. Alf and Gina watch him from the window as he goes through his usual routine of touching the Spurs logo before he turns on the engine.

'He'll need a lot more than luck if he's going to turn things around,' Alf comments with a sigh. Despite always being tough on Cyril, he has only ever wanted to see him succeed. He turns away from the window. Gina worriedly watches Cyril's car disappear down the street.

'I can tell he's lost his confidence. The whole situation has really knocked him for six. Not that he'd admit that, mind you.'

'The problem is, our Cyril is still a wide boy,' Alf calls from the kitchen.

'I suppose we have to let him work it out for himself,' Gina replies, reluctantly tearing her eyes from Cyril's car as it finally turns out of sight.

Cyril collects the post and wanders up the stairs. They mostly look like bills. One stands out from the rest because of its fancy envelope; Cyril opens it. Inside is a huge bill from the lawyer, Maurice Cohen. Cyril is shocked as Maurice is Uncle Lew's friend and had expected him setting up the publishing company to be a favour. In a sudden burst of anger, he rips the invoice into tiny pieces and dumps them in the bin. *Just another thing that didn't work out as planned*, he thinks. Plonking himself down heavily at the desk, Cyril opens the diary. Of course there are no appointments except for a note about working at MJ's later that night. The answer phone is full of people chasing him for payments, and Cyril begins to bite his nails. It is an anxious habit he has developed over the last few weeks. 'You've Lost

That Lovin' Feeling' by The Righteous Brothers plays in the background and Cyril lets out a defeated sigh. He can't help feeling his dream of artist management has run its course. As he turns the radio off, a knock at the door startles him.

'If you're looking for Mandy, Jennifer, Raquel or Sarah they're all downstairs,' Cyril shouts, in no mood to explain the layout of the building to some horny punter.

'Cyril, It's me, am I disturbing you?' a voice calls from behind the door.

'Oh, Uncle Lew, no. Come in. I'm sorry. I've had one too many people knocking on my door looking for the girls. Sometimes I think I'm in the wrong business,' Cyril says.

'I was passing and I wanted to drop in and say how much I appreciated our chat last week. I also want to invite you for lunch as a thank you,' Lew says, sitting down.

'It's fine, Uncle Lew. I'm glad I could help.'

'You did more than lend me your ears. Our little chat gave me the confidence to talk to Sharon about the bedroom situation. We had some of the best sex of our lives over the holiday. She even agreed to beat me about a bit with a wooden spoon. And we kept the light on!' Lew says excitedly.

'Oh my God, she didn't?' Cyril exclaims, caught between intrigue and repulsion.

'You'd better believe it. She even...'

'Come on then. If you insist on buying me lunch we'd best get going,' Cyril interrupts, deciding he can do without the finer details.

They walk together to Frith Street, passing Bar Italia.

'Bianchi's is the best Italian restaurant here in Soho. It's run by Elena Salvini, so I call it "Elena's Place". She's quite a character and she knows all her regulars by their first names. She's almost as famous as her show business patrons.'

As they approach the door, Lew turns to Cyril and adds, 'There's another reason I asked you to lunch. I've invited someone else – someone who can help you with your business.'

'I'm not sure if I'm ready to meet more music people yet. Plus, your contacts are pretty expensive,' Cyril says, remembering the bill from Maurice.

Lew pushes Cyril through the door before he has a chance to make an excuse. The pair are greeted by Elena, a tiny Italian lady with a sweet face. She chats away with Lew as she takes them to the first-floor dining room. They are seated by a window overlooking Frith Street. Lew orders some drinks and they look over the menus. Lew notices that Cyril still looks very down in the dumps.

'It wasn't always easy for your Uncle Brian, you know,' Lew says tentatively.

'I'm sure he didn't make stupid mistakes and lose his biggest artist,' Cyril says huffily. 'I'm probably going to work for a management company for a while, rather than try to run my own. I do still have a few contacts.'

'You'd be surprised. Brian made many mistakes. He gave away the Beatles' merchandise rights for a song. He had his ups and downs like the rest of us. You don't need to work for anyone, Cyril. You have what it takes to make it on your own. You just need a little help from your friends,' Lew smiles.

Lew's words have inspired Cyril and some of his old confidence starts to creep back. Cyril notices Michael, the TV director, walking towards them and tries to hide behind his menu. He hasn't spoken to Michael since that night at Le Gavroche.

'Hello Lew. Oh, and hello Cyril. I had no idea you knew each other.'

'He's my nephew,' Lew says.

'Silly me; I should have seen the resemblance.'

Cyril looks anxiously at Lew, wondering what Michael will say next.

'I'm sorry to hear you lost Roxy to Bea Solomon. You really did a fantastic job in finding her.'

Cyril smiles but remains silent.

'She should have her first number one record by the end of the week. "Waiting for Your Love" went straight to number two last week. Ashley is so excited with the sales that he's throwing a big party to celebrate.'

A chill passes over Cyril at the mention of Ashley Goodman's name.

'If you find any other artists, I'll always make room for them on my show,' Michael says, putting a hand on Cyril's shoulder.

'Thanks, Michael,' Cyril replies.

As Michael walks away, Lew's friend arrives. It's Maurice Cohen, the lawyer who sent Cyril the extortionate bill. Maurice makes his way towards the pair in his trademark three-piece suit and bowtie. Cyril realises that this meeting is probably about the missing payment and wonders whether he can escape through the bathroom window. By the time he has weighed up the odds, it is too late, and Maurice is holding his big hand out to Cyril.

'Nice to meet you, Cyril,' Maurice says with a friendly smile.

'Nice to meet you too, but I don't think I'll be staying for lunch. You see, I don't have any money to pay your ludicrous invoice. I'm brassic; completely broke.'

Maurice laughs. 'I'm not here for your money. I'm here to help.'

Cyril sits down again in confusion.

'Your uncle Lew has told me about your circumstances, and I want to help. How would you like a big fat cheque?'

'I'd be happy with a small, lean one at this moment,' Cyril says. Curiosity has got the better of him, but he is still unsure what is happening. 'Don't tell me you're some fairy godmother who can make magic cheques appear.'

'Over the years I've had many nicknames, but I assure you I'm no fairy.'

'To put it simply: I have a solution to your financial difficulties,' Lew says, joining in the conversation.

'Lew and I started out in business at the same time and we've been friends for many years. It's not easy to know who your friends are in this dog eat dog industry. So I'm going to give you, my good friend's nephew, some free advice. But first, let's order; everything's on me today.'

After they have ordered, Maurice continues: 'What does Tin Pan Alley mean to you?'

'Tin Pan Alley? Never heard of it. Why do I feel like you're about to lecture me on how to run a music business?'

'It's not a lecture, but you could do worse than trying to learn. To start with, you should never represent someone without having secured a contract with them. You should have listened to my advice about this when we spoke about Roxy on the phone.'

Cyril looks sheepishly at the table.

'Do you know where Denmark Street is?'

'Of course. It's off Charring Cross Road, on the edge of Soho, right?'

'Right. Well, it's known as Tin Pan Alley because of the racket coming from people working on their hits. It's home to many music publishing companies. The Rolling Stones, David Bowie, Elton John and his co-songwriter Bernie Taupin all started out writing and recording their songs there. The Sex Pistols even lived on the street!'

'I didn't know that – I'm a big fan of the Sex Pistols. But how does this help with my cash flow?'

'Dick James, the famous music publisher, was also based in Denmark Street. He was contacted in 1963 by Brian Epstein, who was looking for a publisher for The Beatles' song "Please, Please Me". The rest is history.'

Cyril becomes excited at the mention of Brian and listens attentively.

'I took the liberty of speaking on your behalf to some of the top music publishers down on Denmark

Street. I passed on some of Roxy's demo tapes and made sure they knew how she was discovered. With me representing you, I've got three publishing houses who want you to share your publishing rights with them. They see potential in you spotting more successful artists like Roxy, and they're willing to take a chance on you.'

'Do I still have control over the publishing? Or would I be signing everything away?'

'You'd still have control as you will have the majority share in the new company which I will set up for you. In return, they will give you an advance. Then you get down to the business of finding the artists.'

'What kind of advance are we talking?'

'Cyril, in this industry Maurice is known as The Rottweiler,' Lew adds with a wink.

'I think you'll be more than happy with the sum,' Maurice finishes, taking a sip of his champagne.

'I can't thank you both enough,' Cyril says, completely overwhelmed. 'I promise I won't let you down. I'll make the most of this.'

Later that evening, Cyril turns up for work at MJ's club listening to The Eagles' 'One of These Nights' on his Walkman. He has his swagger back and feels great. The club is already bustling with activity and MJ cuts her way through the crowd towards Cyril. She is looking forward to seeing her elderly mother and knows she must leave on time to catch the last train to Wales that evening. MJ is pleased with Cyril's progress; he has taken to his role like a duck to water. Cyril has secretly invited Jazz to stay in Claridge's hotel in Mayfair after his last shift at the club, which is in a few days' time. He has slipped some money to one of his football mates who works at the hotel reception to sneak them in for the night.

'Will you be okay while I'm away?' MJ asks as she prepares to take the stage for her final performance.

'I'll be fine. Don't worry – just enjoy your trip home!' Cyril replies, putting his arms around MJ.

The office phone rings and MJ runs to get it. She returns a few minutes later looking upset and stressed.

'Are you okay? You look like you've seen a ghost,' Cyril asks with concern.

MJ remains quiet for a while, deep in thought. 'You could say that. A ghost from my past.' She walks off and heads straight onto the stage, tapping the microphone to check that it is on.

When the cheers and clapping subside, MJ begins an acapella version of Edith Piaf's 'La Vie en Rose'. She sings as though her life depends on it, pulling on the emotions of every member of the audience as they listen in awe. MJ is in tears as she finishes, which Cyril assumes is part of the act. The audience erupt into applause and they call for an encore, but MJ leaves the stage.

Cyril follows her to the office, calling after her: 'Fucking hell, MJ. That was absolutely beautiful. What an incredible performance.'

'Thanks, Cyril. I just needed to release some of my feelings,' MJ replies, drying her eyes.

'Is this to do with the phone call from earlier?'

MJ nods. 'It was my ex, Simon. The love of my life. I met him when I first arrived in London, seven years ago. I was slim and beautiful back then, and he was a strapping policeman.'

'What happened?'

'We were together for two happy years, but he always talked about wanting a family. Children, to be precise. You know, all that breeder, straight people stuff,' MJ grunts with distain. 'I gave him absolutely everything of myself, but he wanted children. He left me and married a bitch who gave him a son.' MJ has moved from being upset towards anger.

'I'm sorry, MJ. Do you keep in touch?'

'Not really. Sometimes he calls me when he's drunk to tell me how much he still loves me. But the call earlier was to tip me off about a new club and porn squad that will be operating in Soho. I'll probably have to pay them off to avoid raids.'

'What the hell? Paying off the police?'

'Yeah. I'm already paying those Irish bastards, so I need this like I need a hole in the head. Mickey from the market and his cohort are part of the Adams family. They control Soho by harassing clubs and bars to pay them protection money. The current police squad only take money around Christmas, but I don't know what this new one will be like. It sounds like they mean business.'

'I didn't know you had to pay off gangsters, never mind the police!' Cyril exclaims.

'There's a lot you don't know, Cyril. I have to work bloody hard to make enough to pay these bastards as well as saving for my reassignment surgery so I can become a complete woman. Well... a woman who can't bear children,' MJ says dejectedly, bursting into tears again. She storms off to the changing rooms and returns twenty minutes later as John: an overweight bald man in a suit.

Cyril's eyes almost fall out of his head.

'Why are you so shocked, Cyril?'

'I've never seen you as a man before, MJ,' Cyril stutters.

'Well, now you've met the other me – the me my

mother accepts. She's too old to understand who I am and I don't see the need to add any more confusion to her life. I'll see you in four days.'

MJ leaves the club discreetly via the side door.

The next three evenings at the club are busy, but none are as eventful as the night MJ left. Cyril has worked very hard, hustling the clients upstairs to the naughty rooms. On the last night, Cyril is excited about taking Jazz to the hotel. Jazz is pole dancing and keeps looking over at Cyril who is struggling to concentrate as he walks around with a perpetual semi-on. His mind is on one thing and one thing only: sharing a king-sized bed with Jazz for the first time. There is a queue forming and Cyril calls Jazz over to help take the entrance money. One of the clients is a tall man in his late thirties.

'I've booked a room, but I'm not looking for sex, you know. I just want to have a chat with a hostess.'

Cyril is curious, but it's not the first time someone has said they only want to chat.

'Same price either way. I don't care what you do up there.'

'Great.'

'Which girl do you have in mind?' Cyril asks.

'Her,' the man replies flatly, pointing at Jazz who is

standing just behind Cyril.

Cyril isn't too happy and is about to make an excuse when Jazz whispers in his ear: 'Don't make a fuss. It's my job and he's harmless. I've seen him here before.'

Jazz walks away, leading the man upstairs and Cyril watches them go with a pang of jealousy.

Cyril receives a phone call from MJ as she boards the night train back to London.

'How is it going?'

Cyril assures MJ that all is well and wishes her a safe journey home. He glances at his watch, expecting Jazz to come down any minute as the hour the man paid for is up. Cyril is just about to head out for a sneaky cigarette when he hears a scream for help coming from upstairs. Cyril vaults over the bar and grabs the baseball bat on his way, bolting upstairs. He opens the door with the master key but it has been wedged shut from the inside. Without wasting a second, he wrenches the fire extinguisher from the wall and bashes through the thin panelling of the door. He can see Jazz tied up naked on the bed and covered in blood.

'The black slut deserves it,' the man shouts.

Cyril drops the fire extinguisher and picks up the baseball bat as he steps though the broken door. With a burning rage, Cyril swings the bat with full force at the man's head. Unfortunately, the man is quick, leaning back out of Cyril's reach and then dashing forwards, pinning him to the ground. They struggle until Cyril kicks himself free. At this point, the man jumps up and runs out the door. Cyril moves to follow him but Jazz calls out for him to help her.

He helps her get dressed and tries to take her to the hospital, but Jazz refuses. When he realises she won't change her mind, Cyril takes Jazz home. They sit in silence in the car as the radio plays Lisa Stansfield's 'All Woman'. Cyril helps Jazz get cleaned up before putting her to bed. He returns to the club in the early hours of the morning to lock up and then drives home to Stanmore.

On MJ's return to London, Cyril invites her to the upstairs bar at the French House pub for a catch-up drink. Sitting comfortably in the room filled with black and white photos of the pub's celebrity clientele, Cyril tells MJ about a few minor incidents as well as the club's stupendous takings over the last few days. Then he tells her about the attack, and within an hour MJ is at Jazz's flat, only to find her packing to leave for Liverpool.

'MJ, you know this is not the first time I have been attacked at work; I've had it with bruises and black eyes.

If it wasn't for the money I would have left a long time ago,' Jazz complains when MJ enquires how she is.

'What are you going to do?' MJ asks.

'I've saved a pot of money, so I can finally do that beautician course. Who knows, I might even have my own shop one day!'

'You know you are doing the right thing, darling,' MJ tells her. I'll miss you, and I'll be losing my best girl but don't worry about that.'

They hug.

'Thank you, MJ. You saved me once and I'll never forget you and your kindness.'

The women look at each other and tears begin to pool in their eyes. Jazz breaks the silence and tears by turning her attention back to her packing.

'I will miss all the excitement in Soho for sure… and that Cyril especially. I've started to have some feelings for the guy. He's been so sweet and considerate with me.'

'Yes, Cyril's sweet and I know you have a soft spot for him. He's still immature and not sure what he really wants.'

'Oh MJ. The way he looks at me. And the kisses…'

'That's all very well, but he's just a horny little git. Don't be taken in by those puppy dog "come to bed" gorgeous eyes!'

'It's funny, but we've not even had sex yet.'

'Whatever! But don't let what you feel about Cyril influence your future. Maybe later, but not now. He's still in love with that Roxy.'

'The redhead?'

'Yes. I see it every time Cyril is near her, the way he looks at her. He loves her all right, though he's trying to suppress how he feels.'

Jazz gives a rueful smile. She knows MJ is right. She usually is about these things.

MJ returns to the club that evening and finds Cyril touting at the front.

'How's Jazz?' he asks. 'When is she coming back?'

'She leaving London for Liverpool tomorrow.'

'What! Why?'

'She's had it with this trade. She wants to move on and do something else. Something she can respect herself for.'

'I have to go and see her!'

'Don't Cyril! Let the girl go. She's doing the right thing; be happy for her. You going over to her now won't help.'

'But MJ, I must at least say goodbye,' Cyril says, trying to convince himself why he needed to go over.

'I know you like Jazz a lot, but for her sake don't go. You'll only break the girl's heart eventually…'

Cyril knows that what MJ is saying is true. He lights a cigarette and draws in a deep breath.

Chapter Fourteen

'Wild Boys'

Duran Duran

Billy meets Cyril at Bar Italia. He is surprised by Cyril's bruised face, but as always sympathy gives way to humour.

'What happened to you, Knickerman? What did I tell you about picking fights with little girls?' Billy ribs him, trying to prod the bruised side of Cyril's face.

'Oi. Actually, there was an incident at MJ's club a couple of nights ago. I had to fight off this guy who was beating up Jazz.'

'What? Some loony, huh? That lovely black chick?'

'Yeah. We didn't see it coming. The girls said he came in all the time and they thought he was alright.'

'What do you expect from sex addicts?' Billy says.

'I don't know, you tell me,' Cyril laughs. 'Anyway, what do you want? You must want something – I can see it on your face.'

'Can't a guy just meet his mate for coffee?'

Cyril raises an eyebrow.

'Okay, fine. I'm actually doing you a favour. Remember I told you about the new rock band I joined... You probably don't remember because you were off your tits on drugs and crying over Roxy. I talked about you to them.'

'Alright, forgive me for forgetting – it was the lowest point in my life. Don't bring up that episode ever again,' Cyril says huffily. He pauses for a moment before continuing: 'So, what's the band called again?'

'The Lunatics.'

Cyril bursts out laughing and spills his coffee.

'What's so funny? They were called Diamonds before. I convinced them The Lunatics has more of an edge.'

'Only you could convince a bunch of people that the name The Lunatics is an improvement,' Cyril says between loud laughs.

'I'm also the PR and spokesman for the band,' Billy continues to talk over the top of Cyril's laughter, 'because the lads in the band are actually quite shy. Not that you'd know that from listening to their music.'

'Hey, remember where having a big gob got you with your last band?' Cyril warns.

'Do you want to hear my proposal or not?'

'I hope you're not asking me to marry you.'

'We need to replace the idiot Paddy we've got as a manager. I recommended you to the band.'

'You've got to be joking…' Cyril begins before Billy silences him by putting headphones over his ears so he can listen to their music.

'We're playing the Marquee club in Soho in a few weeks for the soft launch of our new album. We just need to offload that awful leprechaun, Murphy. With your experience dealing with the riffraff at MJ's club I'm sure you'll be able to cope with him.'

'What do you mean by that?' Cyril asks, handing the headphones back to Billy.

'Murphy thinks he's some kind of big-time gangster, always boasting about his Irish background. He's full of shit and he never shuts up.'

'Are you sure you're not talking about yourself, Big Gob Billy?'

'Please, do me a favour and just meet the band for a chat.'

'Fine – I'll meet the band. But no promises. The music is quite catchy in its own noisy kind of way.'

'Great! How about I buy you a proper drink?'

'I'm still not touching the sauce, sorry.'

'What's up? Have you become a Muslim?'

'Oh yeah, I'm sure my mother would love that,' Cyril laughs.

Cyril spends the rest of the day in his office thinking about how to approach his new job finding talent for record companies. The twins, Ruby and Cheryl, call to say they have finally recorded some new songs. Cyril arranges to meet them the following day.

As he is about to leave for the evening, Cyril receives an unexpected call from Maurice. He confirms the publishing deal is all agreed and signed off with Polygram, and that a big fat advance cheque is on its way. Cyril is on an almighty high after the call and dances around the office. He only stops when there is a knock at the door a few minutes later and Uncle Lew walks in waving his hands excitedly.

'Cyril, my boy! Look what I've brought you.'

Lew and Cyril jump up and down like little kids. Cyril kisses the cheque over and over again.

'Is this all for me, Lew?'

'Yes. You were promised a big advance, and there you have it. Now all you have to do is find artists and sign them up to your publishing company.'

'We have to celebrate. Let's have a guys' night out. Where should we go? It's on me,' Cyril says, waving the cheque.

They jump into a taxi and Lew asks the driver to

take them to the Playboy Club on Park Lane. Lew is a member of the club and signs Cyril in as his guest. They walk into the Playmate Bar, and Cyril wants to know what they should drink.

'How about champagne?' Lew suggests.

'Ah yes. A bottle of Cristal, please,' Cyril asks the barman. *One or two glasses won't hurt my sobriety*, he thinks.

'Cyril, that's far too expensive,' Lew begins.

'It's a special night.'

They walk into the dining room for dinner, the waiter following behind carrying the Cristal champagne on a silver tray. Cyril can't keep his eyes off the gorgeous Playboy bunnies in their tight-fitting outfits with the famous rabbit tails and ears.

After dinner they watch the live show, which involves a bit of titillating dancing by the bunnies on stage. They both venture into the casino and Cyril buys chips on his credit card.

The pair play a few hands of blackjack and Cyril orders another drink for Lew and a lemonade for himself. As the bunny returns, Cyril passes his business card to her and gives her a big tip.

'I take it you like her?' Lew asks, smirking.

'I'm hoping to score tonight. That bunny keeps wiggling her tail at me. I think she might be up for it.'

'Cyril, there's more chance of Tottenham scoring

a goal than you getting with a bunny. They're paid to flirt, my boy. It's in their job description.'

'I've been meaning to ask, Lew. What's Maurice's deal? He doesn't have a wife, but I know he's not a fairy either.'

Lew laughs drunkenly. 'Spades,' he says with a hiccup. 'And I'm not talking about the playing cards.'

'I'd never have guessed,' Cyril replies.

'Yes, all shapes and sizes. His holidays are always in Africa or the West Indies, but that's between us.'

'To each their own,' Cyril chuckles.

In the early hours of the morning, Lew and Cyril both share a taxi home. Lew is very drunk, and Cyril is just extremely happy.

The next day, Cyril only gets into the office after lunch. He was completely worn out by his night of fun and slept in late. If it wasn't for his meeting with the twins, he would have taken the day off. He makes a strong cup of coffee and turns on the radio which is playing T-Rex's, 'Children of the Revolution'.

The girls turn up a little early, bright and energetic. They can't wait to play the three new songs they have recorded.

'Girls, I love these new songs! Now I can work on getting a record deal for you.'

Ruby and Cheryl clap their hands and celebrate.

'Leave it to me and I'll set up some appointments with the record companies. By the way, did you manage to come up with a new name? Everyone kept telling me that Rub and C sounds too sexual.'

'What about The Sisters?' Cheryl asks.

'Perfect, that's much better,' Cyril replies.

'Cyril, we have something special to show you,' Ruby begins.

'Yeah, remember you wanted us to get some new photographs to show off our style? James from the university took these,' Cheryl continues.

She hands over the photos and Cyril flicks through them. They are extremely suggestive, most of them bordering on pornographic. Some of the pictures remind Cyril of the glossy brochure for MJ's club as the twins hold themselves aloft on poles.

'Was this James' idea?'

Ruby and Cheryl nod in sync.

'I think this is too much. People will think I'm your pimp,' Cyril frowns.

'Oh, come on, Cyril. You're sounding old. We love our new image, and we feel sexy. Why should we be embarrassed to flaunt our bodies?'

'Less of the old, please. I'm only a few years older than you. I know sex sells, but these pictures cross a line.'

'As the great Marvin Gaye would say, "Let's get it on". Crossing lines and breaking boundaries is what sets us apart!' Cheryl says. The twins carry on singing the song.

After the twins have left, Cyril's phone rings.

'Hi Cyril. It's James. How do you like my pictures?'

'Not as much as you liked taking them, I bet. Most of them are unusable – I'll be lucky if I'm able to use three or four!'

'But you said you wanted sexy and new,' James protests.

'Yeah, but not porn, you little perv.'

James starts shouting down the phone, unhappy about being called a pervert. He throws around some abusive language and some slurs relating to offensive Jewish stereotypes.

'I gave you a great opportunity, and you blew it. I'll send you a cheque with a reduced fee in the post,' Cyril shouts, and slams the phone down.

A couple of weeks have flown by, and Cyril has been busy sending out the twins' demos, which have been creating a real buzz within the industry. Mark Jones, who was very keen to sign Roxy before, is now head of A&R for EMI. He has called a meeting with Cyril.

'Cyril, I love their songs; catchy with nice melodies. The sound is very now. What do they look like?' Mark asks.

Cyril hands over three photos of the twins.

'You didn't mention that they're black.'

'Why does it matter?' Cyril says defensively.

'Black artists don't sell records. Well, very few do,' Mark says, holding up the pictures to scrutinise them.

'What are you talking about, Mark? The twins are talented; they write their own songs and they're both born performers.'

'It's the music business, not me, Cyril,' Mark says, spreading his hands apologetically. 'Michael Jackson has just crossed over on MTV as the first black artist to break the mould. This would be my first signing as head of A&R for EMI records, and I don't know if I should be making waves. The managing director, Nigel, is very old school.'

'Wouldn't you prefer to be part of the solution, rather than part of the problem?' Cyril asks directly.

Mark avoids answering. 'Which one is which? They both look the same.'

'They're identical twins, but you can tell them apart when you meet them. Cheryl is more forthcoming and confident, and Ruby is more reserved. I'm telling you, they're going to be the next big thing.'

'It's just so high risk. I do really like them, but…'

'Mark, you don't want EMI to lose out a second time, do you? You know I'm on to another winner here. But I have a few other meetings to get to, so I'll have to leave it with you,' Cyril says, standing up to leave.

'Okay, fine. Sit down. But you'll need to tone down their image. They're hot, but like I said, Nigel is old-school.'

'Sex sells, Mark!'

'Let's get down to the nitty gritty.'

After they have hammered out the details, Cyril offers to shake Mark's hand and asks him to send The Sisters' contract on to Maurice.

'What! You've got The Rottweiler looking after you?' Mark laughs. He takes out a small plastic bag of cocaine and makes a line on the table. After snorting it, he holds the bag out to Cyril, who shakes his head.

As Cyril walks out of the EMI building, he punches his hand in the air, feeling on top of the world. Cyril is relieved that he was able to convince Mark to take a chance on the girls as the other major record companies had already turned him down because they are black.

After his conversation with Mark, Cyril has realised that he needs a hot music producer for The Sisters' tracks to ensure they are a guaranteed success. Mark had mentioned the energetic and fast-talking Pete

Waterman, a superstar in music production with a string of successful records. After calling ten times, however, Cyril is beginning to think contacting Waterman is impossible. Each time, his secretary gives the same robotic answer: 'Mr Waterman is busy right now. I'll let him know you called.' But no one ever calls back.

Cyril doesn't give up easily. It has come to his attention that Waterman is a fan of trains. After speaking to some of his contacts in the industry, it becomes apparent that Waterman is more of a train fanatic than merely a fan. Cyril has a plan to use this to get his attention, and after plotting away for a while he calls The Sisters and Billy in for an urgent meeting.

Billy arrives first. 'What's this about? You sounded all secretive on the phone. Is it a case for Secret Squirrel? Agent 000 reporting for duty.'

'I need to get Pete Waterman's attention. You know who he is?'

'Yeah, of course. He's been working with that hot Aussie bird from the TV, Kylie Minogue.'

'Well, I need you to spy on him for me. Keep a note of his movements about town, that sort of thing.'

'You mean stalking him? Do I get paid for this?'

'Yes, but only if I get what I need out of it.'

Billy gets straight to work. Later on, Cheryl and Ruby arrive at the office expecting some news about a record deal.

'So, Cyril, what's up?' Cheryl asks with a grin. 'You got some good news for us?'

'Good? No… it's great! EMI are on board!'

The girls scream and hug each other before both throwing themselves at Cyril and hugging him too.

'I want you girls to meet one of the hottest music producers, Pete Waterman, and convince him to produce your songs.'

'Pete Waterman? No way! He's going to produce our first record?' Ruby asks.

'Well that's the plan. But I haven't exactly been able to contact him yet. He won't answer my calls.'

The twins look dismayed.

'But don't worry – I'm working on it. When he does meet you, I want it to be impossible for him to say no.'

'So what can we do to help?' the girls ask, desperate to get involved.

'This is going to sound weird, but trust me. I want you to design and make a sexy train uniform to perform in. I'll let you know when I've found a way to meet him. Hopefully it won't take long, so get busy with your costumes.'

'But trains are literally the most un-sexy thing in the world,' Cheryl says, looking confused.

'Just trust me,' Cyril replies with a cheeky grin.

Early in the evening, a few days later, Billy calls Cyril to relay his findings.

'These are the hours that Waterman will be in his office. It's also his birthday tomorrow. His secretary has had a toy train installed in his office to surprise him, so he should be in there for quite a while. Don't ask me how I know all this, but it's gonna cost you more than a few drinks, I tell you that!'

'I'm already doing you a favour by meeting with your band, so I'd say this makes us about even.'

'I don't know about that. I worked my bollocks off these last few days. Literally. And I got rained on.'

'You really took on the secret agent role with vigour. Screwing your way to the information,' Cyril laughs.

'Yeah, but James Bond gets the real beauties. Have you seen Waterman's secretary? Anyway, gotta dash. Agent 000 over and out.'

Cyril laughs again as he puts down the phone. He immediately calls the twins to inform them that their plan will be put into action tomorrow.

The next day the rain continues even heavier than before. Cyril looks nervously out of his office window, the radio playing The Weather Girls 'It's Raining Men'. He has left the girls to carry out Operation Waterman on their own, believing their performance will be more effective if he isn't there watching over them. The twins arrive outside Waterman's office at the planned time, carrying their boombox. They wait until there is no one in reception except a young guy talking on the phone. Cheryl and Ruby stroll up to the desk in their high heeled shoes, wearing the tight-fitting train uniforms they finished making the night before.

'Can I help you?' the receptionist asks.

'We're here to surprise Mr Waterman. It's his birthday.'

'I'm sorry but he doesn't have any appointments scheduled and you need an appointment to see him.'

'It's a surprise. We're kissograms,' Ruby says, worried they might have stumbled at the first hurdle.

'Sorry. I can't let you in.'

'Hey you. Do you know what a kissogram is? Maybe I should just show you,' Cheryl says.

'Well, no. I...' he stutters.

Cheryl leans suggestively over the desk, grabs his tie and pulls him in for a kiss.

'Now that one was on the house. But if I don't see the birthday boy right now, I'll be in big trouble with my boss. And you wouldn't want that, would you?'

The receptionist is stunned into silence and shakes his head.

'Great,' Cheryl smiles.

'His office in on the first floor,' the young man finally manages to say after catching his breath.

The twins high five each other as they head up the stairs. When they reach the office, they see the secretary outside, busy doing paperwork. Thankfully she has already been primed by Billy. The twins become aware of train sounds emerging from behind Waterman's closed door and they try not to snigger. The secretary nods at the girls and they take a deep breath before strolling confidently straight into the office of the superstar record producer. Inside the office, they find Pete sitting on the floor playing with his new miniature train set. He looks up, startled by the twins' sudden entrance. They launch into their routine before he has a chance to ask any questions.

'Hey Mr Waterman. We've come to play with you,' they say together, striking a pose and pointing to Pete.

'What the hell, girls! I love the uniforms!'

Ruby places the boombox on the floor and presses play. They jump into action, thrusting their bodies, dancing and singing 'We want your money.' The performance is a slightly revised version of the one that convinced Cyril to be their manager.

The performance builds towards a frenzied finale as the girls remove their hats and throw them at Pete who is grinning from ear to ear.

'So, how'd you like to hop aboard this train?' Ruby says with a wink.

'This must be my lucky day,' Waterman exclaims, trying to comprehend what he has just witnessed.

After having a chat with the girls, he calls Cyril.

'Is this Cyril Gold? Your antics nearly gave me a bloody heart attack, you crazy fool. You've certainly got my attention though! The twins are going to be massive. I want them to be part of my Hit Factory. Let's meet up to discuss.'

Cyril can't believe his plan worked, and is glad his perseverance paid off. He calls Maurice immediately: 'Waterman is on board, but we'll need more money from EMI to cover his studio costs.'

The following week, Billy arrives at Cyril's office. The other band members trudge in behind him. Cyril already had his doubts about taking the band on, and when they turn up an hour late he is even more certain it would be a waste of his time. They are all wearing black leather jackets with studs, and they all have a small nose ring. Cyril can't help but smirk; they look like an inferior version of KISS, minus the makeup.

'Hi guys, would you like a drink? Tea or Coffee?' asks Cyril much more cheerfully than he feels.

'We need a real fucking drink, not tea,' says the

lead singer, Liam, and the other band members start laughing.

Billy starts by talking about the history of the band and how they've come a long way in five years, beginning as a punk band and then reinventing themselves as a rock band. Liam interrupts.

'We just need to get out of this terrible management deal with that Irish twat, Murphy. The sooner the better.'

'Yeah, and you're the man for the job,' Billy adds.

The other band members join in complaining about Murphy. Money seems to be the biggest issue. They mostly talk amongst themselves, grumbling about their situation. Before Cyril can protest, someone lights up a joint and they pass it around. Cyril sighs and opens all the windows.

'Did you order any food for us?' the guitarist asks.

'No, it's half past eleven,' Cyril replies.

'We always get food when we have meetings at A&M Records,' the bassist adds.

'Well this isn't A&M, and I don't serve breakfast, lunch or dinner here.'

Cyril tries to get to the root of the problem with the band's manager, but the conversation always drifts back to money.

'We have to share the money five ways within the

band,' moans Liam.

'And we have to pay a gigging agent his money up front. The accountant takes his money each month whether we earn or not.'

'We have barely anything to show for it at the end.'

'That bastard does fuck all. He takes a hefty fee for his management but never does anything to improve our earnings,' Liam continues.

'We get a shit weekly wage for doing all the work,' Billy adds.

They all look at Cyril expectantly as though he is going to wave a magic wand and solve all their problems.

'You know I would also take a management fee if I represented you guys?' Cyril says. 'I might be able to get you on another label and negotiate a better deal, but there's really no guarantee.'

The band look at each other for a while before Liam suggests they'll think about it.

'Before we slog it back up the motorway in the Transit, how about getting pissed in the pub?' Liam asks, to which the band members cheer. They hurry out of the office but Billy hangs back.

'They're great guys, don't you think?'

'I don't know, Billy. They don't seem too enthusiastic about the music. Just money, booze and spliffs.'

'We really need help. You owe me one…'

'I know, I know. I'll see what I can do. But I'm not making any promises.'

That evening, Cyril hears from Maurice that he has managed to get more money from EMI to pay Pete Waterman to produce The Sisters' first album. This is on top of the lucrative three-album deal with an advanced payment upfront signed between EMI and The Sisters.'

Cyril stretches out in his office, feeling that things are finally coming together. He gets ready to go home and turns on the answering machine when the door crashes open. Two middle-aged men appear, one a small, stocky white man with a walking stick, and the other a big black man with a fixed smile. Cyril jumps out of his skin.

'The girls are downstairs,' Cyril says meekly.

'It's you I'm looking for, you fuckwit,' the little man says in a heavy Belfast accent. He storms up to Cyril and points the walking stick in his face, shaking it at Cyril's nose.

'I don't have any problems with you. Are you sure you're in the right place?' Cyril says hurriedly.

The man suddenly steps back and laughs loudly and forcefully: 'But I do have a problem with you, Mr Gold. Nobody tries to cross Murphy and gets away with it.'

The little man paces up and down a few times and Cyril watches in bewilderment.

Murphy stops pacing and starts to prod Cyril with his walking stick. 'The Lunatics,' he says narrowing his eyes.

'Excuse me?' Cyril replies, nervously looking between the two men.

'I spent time and money making that band into something. You know what they were like when I found them? Sexually frustrated teenagers with not a pube between them, never mind a brain cell. I made them into The Lunatics. I moulded them. Gave them life,' the man says dramatically.

Cyril realises he could be in for a beating if he doesn't play his cards right.

'They came to me for a chat,' Cyril explains.

'And you think it's okay to stick your big Jewish nose where it doesn't belong? I know your type, Gold. Don't try and play me.'

Murphy gives a quick nod to the other man, who begins to herd Cyril into the corner.

'Take your clothes off,' Murphy shouts.

'Fuck off. No way!'

'My big friend Smiley Sambo has two little friends called right hook and left hook. Unless you want to meet them, I suggest you do as I say.'

Cyril hesitates a fraction too long and Smiley ploughs his fist into Cyril's stomach.

'Okay, okay,' Cyril relents. He quickly undresses and stands shivering, covering himself with his hands.

Murphy strolls over to one of the windows and opens it wide. 'Let's see how you like being hung out to dry.' He turns up the radio to full volume. Duran Duran's 'Wild Boys' is playing.

Before Cyril can react, Murphy and Smiley drag him screaming to the window. They lift Cyril upside down and dangle him head first out of the third-floor window. Ironically it is raining, and Cyril is soaked within seconds.

'So, what do you have to say for yourself, Knickerman?'

'I was never going to take on that stupid band,' Cyril shouts, flailing about.

'Wrong answer,' Murphy bellows.

Cyril, while pleading for his life, still finds a second to curse Billy. Out of all the situations Billy has gotten him into, this is by far the worst.

'I swear I was never going to take them on. Please believe me!'

'Let me think,' Murphy says calmly, letting go of Cyril's right leg. Cyril screams and starts crying.

Smiley speaks for the first time in a low voice: 'Boss,

I'm getting tired here. Can I let go?

'I really don't like Jews. They think they're the chosen ones; what about us poor Catholics? Drop him,' Murphy says walking away from the window.

'No!!!' Cyril screams.

Smiley laughs and drags Cyril back inside, dropping him onto the floor like a wet cat. He trembles and cowers against the wall.

'Stay away from my band or you'll meet some of my other relatives. And trust me, they aren't all as nice as I am,' Murphy says, giving Cyril a final poke with his walking stick.

The two goons walk out the office laughing. Cyril remains on the floor in a state of shock for a few minutes. As the terror drains away, he manages to get dressed. On unsteady legs, he hobbles out of the office and locks it with trembling hands.

Chapter Fifteen

'I Am Woman'

Helen Reddy

After two months in the planning, 'We Want Your Money' by The Sisters is about to be released. Cyril has worked incredibly hard, knowing this could be his make or break. He has an important lunchtime meeting with Mark Jones at EMI's office. Less than ten minutes into the meeting, they get into a heated argument as Cyril requests a budget to make a music video to promote the record.

'Cyril, the budget for The Sisters has rocketed since you got Waterman involved. If the record looks like it's selling well after its release, then we can consider putting money into making a video. I've had Nigel grumbling at me only this morning saying I'm spending too much on an unproven artist,' Mark says tapping his pen on the table irritably.

'I don't understand EMI. The video is the icing on the cake to launch these girls. They need to be seen; they're magnetic on film and they're sure to captivate an audience.'

'I'll give you a bit of free advice, Cyril,' Mark sighs, getting up and closing the door. 'EMI are old school – not like Virgin Records; they take risks with avant-garde artists. It took a lot of convincing to get a black act signed here. But I like you, and I'm glad I stuck my neck out for the girls – I really believe in them. Once The Sisters prove to the guys upstairs that they can bring in the money, they'll be more than happy to make that video.'

Cyril is annoyed and stares blankly at the wall, biting his nails. He is confident that the video is key to the girls' success. He folds his arms indignantly, biting his tongue to stop himself arguing with Mark.

'I've got great press and promotional material lined up for the girls on radio and TV. The money we're spending on them is enormous for a new act. They'll have to sell over a million records to pay for their advance before they even see a penny!'

Cyril lights up a cigarette and leans back in his chair.

'And another thing,' Mark continues, 'EMI, like all record companies, are like banks. We add a large percentage of interest to our loans. Advances are loans and we expect to recoup everything we spend before the artists gets anything, and I mean everything. It's a high-risk business and the interest rates reflect that.'

Cyril remains silent, glancing out the window.

'Come on, it's not all bad. The Sisters are going to be great and you know it! They'll make plenty of money! Do you want to get some lunch?' Mark asks.

'Will that be added to my bill?' Cyril replies sarcastically.

'What do you think?' Mark laughs.

Jerome drops into Cyril's office later that afternoon, looking very smart as usual.

'I was just passing, and I wanted to share my excellent final exam results; I got a two-one! I worked bloody hard and it paid off!' Jerome says, beaming with pride.

'Congratulations! I always knew you were a clever bastard. It's been ages since I've seen you, what with you studying and me working with The Sisters.'

'I'm going to start looking for a proper job in the city now.'

Cyril gives Jerome a well-deserved hug.

'Hey, I bumped into Billy the other day. He said you've been giving him the cold shoulder.'

'Don't talk to me about the big-mouthed idiot. He nearly got me killed,' Cyril complains.

'I didn't think you were one to hold a grudge,' Jerome grins. 'Then again, I guess you didn't have much to hold on to when your danglers were being dangled out the window.' He falls about laughing.

'Not funny, Jerome. That wanker must have filled you in with the details of what happened.'

A silence falls between them and Jerome tries not to think about his friend getting beaten up by a leprechaun for fear it will start him laughing again.

'Are you going to the music awards next month?' Jerome asks, changing the subject.

'Yes, Mark invited me and The Sisters for the EMI table.'

'I'd love to go and spend a night with the stars,' Jerome says dreamily.

'I'll try and get you an invite. Can't promise anything as tickets are like gold dust.'

'Guess where I was this weekend!' Jerome says, suddenly very animated.

'No idea. Out shopping with Mary? Or Ashley? I see you're wearing all the latest stuff.'

'Mary invited me to Elton John's party at his gorgeous mansion in Windsor! I've never seen so many flowers inside a house.'

'Wow, that must have been some bash. So, what's Elton like?' Cyril asks, pretending not to be too interested.

'He's super nice. Roxy and I met him on the night of the TV show, and he remembered us! I even got a chance to check out his ass this time,' Jerome says with a wink.

'Don't tell me you're seeing Elton John now!'

'No, unfortunately I'm not his type. But it was a phenomenal night all the same. There were so many famous people there. Babs even flew in from New York.'

'Babs?'

'Streisand, of course. Liberace was there from LA — he played the piano with Elton. You'd have loved it.'

'I know I would. You could have invited me!' Cyril says, unable to play it cool any longer.

'I know, I'm sorry. But firstly, I was Mary's guest. And secondly, Roxy was there with her boyfriend, Struan,' Jerome pauses to gauge Cyril's reaction at the mention of Roxy's name.

'Jerome, I'm fine. I've moved on. You can bring her up without worrying that I'll break down in tears! I only lost an artist with three number one records in the UK and America,' he says with a sad smile.

'I was more worried that her getting back with Struan would upset you,' Jerome adds.

'Well, he is Tommy's father. I can see why Roxy would have him back, even if he is only here to cash in on her success.'

'Ouch, Cyril. You bitch.'

'Tell me I'm wrong.'

'I wish I could. But I unfortunately think you're spot on. From what I've seen, he's awful. She's just putting up with it for Tommy's sake.'

Cyril shakes his head and shuffles his feet on the carpet.

'Kevin Cash and that backstabbing bitch, Solomon, were too. I just don't trust that pair, especially Solomon. She's a wolf in sheep's clothing.'

'You don't need to tell me. I have first-hand experience with her.'

'On a lighter note – I met someone at the party. He's called Jonathan; a singer Kevin has just signed up. I fell in love with him as soon as I saw him, and from the glances he was giving me, I can tell he's interested too.'

'Are you sure?'

'One hundred percent.'

'So, when do your parents meet him?' Cyril laughs.

'That will never happen. But hopefully I'll see him again soon. Now, how about you take me to that queen's paradise on Greek Street, Patisserie Maison Bertaux, to celebrate my results.'

'Come on then,' Cyril says, grabbing his jacket.

It is a quiet winter's evening, but the atmosphere inside MJ's club is as warm and welcoming as ever. MJ has just finished her rendition of 'I am Woman', by Helen Reddy, accompanied by a routine on the poles from Honey and Dana. MJ walks over to speak with some of her regulars when two men in suits appear at the front door asking to have a chat with her in private.

'Good evening, gentleman. What can I do to make your night sizzle?' she asks in an alluring manner.

'You can drop the act, madam. We're from the club licencing division launched by the Met police. I'm McDonald and this is Campbell.'

'Oh, I've heard about you boys. Are you going to clean up Soho?'

'Well, that depends.'

'Your lads were in here just a few months ago for their yearly visit, and they were perfectly happy with our arrangement.'

'They aren't our lads. We're their replacements. Now, do we understand each other?' McDonald says in a heavy Glaswegian accent.

'We'll be coming around more often than the other guys. If you want to stay in business, we'll be needing a brown envelope at the beginning of each month. Starting today,' Campbell adds.

'This is ridiculous. I can't afford that!' MJ says,

beginning to get in a flap. 'I also have to pay off the Irish gangsters, that fucking Adams Family. Why don't you stop them threatening me for money? They're the real criminals.'

The policemen both shrug; 'Be a good lass and open up. And I mean your safe, not your legs. There's nothing I'm interested in between there,' McDonald smirks.

'We know all about your rooms upstairs – the fucking, the wanking and the spanking. We can close you down just like that,' Campbell continues, snapping his fingers.

MJ has no choice but to take them to the office and pay them.

A few minutes later, Dana walks into the office to find MJ crying in the corner of the room, her eye make-up all smeared and her wig on the floor.

'Oh my God, what happened? Who were those two men? I saw them leaving in a hurry.' Dana asks, picking up the wig.

'Those bent coppers are the worst. Especially that redhead haggis, McDonald. They weren't happy with what I paid them, so they just raided the safe. I tried to stop them and begged them to leave the money I have set aside for my sex-change operation. But they took the whole lot. They pulled off my wig and called me a faggot, shoving me about all over the place to remind me they'll be back again next month.'

'Fucking pigs, they're worse than the gangsters,' Dana says, putting an arm around MJ to comfort her.

The following night, still shaken by the abuse from the police, MJ is confronted by two young Chinese gangsters also demanding protection money. By this time, MJ has had more than enough of people telling her to pay them. Her rage far outweighs her fear, and so MJ mocks the gangsters in a silly Chinese accent.

'You wanna my money, you Chinks? Take this!'

MJ grabs a giant dildo from a nearby shelf and hits one of them over the head, at which point the other starts laughing. The first man finds it less funny and draws a meat cleaver from inside his coat. MJ screams and drops the dildo on the table, holding her hands up to surrender. The man brings the cleaver down, swiftly chopping the dildo in half. Without missing a beat, MJ grabs a baseball bat and swings it in the direction of the gangsters, lumbering towards them menacingly.

'I don't care how big your chopper is. Get the fuck out of here!' she shouts.

The men decide against starting a brawl with the bat-wielding lunatic and run, turning back when they reach a safe distance.

'We'll be back,' one of them shouts.

Cyril walks into Soho on Monday morning

contemplating the upcoming music awards dinner. He is filled with excitement as it has been announced that he is up for manager of the year. The nomination came as a complete surprise. He is pulled from his daydream by the sight of Mickey Sullivan sauntering towards him.

'Hey Cyril, any chance of getting some more underwear from you, what with Christmas coming soon?'

'Sorry, Mickey. I'm not in the underwear business anymore.'

Cyril whistles a tune as he nears the office. 'We Want Your Money' has entered the top thirty in the charts thanks to the number of times it has been played on the air. Mark did a great job organising the PR. Cyril makes a cup of tea and plays back the messages on his answer machine, skipping the irrelevant ones. He comes to a message from MJ, talking at a million miles an hour about the police and the gangsters. The only words that stand out are 'money', 'pricks' and 'dildo'. Cyril calls her back straight away.

'Morning, MJ. You left me a message – is everything okay?'

'It's all over. I can't make my business work anymore; I'm stressed and I'm broke. Over the weekend I was robbed and abused by two rotten pigs!'

'What?'

'As if the bent coppers weren't bad enough, I was then harassed by two gangsters from Chinatown the next day. I've had just about all I can take.'

Sensing MJ is distraught, Cyril agrees to meet her at the club immediately.

'Are you alright? Let's go for a drink at the French House,' Cyril says.

'I don't want a drink. I can't think of food, sorry. I just want to pack up and leave all this behind.'

'Calm down, MJ. Is that really what you want to do? You've worked so hard for everything you have here.' The radio is playing 'Red light Spells Danger' by Billy Ocean in the background. She turns it off.

'Of course, it isn't what I want to do, but what choice do I have? I haven't slept in days for worrying about my finances. Every evening I wonder if this will be the night one of those gangsters finally comes to finish me off. I'm a mess. People always think I'm strong, but behind this independent sarcastic front I'm really lonely and insecure. I'm in desperate need of a little love in my life, Cyril' MJ says, beginning to sob.

Cyril offers her a tissue and tries to comfort her.

'The police and the gangsters are squeezing me to death. I'm going to have a nervous breakdown if I continue to run this place. I told Diamond Geezer to collect the keys later today. This is the end of the road for me,' MJ says, her shoulders slumping sadly.

Cyril feels terrible for MJ and ponders how he can help as he lights up a cigarette for both of them. She was there for him in his darkest moments when he lost Roxy, now he has a chance to return the favour.

'Can you type, MJ?'

'Of course, but only slowly.'

'I need a part time secretary. Why don't you help me out in the office until you decide what you want to do next?'

'Are you offering me a job, Cyril?'

'Yes, you can start tomorrow!' Cyril gives MJ a set of keys to the office, and she gives him a gigantic hug to say thanks. Cyril closes his eyes hoping he has not made a blunder for old time's sake.

Chapter Sixteen

'The Look of Love'

ABC

It is Friday morning, and it's MJ's first day at work. She arrived at the office bright and early to clean the place up. Cyril walks into a spotless office a little while later to find a girl waiting for him, sitting on a chair opposite his desk.

MJ introduces the girl to Cyril, telling him her name, and then goes to make tea in the kitchen. Cyril makes some small talk with the girl and then listens to her demo tape. MJ returns to the office with the tea, making a disapproving face behind the girl's back and miming the word 'No'. Cyril is inclined to agree with MJ's opinion, and gives the girl some pointers on how she might improve her demo. The girl leaves disheartened.

'Thank God for that. She was pretty naff – couldn't sing to save her life. She's all about her image, just trying to look sexy for you. I saw her giving you the eye, showing off those long legs. I know what her game is,' MJ says.

Cyril laughs, finding her remarks entertaining. He hired a secretary but something tells him he got more than he bargained for. He begins to dictate his first letter casually, and MJ is struggling to keep up.

'Slow down, Cyril.

'Slow down? I'm literally going word by word. You said you could type.'

'Yes, but I also said I was slow. Patience is a virtue, darling. Could you start again please?' she asks, with an apologetic face.

Jerome strolls into the office a while later and is surprised to find MJ answering phones.

'Would you like a cup of tea or coffee, Mr Jerome?' MJ asks like a good secretary.

Jerome can't believe how clean and tidy the office looks. He talks non-stop about the music awards which are taking place next Saturday. He loves the idea of spending a night in black-tie attire, rubbing shoulders with the biggest stars.

'Imagine if you got the manager of the year award!' Jerome says, grinning.

'I can't even begin to think what that would feel like,' Cyril replies.

'Everyone expects Roxy to get best new artist for hitting well over a million sales of her single. And her album's gone platinum,' Jerome says, getting swept away with the excitement.

Cyril excuses himself and heads to the bathroom.

MJ shoots Jerome a glare and hurriedly reprimands him for bringing up Roxy when he knows it's such a difficult subject for Cyril. She falls silent as Cyril returns, but not without a final wag of the finger directed at Jerome.

'It wasn't easy to get you onto the EMI table, but I managed to convince them to let me bring you as my plus one,' Cyril says triumphantly.

Jerome looks anxiously between Cyril and MJ. 'Oh, I'm really sorry, but Roxy has already invited me to the CBS table with Ashley. I was just about to tell you.'

MJ looks exasperatedly at Jerome, but Cyril seems to brush over the news with ease. 'So, MJ, what are you doing next Saturday? How would you like to join me and The Sisters on the red carpet?' he asks.

MJ shrieks, and continues to shriek for some time. 'Cyril! That would be amazing, I'd love to join you.'

She rushes over to embrace Cyril and Jerome looks at the floor, feeling a little bad for standing his friend up.

The phone begins ringing and MJ answers it in her high-pitched voice: 'Cyril Gold Artist Management. MJ speaking, how can I help?'

'I'm sorry about the awards. I hope you don't mind me going with Roxy. She asked me a few days ago. Let me make it up to you – I'll buy you dinner tonight and you can meet Jonathan. He's a nice Jewish boy, just like you,' Jerome says with a grin.

'Jonathan?'

'You know, the singer I met at Elton's party. We hooked up, and things have been going well.'

'You old tart!'

'Oi, watch it. It's all hush, hush though. Jonathan is terrified of being found out as gay. He thinks it'd ruin his chances of becoming a pop idol.'

'Yeah, the music industry doesn't seem to like their artists being outside the norm. Gay is taboo; they think it'll drive away the female fans.'

'Does Jonathan know about your part-time job?' Cyril asks.

'No way. Besides, I don't do trade with men anymore. Not with Jonathan in my life,' Jerome says. A look of horror falls upon his face as he realises he has spoken so freely in front of MJ.

MJ, realising Jerome's nervousness, reassures him: 'Don't worry, Jerome. What's said in this office stays in the office.'

'Thanks, MJ. Will you join us for dinner? We're going

clubbing afterwards,' Jerome asks.

'I can't remember the last time I had an evening free to go clubbing; I'd love to join you!'

'We'll have to make it an extra special night then. Let's go somewhere elegant for dinner. How about the Gay Hussar, just off Soho Square, in Greek Street.' Jerome asks, waving his credit card.

'Not another gay place, Jerome.'

'It's not gay; lots of people eat there.'

'Sounds a bit camp to me,' Cyril says hesitantly.

'Believe me, you'll love it.'

Later that night at the Gay Hussar, Jerome and Jonathan are upstairs, sitting in a cosy corner and holding hands under the table. Cyril arrives and walks up to meet them.

'Nice to meet you Jonathan. Jerome has told me a lot about you.'

MJ arrives a little later, all dressed up. The head waiter, in his white jacket, takes her long overcoat. She looks around the restaurant, admiring its dark wooden features. One of the side walls is covered with mirrors, giving the impression that the room is much bigger than it actually is. MJ climbs the stairs, knowing that eyes are following her.

'Hello, boys, sorry I'm late. My hair took ages to set,'

MJ says, greeting them with a glamorous flourish and doing her best Mae West impression.

'That's alright, MJ. We haven't been here that long,' Cyril assures her.

Jerome barely notices MJ's arrival as he is too lost in the eyes of Jonathan. He is clearly besotted by his new tall, blond-haired beau.

The restaurant quickly becomes busier and, after their starter course, MJ excuses herself to go to the bathroom. On her way back, she spots two of her old regulars from the club. They are politicians, both sitting across from their wives smiling and having a nice evening. She glides past their table, careful to be discreet and not make eye contact. When she returns to Cyril and the others, she whispers about all the weird things they paid extra for.

'MJ, I bet you see a fair few famous people in your club,' Jerome says with a grin.

MJ gives a wink and mimes that her lips are sealed.

'You certainly spend a lot of time hanging around famous people, Jerome. I have a feeling you secretly want to be a star yourself,' Cyril teases.

'No, I just want to sleep with them all!' Jerome retaliates with a laugh. Jonathan looks shocked. 'Oh, Jonathan. You'll have to get familiar with my northern sense of humour.'

As promised, Jerome suggests they continue the night at Heaven nightclub. They walk into the club with Frankie Goes to Hollywood's 'Relax' playing, and all four of them can't help but move along to the music. Over the instrumental part of the song, the DJ announces that tonight is talent night.

'For anyone out there with something to show off, come on over to me and sign up. And before anyone asks, no, having a big dick doesn't count!'

MJ pushes her way through the crowd of half-naked bodies, dragging Cyril to the dance floor. Jerome and Jonathan follow closely behind, singing along.

'Relax, don't do it

When you wanna go do it

Relax, don't do it

When you wanna come'

As the evening drifts on, the DJ reminds the crowd that they have fifteen more minutes to sign up for the talent contest. The judge for the contest is Ian Levine, a famous music producer, and the prize for winning is a bottle of champagne.

'Go on Jonathan, you can sing,' Jerome suggests, attempting to drag Jonathan to the DJ.

Jonathan firmly refuses, worried he might be spotted by someone who knows Kevin Cash. It wouldn't look good for him to be spotted in a gay club. Jerome lets go of

Jonathan and heads up to the DJ podium alone. When Jonathan protests, Jerome insists he is going to request a song.

The contest begins and the crowd are delighted by a plethora of different acts, ranging from dancers to drag queens strutting around the stage. The DJ announces the final act: 'For our last entry, please welcome to the stage... MJ!'

The crowd cheer and clap, and MJ looks surprised.

'Jerome, you bastard,' she shrieks.

'Cyril told me you have a stunning voice, and I'd like to hear it for myself,' Jerome grins. 'Go and show them what you've got, girl!'

MJ struts up to the DJ booth, turning around to wag her finger at Jerome. She has a quick word with the DJ before walking onto the middle of the stage. The slow intro to the song begins and the crowd wait in anticipation.

'Spring was never waiting for us, boy

It ran one step ahead

As we followed in the dance...'

The crowd break the calm and cheer for the extraordinary opening.

'MacArthur's Park is melting in the dark

All the sweet, green icing flowing down

Someone left the cake out in the rain

I don't think that I can take it
'Cause it took so long to bake it
And I'll never have that recipe again
Oh no!'

The crowd cheers with excitement as MJ belts out the song like the true diva that she is. The song builds in intensity and MJ shows off her incredible Welsh voice, with a vocal range Donna Summer would be proud of.

As the song finishes, the clubbers are chanting her name. It is obvious that she is the peoples' choice. Ian Levine comes onto the stage and presents MJ with her prize. He escorts her from the stage to the bar, where the rest of her party are jumping for joy.

'Hello, Jerome. Trust you to have a hand in this talented lady,' Ian says, giving Jerome a hug.

'Everyone, meet my friend Ian Levine; successful music producer, songwriter and much, much more,' Jerome says with a slight drunken slur.

'MJ, you have a unique talent and a great voice. I have a new song, and I think you'd be perfect for it.'

'Thank you, Ian. But you'll have to speak to my manager here, Cyril Gold,' MJ says without missing a beat.

Cyril is startled, taken completely by surprise. He's in a daze as Ian begins talking about the song and studio recording dates with him.

It is the night of the yearly music awards. EMI have organised a black limousine to pick up Cyril, MJ and The Sisters. They have already started on the champagne, moving and singing to 'Pull Up to the Bumper' by Grace Jones, while the limousine glides through the streets of the West End and makes for Park Lane. The limo pulls up behind a row of Mercedes, Rolls-Royces and Bentleys, each waiting its turn to drop its VIP passengers at the red carpet leading up to the Grosvenor House ballroom.

When it is finally The Sisters', Cyril's and MJ's turn to walk, they are surrounded by a dozen paparazzi.

'Ruby! Cheryl! Let's see your smiles,' they shout as the cameras flash continuously.

Cyril stands between the twins in front of the main entrance with his arms around their waists. The twins look a million dollars in their tight-fitting, white outfits and expensive gold jewellery hired for the night by the record company. Cyril also looks like a star, all kitted out in a black tuxedo and bow tie. He grins from ear to ear.

The twins are exuding sex appeal, and the paparazzi love them. After the initial commotion has waned slightly, MJ makes her entrance. She steps out of the limo in her extra tall black high heels. Not wanting to be overshadowed by the twins, MJ's outfit is more extravagant than ever. A black leather number with metal studs all over. And to top it off, a leather whip as her prop. She stands out a mile and the paparazzi rush over to her like a swarm of bees.

'What's your name? Who are you? Come on, tell us!' the paparazzi shout. They get no response, which only heightens their interest. MJ only answers them with alluring glances.

As they enter the ballroom, the air is thick with the smell of perfume and smoke. Almost everyone is puffing on a cigar, or elegantly holding a cigarette. The place is packed with celebrities chatting to each other, everyone with a drink in hand. The evening isn't just about awards; it's about networking and playing the field. Everyone is keen to assert their dominance as the kingpins of music.

After an hour, Paul Gambaccini, the host for the evening, invites everyone in the room to take their seat for dinner. There are nine guests on the EMI table: Mark Jones, head of A&R, and his new managing director, Nigel. The head of press and publicity, Isabella-Rose, who speaks with a plum in her mouth, is sitting next to Michael Joshua-Raymond, head of EMI television and radio. Maurice Cohen, The Sisters, Cyril and MJ sit around the other side of the table.

The group Shalamar get up to perform their number, 'A Night To Remember'. After the song ends, the waiters scurry around to serve the first course to the five hundred guests.

'Why do all the senior EMI staff have double-barreled names?' whispers Cheryl in Maurice's ear.

'It's all very old fashioned at the top, my dear,' Maurice whispers back.

'This is the fanciest place I've ever been in my life. Maybe I'll find myself a boyfriend here tonight. What do you think, Cyril? Ruby asks with a grin.

'You'll have a hard time finding a straight one here,' MJ says.

'Not everyone here is gay,' Maurice insists, taking a shine to MJ and her Welsh humour.

'No, but I bet you're into something kinky,' MJ says cheekily.

'You might be surprised if I told you.'

'Nothing surprises me, darling. I've seen it all.'

'I like my women like I take my coffee; black and sweet.'

'Once you've had black, you never go back. Isn't that the saying?' MJ laughs.

Paul Gambaccini is talking about the wonderful year that music has had, pointing out some of the distinguished guests. In walk Roxy and Jerome, looking embarrassed as they head towards the CBS table right in front of the stage. Ashley Goodman and Bea Solomon stand up to greet them. This is the first time Cyril has seen Roxy in person since the fateful evening of the TV talent competition five months ago. She is looking glamorous in a bright canary yellow dress with huge shoulder pads.

'What on earth was Roxy thinking with that bright yellow outfit? She looks like a banana,' MJ lashes out with her acid tongue. 'And those shoulder pads! Are they to keep her afloat in the event of a flood? She's all skin and bone; aren't they feeding her at CBS?'

'Leave her alone,' Cyril says, making a disapproving face. He looks longingly at Roxy, hoping she might turn and notice him.

'Well pardon me!' MJ says sarcastically.

The Sisters can't believe how beautiful Roxy looks, her model-like figure accentuated perfectly in the dress and matching yellow heels. Cyril can see she has lost a lot of weight.

'She must be on drugs. I can tell a druggie from a mile away,' MJ whispers in Maurice's ear. Cyril overhears and winces.

Just as Gambaccini is finishing his presentation, a guy with smooth Mediterranean skin and long brown hair joins Roxy at the table. He stands out from the rest of the room because he is wearing a leather jacket over a white shirt, and blue jeans. The event dress code clearly stipulated black tie only. Cyril watches Roxy and can see her body language change as the man sits down. She clearly isn't comfortable. Jerome finally notices Cyril and gives him a wave. He looks just like a pop star, wedged between Ashley Goodman and Roxy, sporting his new short haircut.

There is a short intermission before the main course, and Cyril walks towards the toilets, imagining the dizzying rush of winning manager of the year. He tries to push the idea from his head so he won't be disappointed. Dan Evans, head of Virgin records, meets him coming from the opposite direction.

'Hey Cyril. You look the business. I hear you're up for an award or two this evening. I love The Sisters. It's a shame you didn't come to me for a deal, especially when we were so close to closing on Roxy.'

'You know what the music business is like, Dan. Nothing personal. But I do have a new artist I want you to consider.' Cyril pulls his business card from his wallet and hands it to Dan. They agree to set up a meeting.

Cyril walks into the toilet to find Jerome washing his hands.

'Well, well, well. You're looking positively dazzling. I just met the lead singer of A-Ha, Morten Harket. He's gorgeous, but my God Cyril, you could give him a run for his money.'

'Stop flirting Jerome. I take it you're enjoying yourself then?'

'Time of my life!'

'How come you and Roxy were late for dinner?'

'Roxy had a huge argument with Struan as we were leaving the house. He's a real tosser. Can turn on the charm when he needs to, but underneath the surface he's just nasty. He wants to get rid of Solomon and become Roxy's manager.'

'But why? I can't see Queen Bea going down without a fight.'

'Money. He thinks he can do her job and keep the fees for himself.'

'What's his hold on Roxy? She's a sensible girl, I thought she would be able to look after herself,' Cyril continues casually.

'Maybe that's love?' Jerome says.

Cyril says nothing and just about manages to keep himself together.

They walk back to the ballroom, chatting, until Cyril realises he has left his wallet on the washbasin. He rushes back to grab it. The group ABC are performing 'Poison

Arrow' on the stage and the sound filters throughout the venue. On his way out of the toilet, Cyril bumps head-on into Roxy. They make eye contact and are both stuck for words. At first, neither of them speaks. Then they both try to speak at the same time. They burst out laughing together.

'How are you, Cyril?' Roxy finally manages to say.

'I'm fine, thank you. You look beautiful,' Cyril stammers. 'How is little Tommy?'

'Thanks. He's good. He hasn't forgotten about you. He asks about you all the time,' Roxy replies, blushing and looking at the floor. She's still the same shy girl he met in the office.

'It looks like your dreams all came true,' Cyril says with a genuine smile.

'I have you to thank for the success. You were the first person who believed in me.'

Cyril moves closer with uncertainty. There are so many things he wants to say. Roxy looks up at him.

'Cyril, I wanted to say...' Roxy begins.

Before she can continue, Struan appears.

'Roxy, I was looking for you all over the fucking place. They're about to announce your category soon. They want you back in your seat.' Without waiting for her to answer, he grabs her arm and pulls her away.

'Hey, no need to be so rough with her mate,' Cyril

says protectively.

'It's okay, Cyril.'

'Wait, you're Cyril? Roxy told me about you. Now fuck off and mind your own business.'

Cyril immediately sees red and pushes Struan against the wall, lifting his fist to his face.

'Stop, Cyril. He's off his head,' Roxy calls out.

Cyril reluctantly pulls back and watches them walk back to the ballroom. Struan is laughing.

Paul Gambaccini asks for the guests to take their seats. The first award goes to Culture Club for most international number one record sales. The awards go on for quite some time before it finally comes to the two that matter.

'This year, we have narrowed down three talented managers. Ms Solomon, Stevo Pearce, and the new kid on the block, Cyril Gold. The award for manager of the year goes to… Stevo Pearce for Soft Cell and Depeche Mode.'

Loud applause follows as Stevo walks to collect his award. Then they announce best new song. The audience wait in anticipation.

'The award goes to… Roxy!!, for "Waiting for Your Love". Congratulations!'

The crowd give Roxy a standing ovation, clapping

and whistling. They calm down as she takes the microphone.

She speaks softly and calmly, emphasising that she is still just a shy girl from south London writing love songs. She thanks everyone who has played a part in her success, and, although she doesn't mention Cyril by name, she looks directly at him when she finishes with: 'And also, for those I may have missed out.'

Roxy is soon surrounded by enthusiastic guests, hoping to speak with her and congratulate her. Cyril and The Sisters have their admirers, too. Maurice leans over and whispers to Cyril.

'You should be proud of yourself. You spotted a true star, and no one can take that away from you.'

An hour later, Cyril heads towards reception to collect his coat. The band ABC is just about to play their hit song 'The Look of Love' live in the ballroom.

'I hear you were the man who discovered Roxy.' Cyril turns around and finds Stevo Pearce offering him his hand.

'Stevo! Congratulations on the win!'

'Thanks, but all this shit means nothing to me,' he replies nonchalantly.

Cyril laughs.

'How come you're leaving so early?'

'I've had a crazy week. I'm not used to all this

excitement. Just need to get home and get some sleep.'
In reality, Cyril just wants to be alone after his emotions
have been stirred by seeing Roxy.

Cyril walks to the exit, only to bump into Roxy in
the cloakroom.

'The woman of the hour can't leave the party early,'
Cyril jokes.

Roxy turns around to reveal a sad face. 'I want to get
back home for Tommy,' she says.

Cyril doesn't know whether he should address the
fact that she is clearly upset.

'So, where is home these days?' he says.

'Chelsea.'

'Very posh. You've come a long way since Peckham,'
Cyril says. He sees her eyes begin to fill with tears. She
turns away.

'What's wrong? Are you okay?'

'I don't want anyone to see me like this.'

Cyril takes her by the shoulders and steers her gently
further into the cloakroom, where they are hidden by
the coats.

'My life is a mess. A total disaster,' Roxy begins. She
starts to sob.

'Come on, what's so bad that we can't fix?' Cyril says,
holding her hands and trying to comfort her. He opens
the door of a cupboard. 'Here. Pop in there for a few

minutes and get yourself together.'

He ushers Roxy inside, and she pulls him in as well, not letting go of his hand. She pulls the door closed and they stand close together, the light falling on their faces through a crack in the door. The silence is only broken by the sound of ABC's song. She stares at Cyril for a few more moments before standing up on her toes and kissing him passionately. Cyril, although surprised and taken aback at first, relaxes into the embrace and kisses her back.

'I thought you didn't like me like that?' Cyril says as they pull apart.

Roxy looks at him with confusion. 'What gave you that idea?'

'Solomon stopped me on the way to your house after the TV show fiasco. She said it'd be best if I left you alone. The truth is, I've wanted to kiss you since they day I met you.'

'Why didn't you?'

'I didn't want to be unprofessional and lose you as a client. Turns out I lost you anyway,' Cyril says with regret.

They continue to stare at each other until Roxy suddenly panics that Struan will be looking for her. She hurries out of the cupboard with her head down, leaving Cyril to contemplate the events that have just unfolded.

When he finally comes out of the cloakroom, Roxy is nowhere to be seen. He heads back to the ballroom and finds Jerome.

'I was looking for you. I'm about to leave for the CBS party. Do you want to come?'

'I don't think Ashley would be particularly pleased to see me.'

'He doesn't hold grudges. He got Roxy in the end, didn't he?' Jerome reassures Cyril while lighting a cigarette.

'Is everything alright with Roxy?' Cyril asks worriedly.

'What do you mean?'

'Is she happy? She looks pretty miserable for someone who just won such an amazing award.'

'Well, she feels like she's made a mistake letting Struan back in her life. You can't get rid of him. He's like a bad smell. From what I can see, he plays a lot of mind games and torments her awfully. He's using drugs to control her too.'

'Why didn't you tell me this sooner? I could have helped!'

'She isn't listening to anyone, Cyril. And you've only just got yourself straight.'

Cyril lets out a huge sigh. He feels stuck between a rock and a hard place. Eventually he decides to make the most of the evening.

'Alright Jerome. Let's go and have a real fucking party.'

Chapter Seventeen

'With or Without You'

U2

It's Sunday morning, and the house phone in Stanmore is ringing loudly. Gina looks groggily at her bedside clock; it's almost eight in the morning. She was supposed to be enjoying a lie in. Reluctantly, she gets out of bed and goes downstairs to answer the phone. In the next room, Cyril is still sleeping peacefully. He didn't get in until the early hours of the morning.

'Cyril! Are you awake? There's a phone call for you,' Gina shrieks at the top of her voice.

'I am now,' Cyril replies with a muffled groan.

'It's Mark Jones from EMI. He wants to talk to you.'

Cyril heaves himself out of bed, wondering why Mark would call at this time.

'Morning Mark. You'd better have a good reason for calling me this early.'

'Have you seen the *News of the World* yet?'

'No, I was in bed until just now. Did I do something scandalous last night?' Cyril jokes.

'Photos of the twins are all over the front page.'

'Shit. What kind of pictures?' Cyril asks hesitantly.

'Stark bollock naked, career down the drain kind of pictures!' Mark shouts down the phone.

'What! Are you sure it's the twins?'

'It's them alright! Someone called James took the pictures and then leaked them to the Sunday newspapers. Nigel is furious and demanding answers, Cyril. Get your arse over to your office and we'll meet there.'

Cyril puts the phone down. It seems James wasn't happy with the fee Cyril sent him for the promotional photos. He hadn't expected the spotty little shit to take revenge. With an exasperated sigh, Cyril dashes out the door to meet Mark.

When Cyril arrives at his office a clearly angry Mark doesn't waste any time before laying out a plan of action. 'Nigel wants to meet us first thing tomorrow in the boardroom,' he says before Cyril has even had a chance to sit down. 'Make sure the twins are there. We need to try and salvage the situation,' Mark continues. He's as worried as Cyril has ever seen him before.

'I can see you're pissed off, Mark. But I think it looks worse than it is, don't you?'

'I don't see how it could be much worse,' Mark says, flapping his hands in panic.

'They were topless, not naked, for a start. There are topless girls all over the newspapers everywhere.' Cyril says, trying to calm the situation.

'Well, not EMI artists! Nigel is going to have to explain this to the CEO as well as the whole EMI board. So, you'd better start taking this seriously.'

'Mark, stop panicking and let me think.'

'I could lose my job over this,' Mark says as he drops himself onto a chair in despair. He immediately jumps back up again. 'I'm going,' he shouts. 'You,' he says, pointing angrily at Cyril, 'have to work out a plan if you want to save The Sisters. I have my mother-in-law's Sunday lunch to get to!' He storms out of the office.

Cyril is left alone to contemplate his next move. His head is pounding as he tries to think of people who might be able to help; he wishes he hadn't partied so heavily last night. The only person that comes to mind is Maurice.

'Hello, Maurice, It's Cyril. Sorry to call you on a Sunday. Are you free to talk?'

'I've got ten minutes, no more.'

Cyril explains the situation and Maurice says he will be at EMI on Monday morning to help out.

Cyril makes himself a cup of tea while he waits for the twins to arrive at the office. He is trying out alternative strategies for the EMI meeting, but none of them seem watertight. His answering machine is filling up with journalist wanting to speak to The Sisters. There is also a message from Pete Waterman, suggesting that Cyril has executed a brilliant media stunt. Cyril isn't so sure that's how EMI will see things.

The twins arrive wearing dark glasses and plain clothes. They aren't their usual confident, bubbly selves. Neither of them can look Cyril in the face.

'Girls, you're late. Do you know how serious this is? Just tell me everything, I need to know how this all happened,' Cyril says, shaking the newspaper in their faces.

'Believe us, we had no idea James was going to sell the photos,' Ruby begins shakily.

'But why did you take off all your clothes for the photoshoot and dance topless for some seedy men in a club? Surely you must have known that wasn't a good idea!' Cyril says, looking between the two of them.

'It was James' idea. He said it would make the artwork more realistic and gritty. He said that's what people want,' Cheryl says.

'What he wants, more like,' Cyril says angrily.

'James said setting it in the club would help us get in the mood for the shoot. Diamond agreed to let us use it privately for an hour.'

'It says in the newspaper that you worked in Diamond's strip club for a while? Is that true?'

'Well we needed to make money somehow. It's not like you were super quick finding us a record deal,' Cheryl complains indignantly.

'He left us his business card, remember? We did it for a laugh and to make some extra cash,' Ruby adds with a more apologetic tone.

'Who's laughing now?' Cyril asks.

'The newspapers lied about us having sex with men at the club. We didn't. We're not whores.'

'This just keeps getting worse and worse,' Cyril says, his head in his hands. 'So, where is that pervy bastard now?'

'We went to his house this morning to confront him. That's why we were late. His mother just told us he's gone overseas on a long holiday.'

Cyril instructs the twins to go home and not speak to any media. He also reminds them under any circumstances not to be late for the meeting with EMI the following day. He glances at his watch and sits down in his chair. The phone rings.

'Hello?'

'Cyril, it's me,' Gina says hurriedly. 'There are reporters and photographers hanging about outside the house. How do they even know where you live?'

'Don't talk to them. Don't even open the door. I'll try and sort it out,' Cyril replies, hoping not to worry his mum.

He decides he can't go home and risk getting implicated further in The Sisters' scandal and so pulls out his contact book.

'Hi Esther. It's Cyril Gold. Do you remember me?'

'No, sorry. Tell me when we last met?' she replies, much to Cyril's surprise. He thought they had quite a bit of chemistry when they exchanged numbers at Virgin Records.

'We met at Virgin Records? We were discussing a deal for my artist, Roxy, about six months ago,' Cyril tries, desperately hoping to jog her memory.

'Never heard of you,' she replies, pausing for a moment and then laughing. 'Cyril, I'm joking. I remember you. I also remember you leaving very quickly after flirting with me the whole time and drinking the champagne.'

'How about I make it up to you? Would you like to go out tonight?'

'Hiding from the media, are we?'

'I take it you've seen the papers?'

'Why don't you come over to my place in Notting Hill? Bring a bottle of wine and you can lay low here.'

Cyril can't quite believe his luck as he drives to Notting Hill, picking up an expensive bottle of red wine on the way.

'This is quite a pad you have here,' he says in awe.

'Thanks. My great aunt left me some money, and I put it towards this place.'

'It's beautiful.'

'So, what brings you here? Business or pleasure?'

Cyril looks confused.

'Are you here to talk about the situation with The Sisters or are you hoping to… relax and unwind?'

'How about both?'

'A man who wants it all; I like it,' Esther says, leading him up to the bedroom.

Cyril heads home in the early hours of the morning after a bottle of wine, some sound advice and an evening of passion. Thankfully, no reporters had decided to camp out in his front garden, and he makes it to bed with no problems.

'Your breakfast is getting cold, Cyril' Gina shouts. Alf peers over the top of his newspaper and sighs as

Cyril clatters down the stairs.

'Never a moment of peace in this house anymore and God knows what our neighbours are thinking,' he complains.

'Sorry, Mum. I don't have time for breakfast,' Cyril says, sipping on his tea.

'Have you worked out what to say to the EMI people this morning? I remember back in my day, nothing like this happened. The world's gone mad,' Alf grumbles, gesticulating at the front page of the newspaper, which is plastered with more pictures of The Sisters.

'More or less,' Cyril replies with a smile. 'I must go. Don't want to be late.' He heads out the door.

'He seems very calm, considering the situation, don't you think?' Gina asks.

'I think our Cyril's matured quite a bit in the last few months. He's solving problems using his head, rather than his emotions,' Alf says holding Gina's hand for a moment before returning to his newspaper.

Cyril arrives at the EMI offices in Manchester Square in a black taxi while the radio plays XTC's 'Making Plans for Nigel'. Cyril is wearing a suit and tie, and has to push his way through a sea of photographers and journalists. The head of EMI press and publicity, Isabella-Rose, is waiting for him in reception. She looks very solemn and has very little to say. Cyril lights a cigarette but Isabella advises him not to smoke as Nigel doesn't like it.

They enter the huge boardroom; the walls are covered with gold and platinum discs. Mark is sitting next to Nigel, both of them looking sulky. Over a cup of tea and some biscuits, Nigel begins the meeting. The twins still haven't arrived. The conversation only seems to be heading in one direction, and nothing Cyril says seems to be pulling it back. Nigel is infuriated with the situation, and it seems like he has already made up his mind to pull the plug. Mark sits there silently, and Cyril is annoyed that he hasn't picked a side. The twins eventually arrive, apologising. Ruby seems especially nervous, whereas Cheryl appears ready for a fight. The pair sit down and the meeting continues.

Isabella-Rose talks about the damage to EMI's image that has been caused by the article. She holds up a copy of the most recent morning papers, which are carrying the story from yesterday.

'I've heard enough of this nonsense,' Nigel butts in. 'You're not the kind of people we want at EMI. This behaviour is unacceptable. You're being dropped.'

'What?' Cyril asks. 'Surely we can turn this to our advantage?'

'I've made up my mind. I don't want anything to

do with The Sisters and I will recommend this to the board. That's the end of it.'

Cyril begins to protest, suggesting ways they could move forwards.

'I'll have to ask you to leave the premises immediately. Don't make a scene,' Nigel says grimly.

Cyril storms into the reception area to find Maurice shouting at a receptionist. He hadn't been allowed into the meeting, under Nigel's instruction. Maurice walks beside Cyril, telling him that things aren't all over yet with EMI and that he has prepared a media statement. They step out of the building into blinding flashes and fifty voices demanding to know what has happened.

'My client is very disappointed with EMI for not standing by the young women, who were duped into a compromising situation. However, The Sisters love making music and they have no intention of quitting the business. We aren't taking any questions at the moment,' Maurice addresses the crowd and then gets into a black taxi with Cyril and the twins.

Later, in Cyril's office, the phones are ringing. Most of the calls are from journalists; he puts the answering machine on to filter them. Some of the messages are interesting, with promoters offering The Sisters live gigs all over the country. He turns on the radio to hear 'With or Without You' by U2 and hums along. Maurice is sitting across from Cyril looking completely bewildered.

'Cyril, what do you know that I don't? Your biggest artists just got dropped and you don't seem to be affected at all. You're cool as a cucumber.'

Cyril smiles. 'You'll see. I'm expecting an important call.'

'Well, I'll leave you to it then. You know where to find me,' Maurice says as he gets up to leave.

Another couple of hours pass and Cyril begins to get nervous. Finally, the call comes through.

'Hello, Cyril. The Sisters are becoming more famous by the hour. EMI dropping them has stirred up lots of attention. We'd like to meet with you at seven, at Morton's in Berkeley Square. See you then.'

Cyril smiles to himself. Everything is going to plan.

When Cyril arrives at the fashionable and exclusive Morton's club, he is escorted up the stairs to a private room. Esther is waiting for him, looking very sexy as usual. A bottle of champagne on ice and a silver tray of glasses sits in front of her. Cyril leans over and kisses her.

'Steady on, tiger. We're expecting company,' she laughs, pulling away.

There is a knock at the door, and Esther's boss, Dan, is shown into the room. Cyril greets him with a firm handshake. Dan skips the pleasantries and cuts straight to the chase.

'I want The Sisters on our label.'

Dan is moving quickly, not wanting to miss out like he did with Roxy. But Cyril still wants to play it cool; he hopes he can play Virgin off with another record company to get more money.

'Why don't we talk business over dinner? There's a table waiting for us downstairs. I'll join you in a few minutes,' Dan suggests.

Cyril and Esther move to the first floor; a corner table for four by the large window overlooking Berkeley Square. Dan joins them several minutes later. As they are looking over the menu, the owner of Virgin Records, Richard Branson, walks in.

'Am I too late to join the party? I'm sure Dan has told you; I'm a big fan of The Sisters,' Richard says pleasantly, extending his hand to an astounded Cyril.

The evening rolls on and the drinks flow. Cyril grows more and more impressed with Richard as he tells rock and roll stories about his time in the business.

'Cyril, this situation reminds me of the Sex Pistols. Two labels dropped them for being too outrageous and always misbehaving. But I wanted them on Virgin Records. I think we can deliver the same kind of success for The Sisters. So, do we have a deal?' Richard finally goes in, hoping to close the deal.

'Yes, as long as Maurice Cohen agrees to the details of the contract.'

'Not the bloody Rottweiler!' Dan exclaims.

Cyril turns to Richard: 'So, tell me one thing. Why did you call it "Virgin" Records? No offence, but it's kind of a weird name.'

'When I started the record company, we had no idea what we were doing. We were all virgins in the business,' he says laughing. 'Waiter, more champagne please.'

The new deal is signed off quickly, and within weeks The Sisters' record hits number one in the charts. It stays there for three weeks. Meanwhile, Maurice is preparing to turn the financial screw on Nigel at EMI for dropping The Sisters.

MJ walks across the legendary crossing on Abbey Road, where The Beatles posed for their famous album cover. As she enters the recording studios she feels a shiver go down her spine; she can hardly believe this is happening. Today is the last day in the studio for the final mix. Ian has allowed MJ to add some of her lyrics to the song, and has changed the song title to 'I Need a Man'.

Cyril arrives and parks his car in front of the Abbey Road recording studios. He looks up the stairs at the entrance and feels a little emotional, thinking back to his late uncle, Brian Epstein, and the Beatles walking up the very same stairs. Cyril is excited to hear the final mix of the record. Ian, being a perfectionist, has not allowed him into the studio until everything is finished.

'This is fantastic. I love the unusual pop sound, and the incredible energy you've given it. It's changed dramatically from your demo,' Cyril says.

'Yes, we had to make it gayer for my diva,' Ian says, looking pleased.

'It's more than just a bit gay. The lyrics are very racy and suggestive. It could be a challenging record to market,' Cyril says gently, not wanting to upset Ian.

Ian laughs. 'Well, I've done my part. The rest is up to you.'

It has been a couple of weeks since Ian delivered MJ's single, and Cyril has been working on record companies, trying to get them to sign MJ. It's proving to be more difficult than he had expected. Cyril is just about to call it a day and head home for his Friday night dinner when Jerome walks into the office. He is absolutely drenched and has obviously been crying.

'Jerome, you look awful.'

'Oh Cyril,' Jerome sighs, grabbing Cyril and hugging him. The radio is playing Cat Stevens' 'The First Cut is the Deepest'.

'What's wrong?'

'It's over,' Jerome says, releasing Cyril from the hug.

'Over? What's over?'

'Jonathan came to see me to say it's all over between us. Kevin Cash found out about us seeing each other and dug up some dirt on me. He told Jonathan I was an escort and said he should drop me if he ever wants to be successful. Kevin is even lining up some girl to be his girlfriend so he looks straight for the newspapers.'

'I'm sorry, Jerome. That's awful,' Cyril says, trying to make sense of what Jerome has told him.

'That's not all. Kevin knows all about the gay pubs and the places I usually hang out in Soho. He threatened me, saying he'd go to the press and leak the story of the Bradford rent boy who caters to music and television executives.'

Jerome begins to cry. 'Can you imagine my family reading about my secret life in London? They're already disappointed in me.'

'Fuck, that nasty bastard really does live up to his reputation as the silent assassin.'

'I need to go home and pack. I've booked a flight to New York tonight,' Jerome says suddenly.

'What? Why?'

'Kevin has given me twenty-four hours to leave.'

'That's crazy. Why New York, though? Can't you just move back north for a while?'

'I need to go as far away as possible to get over Jonathan. I need time to heal. I loved him, Cyril. He was my first real love.'

'I thought I was your first love,' Cyril jokes, trying to lighten the mood.

'You were my first real crush,' Jerome replies with a small smile.

'Time heals everything. You'll get over this, believe me. Do you need any money?'

'No, I'm fine. I have a few contacts out there, so I should be okay.'

Cyril pulls Jerome into a long hug.

'I cannot believe this is happening. You're a great friend and I will miss you…. You old tart!' They both laugh. Finally, they are interrupted by the phone ringing and Gina leaving an angry message about Cyril being late for dinner again.

'You have to call me and let me know when you get settled, alright? You can call me anytime, night or day,' Cyril says outside the office, staring into Jerome's eyes to make sure he know he really cares. He gives Jerome a gentle kiss on the top of his head before they go their separate ways.

Chapter Eighteen

'YMCA'

Village People

Cyril walks into his Berwick Street office with a spring in his step, listening to Chic's 'Good Times' on his Walkman. He is finally starting to relax after a tense few months dealing with The Sisters' fiasco and is working hard to market and promote their record. They are now enjoying their second big hit in the charts, and most likely a top three record by the end of the week. The Rottweiler negotiated a spectacular settlement deal with EMI for dropping them. Cyril and The Sisters were able to keep all the recorded material and their rights without being responsible for any of the studio costs incurred. Maurice has also invoiced Virgin Records for The Sisters' album, which hasn't cost Cyril anything. For the first time ever, Cyril is flush with cash. He is looking to buy himself an apartment in the centre of London.

The only bump in the road is that he hasn't been able to find a record deal for MJ. Not one record company dares take on her record, not even Virgin. They feel uncomfortable signing up a transvestite singing a lewd and lascivious song. Ian Levine still refuses to change the lyrics to make it more marketable.

Cyril hits the playback button on his answer machine and is surprised by an unusual sounding person by the name of Dolly, saying they will be dropping by the office later that morning. From the voice, Cyril can't work out whether the person is a man or a woman, but they end every other sentence with 'dear'.

A while later, Gina calls Cyril for a chat about Lew's up-coming surprise birthday party. So far, the only thing they've agreed on is the date. Neither of them can decide on the other plans; they keep arguing and going around in an endless circle. With only a few weeks left to plan it, Cyril is getting anxious. Suddenly there is a knock at the door.

'I'll have to call you back, Mum. But I really don't think Uncle Lew is a Nouvelle Cuisine kind of guy. Okay… see you soon.'

Cyril opens the door and in strolls a slim, well-groomed man, exuding confidence. He looks Mediterranean; late twenties. His long black hair is swept back and he wears a white open-neck shirt and a waistcoat that matches his seventies-style flared trousers. Cyril wonders whether he has just stumbled into the film *Saturday Night Fever*.

'Nice to meet you, Cyril. I'm Dolly. Disco Dolly to those in the know; famous independent promotional man by day, and infamous dance diva by night,' he says in a camp but personable way.

Dolly immediately reaches out and grabs Cyril's hand, shaking it vigorously. He maintains a fast pace of speech, and laces everything with humour and an infectious smile.

'I was at Bang last night, and my friend Ian Levine was the VIP DJ. He played MJ's record, 'I Want a Man', three times and, my dear... the queens loved it! They went absolutely wild each time. So long story short – I want to promote it.'

'Thanks... mate,' Cyril replies, hesitant to call him Dolly,' but I don't have a record deal for the track yet, and if I'm honest, it not going to happen.'

'I know, I know. Ian told me everything. I have a proposal for you, dear.'

Cyril is all ears, but not entirely sure how this strange disco man will be able to help.

'I'll be your plugger and help you with the marketing for free. Then, when the record becomes a massive hit

– which it will – you can pay me a nice big bonus. What do you say dear?'

'But I told you, I don't have any record labels interested.'

'Create your own independent label. Call it… Gold Records or something. You don't need the big boys, dear. All they want is tried and tested stuff. They don't want to take risks. I know all about Roxy and The Sisters. That's why I came to see you, dear. I know you have what it takes to launch this record off your own back. I can tell you are a risk-taker!'

Cyril starts chuckling, finding it hilarious that Dolly keeps calling him dear.

'What's so funny, dear? You don't believe what I'm telling you?'

'It's not that. But I'm completely new to this – I know nothing about launching my own label.'

'Don't worry, dear. I'll hold your hand the whole way,' Dolly says with a wink. 'The only advantage of having an artist signed to a record label is that they will cover the expense of recording the tracks and have access to lots of contacts for marketing. In MJ's case, the record is already done; you have a deal with Ian, and the mainstream labels don't have access to the gay scene like I do. This record needs a gay plugger to make it happen, and I'm the man for the job.'

Cyril laughs again, shaking his head in disbelief. 'Tell me, where did you get the name Disco Dolly?' he asks.

'I was born in Cyprus and moved to London. No one could pronounce my name, Michalakis, but my friends knew I loved disco music and Dolly Parton. So, there you go, dear: Disco Dolly.'

Dolly isn't shy and doesn't hold back on telling Cyril about all of his past successes, reeling off a list of the most famous acts he has promoted. He name-drops all the DJs, TV producers and directors.

'I'll get the record played in all the gay clubs and bars around the country first, then, on the back of its success there, I'll cross the record over to the mainstream market. How does that sound? Of course, you'll need some money for the initial cost of pressing the record at the EMI factory, and for designing the cover. You think you can handle that?'

'I think I can stretch that far,' Cyril says confidently, trying to keep up.

'Great. Now, do we have a deal, dear?' Dolly holds out his hand.

Cyril looks Dolly in the eye for a moment.

'Yes, why not? I love a challenge, and I like you very much. But I have to tell you now – I'm straight,' Cyril says with a cheeky grin.

'Sorry dear, but you aren't my type,' Dolly replies

dismissively. He pulls out a piece of paper from his jacket. 'Let's get the paperwork out of the way. I've come up with a simple contract.'

Cyril studies the one-page contract and signs it. 'You were obviously very confident I was going to say yes,' Cyril laughs.

'Absolutely dear. I have to dash – got a busy day,' Dolly says, taking the contract from Cyril. He minces out of the office singing Dolly Parton's '9 to 5'.

Later that afternoon, Cyril receives an unexpected phone call from Jerome in New York; he is thrilled to hear his voice.

'I'm so bloody lucky, Cyril. I'm living in New Jersey and loving everything about America. I've made loads of friends and, wait for it… I'm staying in the YMCA,' Jerome says excitedly down the phone, barely pausing for breath. He sings the chorus from the Village People's 'YMCA'.

'I take it you're enjoying yourself?' Cyril says, smiling.

'I've come out to the world, and I feel free to be myself here. I've been to a few of Manhattan's elite parties, and everyone loves my English accent. I'm going to another one on Fifth Avenue tonight.'

'I knew you'd fit right in with the American queens in New York. I'm so happy for you,' Cyril says. He means it, but a part of him is sad that he has lost his friend to a different continent.

Cyril gets Jerome up to speed on everything happening in his life, and they end the phone call with promises to speak again soon.

A few days later, Gina, Sharon, Alf and Cyril are discussing what to do for Lew's birthday; the debate has been endless. Gina thought involving Alf and Sharon would make it easier to decide, but it seems to have created a 'too many cooks spoil the broth' situation.

'What do you give a man who has everything in life?' Sharon sighs.

'We should narrow down the options, at least. Come on, Cyril. This is definitely more your area of expertise,' Gina says exasperatedly.

'If you keep at it you might have finally sorted something out for his eightieth,' Alf interrupts grumpily.

'Oh, shut up, Alf,' Gina shrieks. 'No one's stopping you from helping us decide.'

'Alright, stop shouting,' Sharon says. 'I have an idea. Cyril, can you use your influence to hire a fancy room in the West End with catering for about forty people? It has to be for a good price, though.'

'There are a few places I could have a look at, but

Kettner's on Romilly Street in Soho might be best.'

'Maybe you can get Roxy to perform for us that night.'

'I don't have any contact with Roxy. She doesn't owe me any favours. Anyway, isn't Cliff Richard more Lew's cup of tea?' Cyril says.

'Can't you just ask her? For old time's sake? Lew's friends would be most impressed if we got Roxy to sing at his party,' Sharon asks, pushing her luck.

Cyril glances at Sharon and then at Alf, and Alf shrugs. The two men walk out of the room with Gina shouting after them, demanding they return to sort out the rest of the party.

MJ walks along Frith Street, looking for Bianchi's. She enters the restaurant on the first floor and announces she is here for lunch with Cyril Gold. Elena takes her to Cyril's usual table, by the window overlooking the street.

'Hi MJ,' Cyril says. 'Meet one of the most important and influential television directors, Michael Edwards.'

'Nice to meet you, Mr Edwards,' MJ says sweetly, almost curtsying. She is in awe of the famous director and feels as though she is in the presence of royalty.

'Cyril has told me all about your extraordinary background, and what a voice!' Michael says.

MJ is charmed. She had almost given up hope of anyone taking her singing seriously. 'Thank you, Mr Edwards. That means a lot,' she says.

'I want you on my show, MJ. I'll make you a star!' Michael says with a dramatic hand gesture. He makes a little more small-talk, laying down some vague plans for the show, and then politely excuses himself, leaving MJ and Cyril to have their lunch.

MJ turns to Cyril: 'Is this man for real or what? He's not bullshitting me, is he?'

'No, he's for real. He put Roxy on his show. Now he wants you.'

'Oh my God, Cyril! I can't believe this is happening. You didn't mention my past life… as an accountant, did you?'

'No, I just told him I found you singing in Soho and how you ran the club. And all the extras too. He said you remind him of Bathhouse Bette… Bette Midler, that is. She performed in a bathhouse with Barry Manilow in the seventies.'

'Why are you lecturing me on gay icons? Of course I know all about Bathhouse Betty!' MJ laughs nervously. She goes through the full range of emotions, from fits of panic to joy, finally settling on feeling extremely pleased for herself.

Dolly arrives at the restaurant, stopping off at other

tables to chat with some music executives on his way over to MJ and Cyril.

'MJ, meet Dolly. Dolly, MJ.' The two kiss cheeks and immediately get on like a house on fire.

'I've been so excited to meet you, MJ. You're just as Cyril described, and so much more!'

'Well, I never like to disappoint,' MJ says sexily, pushing back her long blonde hair, loving the admiration.

'To start, no more flowery dresses for you, dear. I saw the photos of you at the music awards, all dressed up in leather. That will be your look for our photoshoot and the cover of the record. Cyril, you launched MJ that night without even realising it. People have been dying to know who the sex bomb with the whip is. Now we can finally let the world know who you are!'

'So you want me to wear exactly the same get up for the photoshoot as I did for the music awards? I'm not usually one for repeating outfits.'

'Don't worry, it'll be perfect,' Dolly reassures.

'I don't want any surprises, okay? No nudity or breast exposing or anything like that,' Cyril says, thinking back to the trouble caused by The Sisters' saucy photoshoot.

'You haven't paid me enough for that,' MJ jokes.

'We'll need to spend some money to get airtime on the radio,' Dolly says looking at Cyril.

'What? More money? How come?'

'You saw those guys I was speaking to on my way over here? They're very influential radio producers, and they have the last say on which records will be played on the radio stations. I'll need to give them an incentive to get our record played.'

'You're having me on,' Cyril says.

'This can't be the first time you've seen inducements and incentives being used in the business, Cyril. Usually it starts with fancy lunches and dinners – nice cars to take them home. Then they bring in sexy women, or men. Or, the old school way, cash. Everyone's at it.'

Cyril nods his head; he is familiar with the hoops you have to jump through to get places in the business.

'Do all the record companies play this game?' MJ asks with surprise.

'Oh yes. It's called Payola,' Dolly whispers.

The following week, it's all hands on the pump to get MJ's record marketed. Dolly bursts into Cyril's office carrying a box of records.

'I just picked these from the pressing plant. The EMI factory will dispatch the rest to record shops all over the country for us. If we get strong airplay from the radio stations, we'll be up and running with record sales.'

Dolly pulls one of the records out of the box and

shows it to Cyril.

'My God, that's amazing!' Cyril says. He is astounded by the impact the imagery has on him.

'I know, dear. I was blown over by how powerful and wicked MJ looks holding that fucking whip. I love it. It'll definitely get people to pay attention.'

MJ saunters into the office and immediately sees the record sleeve. She dashes over and picks up a record, holding it in the air in admiration.

'Is that really me? I absolutely love it!' she exclaims, flinging her arms around Dolly and then Cyril.

'You'd better start believing it! You'll be the talk of the town once you start performing in London's gay venues this week,' Dolly says. 'We have a busy schedule. But first we need to send these records out to all the gay DJs that I know in the country. So, let's start putting these records into the envelopes with your photographs and short bio. Get licking the stamps; we've got a lot to get through.'

MJ makes a face and looks at her perfectly manicured nails.

'Come on, MJ. All hands on deck – you're not a big star yet,' Dolly commands in military style.

The three of them sit around the table and start putting together promotional packs. They chat and laugh together, then MJ starts singing.

'Just whistle while you work…'

Cyril joins in with the whistling, and Dolly falls about laughing. MJ and Cyril quickly join him, giggling like children.

Three days later, Dolly, MJ and Cyril arrive at Heaven nightclub to launch MJ's record; it will be her live debut. The venue is heaving with clubbers standing shoulder to shoulder. At midnight, the DJ introduces MJ. The crowd go wild when four topless muscle men in jeans take their position on the dimly lit stage.

'I didn't know we had dancers. Great idea! But where's MJ?' Cyril asks

'The queens all like a bit of eye candy. And you'll see, dear. Just watch,' Dolly replies, never taking his eyes from the stage.

Cyril wonders at the cost of all this but decides against probing Dolly any further; this is MJ's night after all.

The lights go down and the music starts. The spotlight picks out a silhouette; the figure of a large woman with big hair and high heels, holding a whip. MJ turns around and walks forwards towards the crowd, cracking the whip several times before she begins singing 'I Want a Man'. The performance is wild, sexy and over the top; everything that MJ embodies. She works the crowd expertly, holding them in the palm of her hand. The song goes down a storm.

Within weeks, the record enters the bottom of the top thirty music charts, and MJ continues to promote it, going from one gay venue to another every night. Cyril stumps up some Payola and the record gets some play on the mainstream radio stations. The song clearly strikes a chord with listeners as record sales shoot up, taking many in the music business by surprise. It seems like everything is going swimmingly. Then Dolly stomps into Cyril's office with a face like thunder. Cyril is on the phone, but hurriedly ends the call.

'Bad news. Our record has been banned by the authorities. They've stopped playing it on all the stations.'

'What?' Cyril shouts.

'They called the song immoral and filthy and said MJ is a travesty to wholesomeness and good family values.'

'Fuck the authorities. The lyrics have definitely come back to bite us,' Cyril kicks over one of the chairs in frustration. 'Right, I'll get on the phone and cancel all MJ's gigs.'

'Hang on, Cyril. I was thinking on my way over here that we might be able to use this as publicity. It could be a headline in the newspapers. Let's turn it to our advantage and continue with the promotion.'

Cyril can see where Dolly is coming from and, since they have nothing to lose, agrees. He decides he needs a drink and heads to The Star and Garter. As Cyril walks through the door, he sees Billy leaning on the bar. Cyril still hasn't forgiven Billy for dropping him in it with a dangerous gangster. He turns to leave.

'Cyril!' Billy calls out, running up to him. 'Don't go. I need to speak to you.'

Cyril wheels around. 'I don't have anything to say to you, Billy. You nearly got me killed by that fucking Irish leprechaun. Bet you thought it was really funny too,' Cyril growls, grabbing Billy by the coat.

'I'm sorry. I had no idea that would happen,' Billy pleads.

'My mum always said you were trouble. She's right. I'm going now, before I sock you one.'

'Come on, Cyril. It's Christmas soon. You know, peace and goodwill?'

Cyril glares in disbelief and shakes his head. He turns to leave.

'I can explain about Murphy coming to your office. It was Liam, the singer. He set you up. He told Murphy you wanted to be our manager even though you said you didn't. Liam thought that would be the quickest way to get rid of him. It worked; we got out of our contract with him, but not before Murphy slashed Liam in the face with a broken bottle. He needed thirteen stitches and now he's got a huge scar.'

'You're all fucking nutters,' Cyril says, again going to leave.

'Roxy's in a bad way, Cyril. That Struan bloke has videos of her taking coke and he's using them to blackmail her.'

'Are you being serious?'

'Roxy wanted him to leave the house but he demanded a huge payoff. It was Struan who got her into drugs in the first place.'

'How do you know all this?' Cyril asks, forgetting to be angry for a second.

'I have friends,' Billy says, holding out a piece of paper to Cyril with a phone number and an address on it. 'Speak to her. She needs you.'

Billy walks out of the pub, leaving Cyril standing there in bewilderment. The Beatles' 'Lucy in the Sky with Diamonds' is playing on the jukebox. Cyril looks at the piece of paper and stuffs it into his pocket with a sigh.

The following morning, Cyril comes downstairs to find Alf in the kitchen reading the morning paper and Gina making breakfast.

'Look what's made the front page of the newspapers. You never told me MJ used to be an accountant… and a man.'

Gina looks at Alf. 'Surely you knew MJ was a man. Even I know that.'

'MJ is a kind, beautiful and talented person, Dad. Her life would have been a lot easier if she had been born a woman. She might have been born a man, but there was always a woman inside, screaming to get out.'

The newspaper features a photo of MJ with a story about how the song 'I Want a Man' has been banned for its suggestive lyrics. It also contains further details about MJ running a sadomasochism club in Soho.

'What's new? The papers are always exaggerating,' Cyril says. 'MJ just runs a club.'

Alf raises an eyebrow suspiciously as Cyril dashes towards the door.

'What about your breakfast?' Gina calls out.

'I'm not hungry,' Cyril replies, closing the front door behind him.

Dolly is waiting impatiently outside the office when Cyril arrives with a bottle of milk in his hand.

'Cyril, get a move on! You won't believe what's happened, dear. Hurry up; your phones have been ringing like mad.'

He scurries up the last few steps and unlocks the office. 'What is it now, Dolly? I don't know if I can take any more mishaps.'

'It's good news, dear, don't panic. Fucking incredible news, actually. The record is selling like hotcakes. The pressing plant have been inundated with orders from record shops all over the country. The way things are going, we'll have a number one record for Christmas!'

'You're kidding me!' Cyril laughs. He gives Dolly a hug and they start jumping up and down.

'I'm off to meet MJ for a day of interviews in TV studios. She's in very high demand; everyone wants to know her life story. I'll call you later when I get the new chart positions,' Dolly says, rushing out of the office with a box of records under his arm.

Cyril makes himself a cup of tea and does a celebratory dance. How things can change in twenty-four hours, he thinks. He plays back the messages on his answering machine. Most of them are requests for interviews with MJ. One message takes him completely by surprise; a friend of Jerome's calling from America asking Cyril to ring back urgently. Cyril dials the number and waits anxiously.

'Hello? This is Cyril Gold from London. You left a message about Jerome?'

'Yes, thanks for calling back. I have some bad news. Jerome, or Georgie as everyone calls him round here…'

'Just tell me what happened,' Cyril interrupts.

'He was walking home along the boulevard on fifty-third and third. A New Jersey gang followed him. They jumped him. One of them had a switchblade… Jerome was always talking about you. We didn't know how to contact his family, so we thought we should call you.'

In utter disbelief, Cyril ends the call. He runs to the kitchen sink and throws up. On his way back into the office, he hears Dolly leaving a message.

'It's better than we thought! MJ's record has gone straight to number one! And The Sisters are at number two! Can you believe it? Number one and number two! Fucking amazing, dear. We absolutely have to celebrate!'

Cyril sinks down in his office chair feeling numb.

After a while sitting in silence, Cyril leaves the office and walks onto Berwick Street. His mind is so far away that he almost doesn't notice Mickey Sullivan calling out to him, congratulating him on his success. Cyril manages a smile and a wave. Mickey's radio is playing Rod Stewart's, 'The Killing of Georgie.' Cyril continues to walk, completely oblivious to the world swirling around him. Suddenly, he stops and hails a taxi.

'Can you take me to this address in Chelsea, please?' Cyril asks, showing the driver the piece of paper Billy gave him.

The taxi pulls up to an enormous three-story house with a 'Sold' sign hanging outside. Still in a daze, Cyril presses the doorbell. A familiar voice comes over the intercom.

'Hello?'

'Roxy? It's Cyril.'

The buzzer sounds and the door springs open. Roxy is standing in the reception hall. Cyril finds himself once again lost for words.

Roxy breaks the silence: 'What brings you here?'

'It's a lovely place. How come you're moving?' Cyril says.

'You didn't come here to view the house, did you? It's sold.'

'Billy told me you are in trouble', Cyril interrupts.

'I hate the house, Cyril. Nothing but bad memories here. It was a mistake to let Struan back into my life.'

'You were just doing what was best for Tommy,' Cyril says sympathetically.

'Tommy means everything to me. But by the time I realised what a truly terrible person Struan is, it was too late. I just needed help to deal with the pressures of overnight success. His answer to everything is drugs. Bea was no use either. As long as I was still bringing in the money she didn't care. I was completely exhausted from a non-stop schedule of promoting records; I just needed a break.'

'Jerome told me things weren't going great, but I had no idea it was this bad.'

'I spent some time in rehab too,' Roxy says hesitantly. 'The Priory. I was a total mess. Besides dealing with the drug problem, I was glad just to have some rest! I was burning the candle at both ends. You know how nervous I was about performing – that never went away.'

'I'm so sorry. I should have been there for you,' Cyril begins apologetically.

'It's not your fault, Cyril. Besides, it seems like you've had your hands full with MJ and The Sisters,' Roxy replies with a wry smile.

They both laugh.

'I knew you had my best interests at heart. Jerome told me what you did to get me on Michael's TV show…'

'He never could keep a secret,' Cyril says with a sad smile.

Just then, Tommy comes running up, calling out Cyril's name.

'Have you come to take me to the zoo?' he asks, looking up at Cyril.

'They don't let you forget your promises, do they?' Cyril chuckles, crouching down to give Tommy a hug.

'Come and see our Christmas tree,' Tommy says, pulling Cyril into the living room. The sound of Wham's 'Last Christmas' drifts to meet him. Cyril is suddenly overtaken by emotions hearing the song. He falls to his knees and Roxy runs over to sit next to him, holding his hand. 'What's wrong Cyril?' she asks.

'Well, I missed you both… and…,' Cyril's voice cracks and he breaks down in tears.

'What's the matter? Tell me,' she asks with concern.

Cyril whispers in her ear, telling her what has happened to Jerome.

'Oh God, no,' Roxy says, holding her hand to her mouth in disbelief.

Tommy then decides to join in their embrace and have a group hug. There are a few moments of silence.

'Can we go to the zoo now?' Tommy's little voice pipes up.

Roxy's and Cyril's tears turn to half-hearted laughter.

'Sure! We could all do with some fresh air. You can have a look at all the animals and your mummy and I can have a nice long chat. We've got a lot to catch up on,' Cyril says looking at Roxy with a smile.

Roxy grabs her jacket and goes to turn off the TV, which is playing the music video for Starship's 'Nothing's Gonna Stop Us Now'. Cyril reaches out and turns Roxy to him and they gaze deeply into each other's eyes.

'Just let the music play, Roxy.'

She smiles and nods.

Tommy taps Cyril's leg and the three of them leave the house, hand in hand.

THE END

www.sohohustle.com

Printed in Great Britain
by Amazon